THIS BOO[K]
BELONGS

_____

_____

VINTAGE CLASSICS

The Brothers Grimm

Grimms' Fairy Tales

VINTAGE BOOKS

London

Published by Vintage 2013

4 6 8 10 9 7 5 3

Translation copyright © Jack Zipes 1987, 1992, 2002
Chapter heading illustrations copyright © Luisa Crosbie 2013

This translation was first published in the USA by Bantam in 1987
These stories first published in Great Britain in *The Complete Fairy Tales*
by Vintage Classics in 2007

Vintage
Random House, 20 Vauxhall Bridge Road, London SW1V 2SA

www.vintage-classics.info

Addresses for companies within The Random House Group Limited can
be found at: www.randomhouse.co.uk/offices.htm

The Random House Group Limited Reg. No. 954009

A CIP catalogue record for this book
is available from the British Library

ISBN 9780099582557

The Random House Group Limited supports The Forest Stewardship
Council® (FSC®), the leading international forest-certification organisation.
Our books carrying the FSC label are printed on FSC®-certified paper.
FSC is the only forest-certification scheme supported by the leading
environmental organisations, including Greenpeace. Our
paper procurement policy can be found at
www.randomhouse.co.uk/environment

Printed and bound in Great Britain by Clays Ltd, St Ives plc

Contents

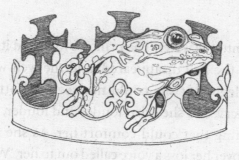

1

The Frog King, or Iron Heinrich

IN OLDEN times, when wishing still helped, there
lived a king whose daughters were all beautiful,
but the youngest was so beautiful that the sun itself,
which had seen so many things, was always filled with
amazement each time it cast its rays upon her face. Now,
there was a great dark forest near the king's castle, and
in this forest, beneath an old linden tree, was a well.
Whenever the days were very hot, the king's daughter
would go into this forest and sit down by the edge of
the cool well. If she became bored, she would take her
golden ball, throw it into the air, and catch it. More than
anything else she loved playing with this ball.

One day it so happened that the ball did not fall
back into the princess's little hand as she reached out
to catch it. Instead, it bounced right by her and rolled

straight into the water. The princess followed it with her eyes, but the ball disappeared, and the well was deep, so very deep that she could not see the bottom. She began to cry, and she cried louder and louder, for there was nothing that could comfort her. As she sat there grieving over her loss a voice called out to her, 'What's the matter, Princess? Your tears could move even a stone to pity.'

She looked around to see where the voice was coming from and saw a frog sticking his thick, ugly head out of the water. 'Oh, it's you, you old water-splasher!' she said. 'I'm crying because my golden ball has fallen into the well.'

'Be quiet and stop crying,' the frog responded. 'I'm sure I can help you. But what will you give me if I fetch your plaything?'

'Whatever you like, dear frog,' she said. 'My clothes, my pearls and jewels, even the golden crown I'm wearing on my head.'

'I don't want your clothes, your pearls and jewels, or your golden crown,' the frog replied. 'But if you will love me and let me be your companion and playmate, and let me sit beside you at the table, eat from your little golden plate, drink out of your little cup, and sleep in your little bed—if you promise me all that, I'll dive down and retrieve your golden ball.'

'Oh, yes,' she said. 'I'll promise you anything you want if only you'll bring back the ball!' However, she thought, What nonsense that stupid frog talks! He just sits in the water croaking with the rest of the frogs. How can he expect a human being to accept him as a companion?

Once the frog had her promise, he dipped his head under the water, dived downward, and soon came paddling back to the surface with the ball in his mouth. When he threw it onto the grass, the princess was so delighted to see her beautiful plaything again that she picked it up and ran off with it.

'Wait, wait!' cried the frog. 'Take me with you. I can't run like you.'

He croaked as loudly as he could, but what good did it do? She paid no attention to him. Instead, she rushed home and soon forgot about the poor frog, who had to climb back down into his well.

The next day, as she sat at the table with the king and his courtiers and ate from her little golden plate, something came crawling *splish, splash, splish, splash* up the marble steps. When it reached the top, it knocked at the door and cried out, 'Princess, youngest daughter, open up!'

She ran to see who was outside. But when she opened the door and saw the frog, she quickly slammed the door shut and went back to the table in a state of fright. The king could clearly see her heart was thumping and said, 'My child, what are you afraid of? Has a giant come to get you?'

'Oh, no,' she answered. 'It's not a giant, but a nasty frog.'

'What does a frog want from you?'

'Oh, dear Father, yesterday when I was sitting and playing near the well in the forest, my golden ball fell into the water, and because I cried so much, the frog fetched it for me, and because he insisted, I had to promise he could be my companion. But I never thought he'd get out of the water. Now he's outside and wants to come in and be with me.'

Just then there was a second knock at the door, and a voice cried out:

'Princess, Princess, youngest daughter,
open up and let me in.
Have you forgotten
what you promised
down by the well's cool water?
Princess, Princess, youngest daughter,
open up and let me in.'

Then the king said, 'If you've made a promise, you must keep it. Go and let him in.'

After she went and opened the door, the frog hopped into the room and followed her right to her chair, where he plopped himself down and cried out, 'Lift me up beside you!'

She refused until the king finally ordered her to do so. Once the frog was on the chair, he wanted to climb onto the table, and when he made it to the table, he said, 'Now push your little golden plate nearer to me so we can eat together.'

To be sure, she did this, but it was quite clear that she did not like it. The frog enjoyed his meal, while each bite the princess took got stuck in her throat. Finally he said, 'I've had enough, and now I'm tired. Carry me upstairs to your room and get your silken bed ready so we can go to sleep.'

The princess began to cry because the cold frog frightened her. She did not even have enough courage to touch him, and yet, now she was supposed to let him sleep in her beautiful, clean bed. But the king gave her an angry look and said, 'It's not proper to scorn someone who helped you when you were in trouble!'

So she picked up the frog with her two fingers, carried him upstairs, and set him down in a corner. Soon after she had got into bed, he came crawling over to her and said, 'I'm tired and want to sleep as much as you do. Lift me up, or I'll tell your father!'

This made the princess extremely angry, and after she picked him up, she threw him against the wall with all her might.

'Now you can have your rest, you nasty frog!'

However, when he fell to the ground, he was no longer a frog but a prince with kind and beautiful eyes. So, in keeping with her father's wishes, she accepted him as her dear companion and husband, whereupon the prince told her that a wicked witch had cast a spell over him and no one could have got him out of the well except her, and now he intended to take her to his kingdom the next day. Then they fell asleep, and in the morning, when the sun woke them, a coach drawn by eight white horses came driving up. The horses had ostrich plumes on their heads and harnesses with golden chains. At the back of the coach stood Faithful Heinrich, the young king's servant. He had been so distressed when he had learned his master had been turned into a frog that he had ordered three iron bands be wrapped around his heart to keep it from bursting from grief and sadness. But now the coach had come to bring the young king back to his kingdom, and Faithful Heinrich helped the prince and princess into it and then took his place at the back again. He was overcome by joy because his master had been saved.

When they had travelled some distance, the prince

heard a cracking noise behind him, as if something had broken. He turned around and cried out:

> 'Heinrich, the coach is breaking!'
> 'No, my lord, it's really nothing
> but the band around my heart,
> for it nearly fell apart
> when the witch did cast her spell
> and made you live as a frog in a well.'

The cracking noise was heard two more times along the way, and the prince thought each time that the coach was breaking, but the noise was only the sound of the bands snapping from Faithful Heinrich's heart, for he knew his master was safe and happy.

2
The Marvellous Minstrel

ONCE upon a time there was a marvellous minstrel who walked through a forest all alone and thought about all kinds of things. When there was nothing more to think about, he said to himself, 'I'm getting bored here in the forest, and I need to get myself a good companion.'

He took his fiddle from his back and began playing a tune that resounded through the trees. It was not long before a wolf came trotting through the thicket.

'Ah, here comes a wolf! I don't have any desire to see a wolf,' said the musician.

But the wolf came closer and said to him, 'Oho, dear musician, what's that lovely tune you're playing? I'd like to learn to play that way too.'

'You can easily do it,' responded the minstrel. 'You only have to do as I say.'

'Oh, minstrel,' the wolf said, 'I'll obey you just as a pupil obeys his teacher.'

The minstrel told him to come along, and after they had walked some distance together, they came to an old oak tree that was hollow inside and split down the middle.

'Look here,' said the minstrel, 'if you want to learn how to fiddle, you must put your front paws into this crack.'

The wolf obeyed, but the minstrel quickly picked up a stone, and with one blow he wedged the wolf's front paws in so tightly that the beast was forced to stay there like a prisoner.

'Wait here until I get back,' the minstrel said, and he went his way.

After a while he said to himself once more, 'I'm getting bored here in the forest, and I need to get myself another companion.'

He took his fiddle and played another tune that was heard throughout the forest. It was not long before a fox came slinking through the trees.

'Ah, here comes a fox!' said the minstrel. 'I don't have any desire to see a fox.'

The fox came up to him and said, 'Oho, dear minstrel, what's that lovely tune you're playing? I'd like to learn to play that way too.'

'You can easily do it,' said the minstrel. 'You only have to do as I say.'

'Oh, minstrel,' the wolf said, 'I'll obey you just as a pupil obeys his teacher.'

'Follow me,' said the minstrel.

After they had walked some distance, they came to a footpath with tall bushes on either side. The minstrel stopped, grabbed hold of a little hazel tree, and bent it down to the ground. Then he held the top down with his foot while he bent another little hazel tree down from the other side.

'Well now, my little fox,' he said, 'if you want to learn something, give me your left front paw.'

The fox obeyed, and the minstrel bound the paw to the tree on the left.

'Little fox,' he said, 'now give me your right paw.'

He bound this one to the tree on the right. After he made sure that the knots were tight enough, he let go, and the little trees shot up into the air and jerked the fox up high so he was left dangling in the air.

'Wait here till I get back,' said the minstrel, and he went his way.

Once again he said to himself, 'I'm getting bored in the forest and need to get another companion.'

So he took his fiddle, and the sounds reverberated

through the forest. Then a little hare came hopping toward him.

'Ah, here comes a hare!' said the minstrel. 'I didn't want a hare.'

'Oho, dear minstrel,' the little hare said, 'what's that lovely tune you're playing? I'd like to play that way too.'

'You can easily do it,' said the minstrel. 'You only have to do as I say.'

'Oh, minstrel,' the little hare answered, 'I'll obey you just as a pupil obeys his teacher.'

They walked some distance together until they came to a clearing in the forest where an aspen tree was standing. The minstrel tied a long cord around the little hare's neck and attached the other end to the tree.

'Move lively, little hare,' the minstrel cried out. 'I want you to run around the tree twenty times.'

The little hare obeyed, and after he had done that twenty times, the cord was wrapped around the tree twenty times, and the little hare was trapped. No matter how much he pulled or tugged, he only made the cord cut deeper into his soft neck.

'Wait here till I get back,' said the minstrel, and he went off.

In the meantime, the wolf had yanked and pulled and bitten on the stone. He kept working at it until he finally freed his paws and drew them out of the crack. Bursting with anger and fury, he rushed after the minstrel, intending to tear him to pieces. When the fox saw him running along, he began to wail and scream with all his might, 'Brother wolf, come help me! The minstrel has tricked me!'

The wolf pulled the little trees down to the ground, bit the rope in two, and freed the fox, who went with him to get revenge on the minstrel. They found the little hare tied up and released him as well. Now all three began searching for their enemy.

As the minstrel walked along his way he played his fiddle once again, but this time he was more fortunate. The sounds reached the ears of a poor woodcutter who was instantly compelled to stop working whether he wanted to or not, and he went to listen to the music with his axe under his arm.

'Here comes the right companion at last!' said the minstrel. 'I never wanted beasts in the first place, just humans.'

Now he began to play so beautifully and so delightfully that the poor man stood there as if he were under a magic spell, and his heart leapt for joy. As he was standing there, the wolf, the fox, and the little hare came running up, and he could see that they had something evil in mind. So he raised his glittering axe and stood in front of the minstrel as if to say, 'Whoever wants him had better watch out, because he'll have to deal with me first.'

The animals were frightened by this and ran back into the forest, while the minstrel played one more tune for the woodcutter out of gratitude. Then he moved on his way.

3
Riffraff

THE rooster said to the hen, 'Now's the time the nuts are ripe. Let's go up to the hill and for once eat our fill before the squirrel hauls them all away.'

'All right,' responded the hen. 'Let's go and have a good time.'

They went up the hill, and since it was such a bright cheery day, they stayed till evening. Now, I do not know whether it was because they had stuffed themselves too much, or whether they had become too high and mighty, but they did not want to return home on foot, so the rooster had to build a small carriage out of nut shells. When it was finished, the hen got in and said to the rooster, 'Now you can just harness yourself to it.'

'You have some nerve!' said the rooster. 'I'd rather go home by foot than let myself be harnessed to this carriage. No, that wasn't part of our bargain. I'd gladly be coachman and sit on the box, but I refuse to pull the carriage!'

As they were quarrelling, a duck came by quacking 'You thieves! Who said you could come up on my nut hill? Just you wait! You'll pay for this!'

She charged at the rooster with a wide-open beak, but the rooster was on his toes and threw himself at the duck nice and hard. Then he dug his spurs into her so violently that the duck begged for mercy and willingly let herself be harnessed to the carriage as punishment. Now the rooster sat down on the box as coachman, and when they set out, he shouted, 'Giddyap, duck! Run as fast as you can!'

After they had gone some distance, they encountered two travellers on foot, a needle and a pin.

'Stop! Stop!' the two cried out. It would soon be very dark, they said, and they would not be able to go one step further. Besides, the road was dirty. So they asked if they could have a ride. They had been at the tailor's tavern outside the town gate and had had one beer too many, which made them late as well.

Since they were thin and did not take up much room, the rooster let them both get in, but they had to promise not to step on his or the hen's feet. Later that evening they came to an inn, and as they did not want to travel any farther, and as the duck was not walking well but swayed from side to side, they decided to stop there. At first the innkeeper raised a lot of objections and said his inn was already full. Moreover, he thought they were not a very distinguished looking group. However, they used some sweet talk and offered him the egg that the hen had laid along the way and told him that he could also keep the duck, who laid an egg a day. So finally he relented and said they could spend the night.

Now they ordered some good hot food and had a merry time of it. Early the next morning, as the sun was rising and everyone was asleep, the rooster woke the hen, fetched the egg, pecked it open, and together they devoured it. After throwing the shells on the hearth, they went to the needle, who was still asleep, grabbed him by the head, and stuck him into the innkeeper's easy chair. Then they stuck the pin into his towel. Finally, without much ado, they flew away over the heath.

The duck, who liked to sleep in the open air and had spent the night in the yard, heard the flapping of their wings. So she roused herself, found a brook, and swam off. That went much faster than being harnessed to a carriage. A few hours later the innkeeper got out of bed, washed himself, and took the towel to dry himself. However, the pin scratched his face, leaving a red mark from ear to ear. Then he went into the kitchen and wanted to light his pipe. But, as he leaned over the hearth, the eggshells popped into his eyes.

'Everything's after my head this morning,' he said, and went to sit down in his easy chair to settle his bad mood, but he jumped up immediately and screamed, *'Oww!'* The needle stuck him worse than the pin and not in the head. Now he was completely angry and suspected the guests who had arrived so late the night before. But when he went looking for them, they were gone. Then he swore he would never again let riffraff stay at his inn, especially when they eat so much, pay nothing, and play mean tricks on top of it all.

4

Brother and Sister

A LITTLE brother took his little sister by the hand and said, 'Since our mother died, we've not had one moment of happiness. Our stepmother beats us every day, and when we come near her, she kicks us away with her foot. We get nothing but hard crusts of bread, just leftovers for food, and the dog under the table is better off. At least he gets a good chunk of meat to eat every now and then. Lord have mercy on us, if our mother only knew! Come, let's go off together into the wide world.'

They walked over meadows, fields, and stones the entire day, and when it began to rain, the sister said, 'God and our hearts are weeping at the same time.'

In the evening they came to a great forest and were so exhausted from their grief, hunger, and long journey that they crept into a hollow tree and fell asleep. When they woke up the next morning, the sun was already high in the sky and warmed the tree with its rays.

'Sister,' said the brother, 'I'm thirsty. If only I knew where to find a spring, I'd go and have a drink right away. Listen, I think I hear one gurgling.'

The brother stood up, took his sister by the hand, and set out to look for the spring. However, the evil stepmother, who was a witch, had noticed that the children had run away. She had gone slinking after them in secret, as witches often slink, and had put a curse on all the springs in the forest. So, when they found a spring rushing and leaping over stones, the brother wanted to take a drink, but the sister heard the gurgling spring say, 'Whoever drinks of me will be turned into a tiger.'

Then the sister exclaimed, 'Please, brother, don't drink, or else you'll turn into a wild beast and tear me to pieces!'

Even though he was very thirsty, the brother did not drink. Instead he said, 'I'll wait until we reach the next spring.'

When they reached the next spring, once again the sister heard what it was babbling. 'Whoever drinks of me will be turned into a wolf. Whoever drinks of me will be turned into a wolf.'

'Brother!' the sister exclaimed. 'Please don't drink, or else you'll be turned into a wolf and eat me up.'

The brother did not drink and said, 'I'll wait until we reach the next spring, but then I must drink no matter what you say. My thirst is much too great.'

When they came to the third spring, the sister heard the babbling of the spring. 'Whoever drinks of me will be turned into a deer. Whoever drinks of me will be turned into a deer.'

'Oh, brother!' the sister exclaimed. 'Please don't drink, or else you'll be turned into a deer and run away from me.'

But the brother, who was already kneeling at the spring, leaned over and drank some of the water. Immediately after a few drops had touched his lips, he lay there in the form of a fawn. The sister began weeping over her poor bewitched brother, sitting sadly at her side, and the little fawn wept too. Finally, the girl said, 'Hush, my dear little fawn. I shall never forsake you.'

She took off her golden garter and put it around the fawn's neck. Then she pulled up some rushes and wove them into a soft rope, which she attached to the little animal. Afterward she led him onward and deeper into the forest. When they had gone a long, long way, they came to a little house, and the girl looked inside. Since it was empty, she thought, We might as well stay and live right here. So she looked for leaves and moss and made a soft bed for the fawn. Every morning she went out and gathered roots, berries, and nuts for herself, and for the fawn she brought back tender grass, which he ate out of her hand. This made him content, and he would romp around her in a playful fashion. At night, when the sister was tired and had said her prayers, she would lay her head on the back of the fawn. That was her pillow, and she would fall into a sweet sleep. If only the brother could have regained his human form, it would have been a wonderful life.

For a long time they lived like this, all alone in the wilderness. However, it came to pass that the king of the country held a great hunt in the forest, and soon horns could be heard along with the barking of dogs and the merry cries of the huntsmen. The fawn listened to the sounds and longed very much to be a part of it all.

'Ah,' he said to his sister, 'let me go and join the hunt. I can't bear it any longer!' He kept pleading until she gave her consent.

'But make sure you're back here by evening,' she said to him. 'I'm going to lock the door to keep the brutal hunters out, and when you return, I want you to knock on the door and say, "My little sister, let me in." That way I'll recognize you. If you don't say this, I won't open the door.'

Then the fawn ran off, glad and merry to be out in the open air. The king and his hunstsmen saw the beautiful creature and set out in pursuit, but they could not catch up with him. Whenever they thought they had him for sure, he would burst through the bushes and disappear. When it got dark, he ran back to the little house, knocked, and said, 'My little sister, let me in.'

The little door was opened for him, and he jumped inside. Then he rested the entire night on his bed. The next morning the hunt began anew, and when the fawn heard the horn again and the *'Tallyho!'* of the huntsmen, he became very restless and said, 'Sister, open the door. I must be off!'

The sister opened the door for him and said, 'Remember, you must be back by evening and say the passwords.'

When the king and his hunstsmen saw the fawn with the golden collar once more, they all pursued him, but he was still too swift and nimble for them. All day long they chased him, but finally by evening they had surrounded him. Then one huntsman wounded him slightly on his foot, and as the fawn slowly ran away he was limping. This allowed a huntsman to trail him all the way to the house, and he heard the fawn cry out, 'My little sister, let me in.' He watched the door open and close quickly and took note of all that happened. Then the huntsman went back to the king and told him about everything he had seen and heard.

'Tomorrow we shall hunt again,' the king said.

Meanwhile, the sister was greatly distressed when she saw her little fawn was wounded. She washed off the blood, placed herbs on the wound, and said, 'Now, go to bed, my dear fawn. You must let your wound heal.'

Actually the wound was so slight that the fawn did not even feel it the next morning. And, once again, when he heard the merry cries of the hunt outside, he said, 'I can't bear it. I've got to be there! I won't make it easy for them to catch me.'

The sister wept and said, 'Now they'll kill you, and I'll be left alone in the forest, forsaken by the whole world. I'm not going to let you out.'

'Then I'll die of misery,' responded the fawn. 'Whenever I hear the sounds of the hunting horn, I feel as if I were going to burst out of my skin.'

After he said that, his sister could no longer refuse, and with a heavy heart she opened the door for him. The fawn bounded cheerfully and sprightfully into the forest. When the king caught sight of him, he said to his huntsmen, 'Now, I want you to chase him the whole day long and into the night, but make sure that you don't harm him.'

Later, as the sun began to set, the king turned to the huntsman and said, 'All right, take me and show me the little house in the forest.'

After the king arrived at the front door, he knocked and called out, 'Dear little sister, let me in.'

The door opened, and upon entering, the king stood face-to-face with the most beautiful maiden he had ever seen in his life. The maiden was frightened when she saw it was a man with a golden crown on his head and not her fawn. Yet, he looked at her in a kind way, and after extending his hand, he said, 'Would you like to come with me to my castle and be my dear wife?'

'Oh, yes,' responded the maiden. 'But the fawn must come with me too. I won't ever forsake him.'

'He can stay with you as long as you live,' said the king, 'and he shall want for nothing.'

Just then the little fawn came running in, and the sister attached the rope of rushes to him, took the rope in her own hand, and led him out of the house. The king lifted the beautiful maiden onto his horse and brought her to his castle, where the wedding was celebrated with great splendour. Now the sister was queen, and for a long time they all lived together in happiness. The fawn was well tended and ran about the castle garden.

In the meantime, the evil stepmother, who had caused

the children to run away in the first place, thought that the sister had been torn to pieces by wild beasts and that the brother, as a fawn, had been shot to death by huntsmen. When she learned instead how happy they were and how well everything was going for them, jealousy and resentment stirred in her heart and gave her no peace. Her one and only thought now was to find a way to bring about their misfortune again. Her own daughter, who was as ugly as sin and had only one eye, reproached her by saying, 'I'm the one who should be queen! Why don't I have any luck?'

'Just be quiet!' said the old woman, who gave her reason to be satisfied. 'When the right time comes, I'll know what to do.'

Finally, the right time came: the queen gave birth one day to a baby boy while the king was out hunting. So the old witch assumed the form of the chambermaid, went into the room where the queen was lying, and said to the convalescent, 'Come, your bath is ready. It will make you feel better and give you fresh strength. Quick, before it gets cold.'

The witch's daughter had come too. Together they carried the frail queen into the bathroom, put her into the tub, locked the door, and ran away, for they had made such a terrible fire in the bathroom that the queen was soon suffocated to death.

When that was done, the old woman took her daughter, put a nightcap on her, and laid her in bed in place of the queen. She also gave her the shape and features of the queen. However, she could not replace the eye that the daughter had lost. Therefore, the daughter had to lie on the side where she had no eye. That way the king would not notice anything amiss. In the evening, when he returned home and heard his wife had given birth to a baby boy, he was very happy and wanted to go to his dear wife's bedside and see how she was doing. But the old woman cried out quickly, 'For goodness sake, keep the curtains closed! The queen must not be exposed to light. She needs peace and quiet.'

The king stepped back and was thus prevented from discovering the false queen lying in the bed. However, at midnight, when everyone was asleep except the nurse, who was sitting by the cradle in the nursery and watching over the baby all by herself, the door opened, and the true queen entered. She lifted the baby out of the cradle, took him in her arms, and suckled him. Then she puffed up his little pillow, put him back in the cradle, and covered him with a little blanket. Nor did she forget the fawn. She went to the corner where he was lying and stroked his back. Then she silently left the room, and when morning came, the nurse asked the guards whether they had seen anyone enter the castle during the night.

'No, we didn't see a soul,' they replied.

Thereafter the queen came many nights and never uttered a word. The nurse always saw her, but she did not dare tell anyone about it. After some time had passed, the queen began to speak, and one night she said:

'How's my child? How's my fawn?
Twice more I'll come, then I'll be gone.'

The nurse did not answer her, but when the queen disappeared, she went to the king and told him everything.

'Oh, God!' he exclaimed. 'What's going on? Tonight I'll keep watch over the child myself.'

In the evening he went into the nursery, and at midnight the queen reappeared and said:

'How's my child? How's my fawn?
Once more I'll come, then I'll be gone.'

She nursed the child as she usually did and then disappeared. The king did not dare to speak to her, but he kept watch the following night as well. Once again she said:

27

'How's my child? How's my fawn?
There's no more time. Soon I'll be gone.'

The king could no longer restrain himself. He sprang forward and said, 'You can be no one else but my dear wife!'

At that very moment life was restored to her by the grace of God. Indeed, she was alive and well, and the rosy colour came back to her cheeks. She then told the king how the evil witch and her daughter had committed cruel crimes against her. So the king had them led before the court, and they received their sentences. The daughter was taken into the forest, where wild beasts tore her to pieces, while the witch was thrown into a fire and miserably burned to death. When there was nothing left of her but ashes, the fawn was transformed and regained his human form. From then on sister and brother lived happily until the end of their days.

5

Rapunzel

ONCE upon a time there was a husband and wife who for quite some time had been wishing in vain for a child. Finally, the dear Lord gave the wife a sign of hope that their wish would be fulfilled. Now, in the back of their house the couple had a small window that overlooked a splendid garden filled with the most beautiful flowers and herbs. The garden, however, was surrounded by a high wall, and nobody dared enter it because it belonged to a sorceress who was very powerful and feared by all. One day when the wife was standing at the window and looking down into the garden, she noticed a bed of the finest rapunzel lettuce. The lettuce looked so fresh and green that her mouth watered, and she had a great craving to eat some. Day by day this craving increased, and since she knew she could not get any, she began to waste away and look pale and miserable.

Her husband became alarmed and asked, 'What's wrong with you, dear wife?'

'Ah,' she responded, 'I shall certainly die if I don't get any of that rapunzel from the garden behind our house.'

Her husband, who loved her, thought, Before I let my wife die, I'll do anything I must to make sure she gets some rapunzel.

That day at dusk he climbed over the wall into the garden of the sorceress, hastily grabbed a handful of rapunzel, and brought them to his wife. Immediately she made them into a salad and ate it with great zest. But the rapunzel tasted so good to her, so very good, that her desire for them was three times greater by the next day. If she was to have any peace, her husband knew he had to climb into the garden once more. So at dusk he scaled the wall again, and just as he landed on the other side, he was given a tremendous scare, for he stood face-to-face with the sorceress.

'How dare you climb into my garden and steal my rapunzel like a thief?' she said with an angry look. 'You'll pay for this!'

'Oh,' he cried. 'Please, let mercy prevail over justice. I did this only because I was in a predicament: my wife noticed your rapunzel from our window, and she developed such a great craving for it that she would have died if I hadn't brought her some to eat.'

Upon hearing that, the anger of the sorceress subsided, and she said to him, 'If it's truly as you say, then I shall permit you to take as many rapunzel as you like, but only under one condition: when your wife gives birth, I must have the child. You needn't fear about the child's well-being, for I shall take care of it like a mother.'

In his fear the man agreed to everything, and when his wife had the baby, the sorceress appeared at once. She gave the child the name Rapunzel and took her away.

Rapunzel grew to be the most beautiful child under the sun.

But when she was twelve years old, the sorceress locked her in a tower that was in a forest. It had neither door nor stairs, only a little window high above. Whenever the sorceress wanted to get in, she would stand below and call out:

'Rapunzel, Rapunzel,
let down your hair for me.'

Rapunzel's hair was long and radiant, as fine as spun gold. Every time she heard the voice of the sorceress, she unpinned her braids and wound them around a hook on the window. Then she let her hair drop twenty yards, and the sorceress would climb up on it.

A few years later a king's son happened to be riding through the forest and passed by the tower. Suddenly, he heard a song so lovely that he stopped to listen. It was Rapunzel, who passed the time in her solitude by letting her sweet voice resound in the forest. The prince wanted to climb up to her, and he looked for a door but could not find one. So he rode home. However, the song had touched his heart so deeply that he rode out into the forest every day and listened. One time, as he was standing behind a tree, he saw the sorceress approach and heard her call out:

'Rapunzel, Rapunzel,
let down your hair.'

Then Rapunzel let down her braids, and the sorceress climbed up to her.

'If that's the ladder one needs to get up there, I'm also going to try my luck,' the prince declared.

The next day, as it began to get dark, he went to the tower and called out:

'Rapunzel, Rapunzel,
let down your hair.'

All at once the hair dropped down, and the prince climbed up. When he entered the tower, Rapunzel was at first terribly afraid, for she had never laid eyes on a man before. However, the prince began to talk to her in a friendly way and told her that her song had touched his heart so deeply that he had not been able to rest until he had seen her. Rapunzel then lost her fear, and when he asked her whether she would have him for her husband, and she saw that he was young and handsome, she thought, He'll certainly love me better than old Mother Gothel. So she said yes and placed her hand in his.

'I want to go with you very much,' she said, 'but I don't know how I can get down. Every time you come, you must bring a skein of silk with you, and I'll weave it into a ladder. When it's finished, then I'll climb down, and you can take me away on your horse.'

They agreed that until then he would come to her every evening, for the old woman came during the day. Meanwhile, the sorceress did not notice anything, until one day Rapunzel blurted out, 'Mother Gothel, how is it that you're much heavier than the prince? When I pull him up, he's here in a second.'

'Ah, you godless child!' exclaimed the sorceress. 'What's this I hear? I thought I had made sure you had no contact with the outside world, but you've deceived me!'

In her fury she seized Rapunzel's beautiful hair, wrapped it around her left hand several times, grabbed a pair of scissors with her right hand, and *snip, snap* the hair was cut off, and the beautiful braids lay on the ground. Then the cruel sorceress took Rapunzel to a desolate land where she had to live in great misery and grief.

On the same day that she had banished Rapunzel, the sorceress fastened the braids that she had cut off to the hook on the window, and that evening, when the prince came and called out:

> 'Rapunzel, Rapunzel,
> let down your hair,'

she let the hair down.

The prince climbed up, but instead of finding his dearest Rapunzel on top, he found the sorceress, who gave him vicious and angry looks.

'Aha!' she exclaimed with contempt. 'You want to fetch your darling wife, but the beautiful bird is no longer sitting in the nest, and she won't be singing anymore. The cat has got her, and it will also scratch out your eyes. Rapunzel is lost to you, and you will never see her again!'

The prince was beside himself with grief, and in his despair he jumped off the tower. He escaped with his life, but the thorns he fell into pierced his eyes, so he became blind. Now he strayed about in the forest, ate nothing but roots and berries, and did nothing but mourn and weep about the loss of his dearest wife. Thus he wandered for many years in misery. Eventually, he made his way to the desolate land where Rapunzel was leading a wretched existence with the twins, a boy and a girl, to whom she had given birth. When he heard a voice that he thought sounded familiar, he went straight toward it, and when he reached her, Rapunzel recognized him. She embraced him and wept, and as two of her tears dropped on his eyes they became clear, and he could see again. Then he escorted her back to his kingdom, where he was received with joy, and they lived happily and contentedly for a long time thereafter.

6

The Fisherman and His Wife

ONCE upon a time there was a fisherman who lived with his wife in a dirty hovel near the sea. Every day the fisherman went out to fish, and all he did was fish and fish. One day he was sitting with his line and gazing into the clear water. And all he did was sit and sit. Suddenly his line sank deep down to the bottom, and when he pulled it up, he had a large flounder on the line, and the flounder said to him, 'Listen here, fisherman, I beg of you, let me live. I'm not a real flounder but an enchanted prince. So what would it benefit you to kill me? I certainly wouldn't taste very good. Put me back into the water, and let me go.'

'Hold on,' said the man. 'You don't have to waste your words on me. I would have thrown a talking fish back into the water anyway.'

He then put the fish back into the clear water, and the flounder swam to the bottom, leaving behind a long streak of blood. Then the fisherman stood up and went to the hovel to be with his wife.

'Husband,' asked the wife, 'didn't you catch anything today?'

'No,' said the man. 'I caught a flounder, but he said he was an enchanted prince, and I let him go.'

'Didn't you wish for anything?' asked the wife.

'No,' said the husband. 'What should I have wished for?'

'Ah,' said the wife. 'Don't you think it's awful that we've got to keep living in such a hovel? It stinks, and it's disgusting. You should have wished for a little cottage. Go back and call him. Tell him we want a little cottage. I'm sure he'll give us one.'

'But there's no reason to go back,' said the husband.

'Of course there is,' said the wife. 'Look, you caught him and let him go. That's why he's bound to give it to us. Now go at once!'

The man really did not want to go, but neither did he want to oppose his wife. So he went back to the sea.

When he got there, the sea was very green and yellow and no longer so clear. He stood on the shore and said:

'Flounder, flounder, in the sea,
if you're a man, then speak to me.
Though I do not care for my wife's request,
I've come to ask it nonetheless.'

The flounder came swimming up to him and said, 'Well, what does she want?'

'Oh,' said the man. 'My wife thinks I should have wished for something because I caught you. Since she doesn't want to live in a hovel, she'd like to have a cottage.'

'Just go home,' said the flounder. 'She's already got it.'

When the fisherman arrived at home, his wife was no longer sitting in a hovel. Instead, she was sitting on a bench before the door to a little cottage. His wife took him by the hand and said, 'Come inside, husband. Look! Now, isn't this better?'

They went inside, and in the house he found a little hallway, a splendid parlour, and a bedroom. There was also a kitchen and a pantry furnished with all the best dishware and utensils, tinware and brass, everything that one could possibly need. Behind the cottage was a little yard with chickens and ducks and a garden with vegetables and fruit.

'You see,' said the wife, 'isn't this nice?'

'Yes,' said the husband. 'Hopefully, it will stay that way. Now we can live quite happily.'

'That's something we've got to think about,' said the wife.

Thereupon they had something to eat and went to bed.

Everything went well for about a week or two, and then the wife said, 'Listen, husband, the cottage is much too cramped, and the yard and garden are too small. The flounder could have given us a larger house. I'd very much like to live in a great stone castle. Go back to the flounder and tell him to give us a castle.'

'Ah, wife,' the husband said, 'the cottage is good enough. Why should we want to live in a castle?'

'My goodness!' said the wife. 'Just go back to him! The flounder can do this without any trouble.'

'No, wife,' said the husband. 'The flounder has just given us a cottage, and I don't want to go back again so soon. He might be insulted.'

'Just go!' said the wife. 'He can easily do it, and he'll be glad to do it. Just go back to him!'

The husband's heart grew heavy, and he did not want to go. He said to himself, 'It just isn't right.' Nevertheless, he went.

When he got to the sea, the water was purple, dark blue, grey, and dense. It was no longer green and yellow, though it was still calm. Then he stood there and said:

> 'Flounder, flounder, in the sea,
> if you're a man, then speak to me.
> Though I do not care for my wife's request,
> I've come to ask it nonetheless.'

'Well, what does she want?' the flounder asked.

'Oh,' said the man, somewhat distressed. 'She wants to live in a great stone castle.'

'Just go home. She's already standing at the gate,' the flounder said.

The man went back, thinking he was going home, but as he approached the spot where the house had been, he found a great stone palace, and his wife was standing on the steps just about to enter. She took him by the hand and said, 'Come inside.'

He went in with her and found a big front hall with a marble floor and numerous servants who opened the large doors for them. The walls were all bright and covered with beautiful tapestries. All of the chairs and tables in the rooms were made of gold. Crystal chandeliers hung from the ceilings, and all the rooms and chambers had carpets. Furthermore, the tables sagged under the weight of food and bottles of the very best wine. Behind the palace was a huge yard with stables for horses and cows and the finest carriages. There was also a wonderful large garden with the most beautiful flowers and fine fruit trees, as well as a pleasure park about half a mile long, which had stags, deer, hares, and everything else in it that one could wish for.

'Well,' said the wife, 'isn't that beautiful?'

'Oh, yes,' said the husband. 'Hopefully, it will stay that way. Now let's live in the beautiful castle and be content.'

'We'll have to think about that,' said the wife, 'and sleep on it.'

Then they went to bed.

The next morning the wife woke up first. It was just daybreak, and from her window she could see the glorious countryside lying before her. As her husband began stretching she poked him in the side with her elbow and said, 'Husband, get up and look out the window. Listen, don't you think you can be king over all this country? Go to the flounder and tell him that we want to be king.'

'Ah, wife,' said the husband. 'Why should we be king? I don't want to be king.'

'Well,' said the wife, 'you may not want to be king, but I do. Go to the flounder, and tell him I want to be king.'

'Oh, wife,' said the husband, 'why do you want to be king? I don't want to tell him that.'

'Why not?' said the wife. 'Go to him at once and tell him I must be king!'

The husband went but was most distressed that his wife wanted to be king. It's not right. It's just not right, he thought, and he did not want to go but went just the same.

When he got to the sea, it was completely grey and black, and the water was twisting and turning from below and smelled putrid. The fisherman stood there and said:

'Flounder, flounder, in the sea,
if you're a man, then speak to me.
Though I do not care for my wife's request,
I've come to ask it nonetheless.'

'Well, what does she want?' asked the flounder.

'Oh,' said the man. 'She wants to be king.'

'Go back home,' said the flounder. 'She's already king.'

Then the man went home, and as he approached the palace, he saw that the castle had become much larger, with a huge tower and glistening ornaments on it. There were sentries standing in front of the gate, along with many soldiers, drums, and trumpets. When he entered the palace, he found that everything was made of pure marble and gold and had velvet covers with large golden tassels. The doors to the hall were opened, and he could see the whole court. His wife was sitting on a high throne of gold and diamonds, and on her head she had a big golden crown and in her hand a sceptre of pure gold and jewels. Two rows of ladies-in-waiting were standing on either side of her, each lady a head shorter than the next. The fisherman stepped forward and said, 'Oh, wife, now you're king, aren't you?'

'Yes,' said his wife, 'now I am king.'

He stood there and looked at her, and after he had gazed at her for some time, he said, 'Oh, wife, it's wonderful that you're king! Now let's not wish for anything more.'

'No, husband,' the wife said as she became very restless. 'I have too much time on my hands, and I can't stand it anymore. Go back to the flounder and tell him I'm king, but now I must become emperor as well.'

'Oh, wife,' said the husband, 'why do you want to become emperor?'

'Husband,' she said. 'Go to the flounder. I want to be emperor!'

'Oh, wife,' the husband said. 'He can't make you emperor. I don't want to tell that to the flounder. There's only one emperor in the empire. The flounder can't make you emperor. He definitely can't do that.'

'What!' said the wife. 'I'm king, and you're just my husband. I want you to go there at once! And I mean, at once! If he can make a king, he can also make an emperor. Go to there at once!'

The husband had to return, but as he walked along, he became scared and thought to himself, This won't turn out well at all. Such arrogance, to want to be emperor! The flounder's going to get sick and tired of this.

When he got to the sea, it was all black and dense, and it began to twist and turn from below so that bubbles rose up, and a strong wind whipped across the surface and made the water curdle. The man became frightened, but he stepped forward and said:

> 'Flounder, flounder, in the sea,
> if you're a man, then speak to me.
> Though I do not care for my wife's request,
> I've come to ask it nonetheless.'

'Well, what does she want?' asked the flounder.

'Oh, flounder,' he said. 'My wife wants to be emperor.'

'Go back home,' said the flounder. 'She's already emperor.'

Then the man went home, and when he arrived, the entire castle was made of polished marble with alabaster figures and golden ornaments. Soldiers were marching in front of the gate, and they were blowing trumpets and beating cymbals and drums. Meanwhile, barons, counts, and dukes were inside the palace walking around like servants. They opened the doors of pure gold for him, and as he entered, he saw his wife sitting on a two-mile-high throne made from a single piece of gold. She was wearing a golden crown three yards tall and covered with diamonds and garnets. In one hand she held the sceptre and in the other the imperial globe. She was flanked on either side by two rows of bodyguards, each man shorter than the next, beginning with a tremendous giant two miles tall and ending with the tiniest dwarf, who was no bigger than my pinky. There were also many princes and dukes standing before her, and her husband stepped up and said, 'Wife, now you're emperor, aren't you?'

'Yes,' she said, 'I'm emperor.'

Then he stood there and took a good look at her, and after gazing at her for some time, he said, 'Oh, wife, it's wonderful that you're emperor. Let's keep it that way.'

'Husband,' she said. 'Why are you standing there? It's true that I'm emperor, but now I want to be pope. Go and tell this to the flounder.'

'Oh, wife,' said the husband. 'What, in heaven's name, don't you want? You can't be pope. There's only one pope in Christendom. The flounder can't make you pope.'

'Husband,' she said. 'I want to be pope! Go there at once and tell him I must be pope.'

'No, wife,' said the husband. 'I don't want to tell him that. It won't turn out well. That's too much to ask. The flounder can't make you pope.'

'Stop talking nonsense, husband!' said the wife. 'If he can make me emperor, he can also make me pope. Go there at once! I'm the emperor, and you're just my husband. So, do as I say!'

The man became frightened and went, but he felt rather queasy. He was trembling and shaking, and his knees began to wobble. A strong wind swept across the land. Dark clouds flew by as evening came. Leaves were falling from the trees, and the sea rose up in waves and roared as if it were boiling, and the waves splashed against the shore. In the distance the fisherman could see ships firing guns in distress as they were tossed up and down by the waves. Though there was still a little blue in the middle of the sky, the horizon was completely red, as if a heavy thunderstorm were coming. Then he stepped forward, filled with fear and dread, and said:

'Flounder, flounder, in the sea
if you're a man, then speak to me.
Though I do not care for my wife's request,
I've come to ask it nonetheless.'

'Well, what does she want?' asked the flounder.

'Oh,' the man said, 'she wants to be pope.'

'Go back home,' said the flounder. 'She's already pope.'

Then the man went home, and when he arrived, he found a great church with nothing but palaces surrounding it. He forced his way through crowds of people and found everything inside illuminated by thousands and thousands of candles. His wife was sitting on a throne even higher than the one before, and she was dressed in pure gold with three big golden crowns on her head. Numerous bishops and priests were standing around her, and there were two rows of candles on either side of her. The biggest candle was as thick and as large as the highest tower, and the tiniest was a church candle. And all the emperors and kings were taking their turn kneeling before her and kissing her slipper.

'Wife,' the man said as he looked at her carefully, 'now you're pope, aren't you?'

'Yes,' she said, 'I'm pope.'

Then he stepped forward and took a good look at

her, and it was as if he were looking into the bright sun. After gazing at her for some time, he said, 'Oh, wife, it's wonderful that you're pope. Let's keep it that way.'

But she sat stiff as a board and neither stirred nor moved. Then he said, 'Wife, be satisfied. Now that you're pope, you can't become anything greater.'

'I'll think about it,' said the wife.

Then they both went to bed, but she was not satisfied, and her ambition did not let her sleep. She kept thinking of ways she might become greater than she was, while her husband slept soundly, for he had run around a good deal that day. She could not get to sleep at all and tossed and turned from side to side the whole night, trying to think of ways she might become greater than she was. However, nothing whatsoever occurred to her. When the sun began to rise and she saw the red glow of the dawn, she sat up in bed and watched the sun rise from her window. Then the thought occurred to her: Aha, I could also make the sun and the moon rise! She poked her husband in the ribs with her elbow and said, 'Husband, wake up and go to the flounder. Tell him I want to be like God.'

The husband was still half asleep, but he was so shocked by what she had said that he fell out of the bed. He thought that he had misheard her and rubbed his eyes.

'Oh, wife,' he said. 'What did you say?'

'Husband,' she said, 'if I can't make the sun and the moon rise, I won't be able to bear it. Do you think I want to just watch? No, I won't have any more peace until I myself can make them rise.'

She gave her husband such an awful look that a shudder ran through his bones.

'Go there at once! I want to be like God.'

'Oh, wife!' the husband said, and fell down on his knees. 'The flounder can't do that. He can make you an emperor and pope, but I beg you, be content and stay pope.'

She immediately became furious, and her hair flew wildly about her head. She tore open her bodice, gave him a kick with her foot, and screamed, 'I won't stand for it and can't stand it any longer! I want you to go at once!'

He slipped into his trousers then and ran off like a madman. Outside a great storm was raging, so he could barely keep on his feet. Houses and trees were falling, mountains were trembling, and large boulders were rolling into the sea from the cliffs. The sky was completely pitch black, and there was thunder and lightning. Black waves rose up in the sea as high as church steeples and mountains, and they all had crests of white foam on top. Then the fisherman

49

screamed, but he could not even hear his own
words:

> 'Flounder, flounder, in the sea,
> if you're a man, then speak to me.
> Though I do not care for my wife's request,
> I've come to ask it nonetheless.'

'Well, what does she want?' the flounder asked.
'Oh,' he said, 'she wants to be like God.'
'Go back home. She's sitting in your hovel again.'
And there they are still living this very day.

7

The Brave Little Tailor

ONE summer morning a little tailor was sitting on his table by his window. He was in good spirits and was sewing with all his might. Just then a peasant woman came down the street and cried out, 'Good jam for sale! Good jam for sale!'

That sounded lovely to the little tailor's ears. He stuck his tiny head out the window and called, 'Up here, my dear woman, you're sure to make a good sale with me!'

The woman, with her heavy basket, climbed the three flights of stairs to the tailor's place and had to unpack all her jars in front of him. He inspected each one of them by lifting and sniffing the jam. Finally, he said, 'The jam seems good to me. I'll take three ounces, dear woman, but if it comes to a quarter of a pound, it won't matter.'

The woman, who had hoped to sell a great deal, gave him what he wanted but went away very annoyed and grumbling.

'Now, may God bless my jam!' the little tailor exclaimed. 'Let it give me energy and strength!' He fetched a loaf of bread from the cupboard, cut a full slice for himself, and spread it with the jam. 'This certainly won't have a bitter taste,' he said. 'But first I want to finish the jacket before I take a bite.'

He put the bread down beside him and continued sewing, making bigger and bigger stitches due to his joy. Meanwhile, the smell of the sweet jam rose to the wall, where lots of flies had gathered and were now enticed by the smell to swarm and settle on the jam.

'Hey, who invited you?' the little tailor said, and chased the unwelcome guests away. But the flies did not understand German, nor would they let themselves be deterred. Rather, they kept coming back in even larger numbers. Finally, the little tailor had been needled enough, as they say, and he grabbed a piece of cloth from under his worktable.

'Wait, I'll give you something!' he said, swinging at them mercilessly. When he let up and counted, there were no less than seven flies lying dead before him with their legs stretched out.

'You're quite a man!' he said to himself, and could

not help but admire his bravery. 'The entire city should know about this!' And the little tailor hastily cut out a belt for himself, stitched it, and embroidered large letters on it: 'Seven with one blow!'

'But why just the city?' he continued. 'Why shouldn't the whole world know about it?' And his heart wagged with joy like a lamb's tail.

The tailor tied the belt around his waist, and since he now thought that his bravery was too great for his workshop, he decided to go out into the world. Before he left, he searched his house for something to take with him, but he found only a piece of old cheese, which he put in his pocket. Outside the city gate he noticed a bird caught in the bushes, and the bird too found its way into his pocket. Now he bravely hit the road with his legs and pushed on. Since he was light and nimble, he did not become tired. His way led him up a mountain, and when he reached the highest peak, he came across a powerful giant who was sitting there comfortably and gazing about. The little tailor went up to him, addressed him fearlessly, and said, 'Good day, friend, you're sitting there and gazing at the great wide world, right? Well, I happen to be on my way into the world to try my luck. Would you like to come along?'

The giant looked at the tailor contemptuously and said, 'You crumb! You miserable creature!'

'Is that so!' the little tailor responded, and opened his coat to show the giant his belt. 'You can read for yourself what kind of man I am!'

The giant read 'Seven with one blow!' and thought that it meant the tailor had slain seven men. Therefore, he began to show some respect for the little fellow. Nevertheless, he wanted to test him first. So he took a stone in his hand and squeezed it until water began to drip from it.

'Do the same,' said the giant, 'if you have the strength.'

'Is that all?' the little tailor said. 'That's just child's play for a man like me.'

He reached into his pocket, took out the soft cheese, and squeezed it until the liquid ran out.

'That beats yours, doesn't it?' the tailor declared.

The giant did not know what to say, for he could not believe that such a little man was so strong. Next he picked up a stone and threw it so high that it could barely be seen with the naked eye.

'Now, you do the same, you midget!'

'That was a good throw,' said the tailor, 'but even so, the stone had to return to the ground in the end. Now, I'm going to throw one that won't ever come back.'

He reached into his pocket, took out the bird, and

threw it into the air. The bird was glad to be free and just kept climbing high in the sky and never returned.

'How did you like that little show, friend?' the tailor asked.

'You certainly can throw,' the giant said. 'But let's see if you can carry a decent load.'

He led the little tailor to a tremendous oak tree that had been cut down and was lying on the ground.

'If you're strong enough,' he said, 'help me carry the tree out of the forest.'

'Gladly,' answered the little man. 'You take the trunk on your shoulder, and I'll carry the branches and the twigs. After all, they're the heaviest.'

The giant lifted the trunk onto his shoulder, while the tailor sat down on a branch. Since the giant could not turn to look around, he had to carry the entire tree and the little tailor as well. Of course, the tailor was feeling good and was quite merry in the rear, so he began to whistle a little song called 'Three Little Tailors Who Went Out for a Ride,' as if carrying a tree were child's play. After the giant had carried the heavy load a good part of the way, he could go no further and cried out, 'Listen, I've got to let the tree drop.'

The tailor quickly jumped down, grabbed the tree with both his arms as if he had been carrying it, and said to the giant, 'You're such a huge fellow, and yet you can't even carry the tree!'

They walked on together, and when they came to a cherry tree, the giant seized the top, where the fruit was ripest. He bent it down, handed it to the tailor, and told him to eat some of the fruit. But the little tailor was much too weak to hold on to the treetop, and when the giant let go of it, the tailor was catapulted into the air. After he came down again, unharmed, the giant said, 'What's this? Don't tell me that you're not strong enough to hold on to that measly twig!'

'Don't worry, I've got plenty of strength,' the tailor responded. 'Do you think that something like that is really difficult for a man who's slain seven with one blow? I jumped over the tree because some huntsmen were shooting there in the bushes. Let's see if you can jump over it yourself.'

The giant tried but could not make it over the tree. He got stuck in the branches, so the little tailor got the better of him once again.

'Well, if you're such a brave fellow,' the giant said, 'come along with me to our cave and spend the night with us.'

The little tailor agreed and followed him. When they arrived in the cave, the other giants were still sitting by the fire, and each one had a roasted sheep in his hand and was eating it. The little tailor looked around and thought, It's certainly roomier in here than in my workshop.

The giant showed him to a bed and told him to lie down and have a good sleep. But the bed was too big for the little tailor, so he did not get into it but crept into a corner of the cave. When midnight came and the giant thought the little tailor was sound asleep, he got up, took a large iron bar, smashed the bed in two with one stroke, and thought he had put an end to the grasshopper. At dawn the next day the giants went into the forest and forgot all about the little tailor. But all of a sudden he came walking along quite merrily and boldly. The giants were horrified, for they feared he might slay them all. So they ran away as fast as they could.

The tailor just followed his pointed nose and kept going. After he had travelled about for a long time, he came to the courtyard of a royal palace. Since he felt tired, he lay down in the grass and fell asleep. While he was lying there, some people came, examined him from all sides, and read on his belt 'Seven with one blow.'

'Ah!' they said. 'What can a great warrior be doing here during peacetime? He must be a mighty lord.'

They went and reported it to the king and advised him that the warrior would be an important and useful man to have if war broke out and that the king should try to keep him there at all costs. The king appreciated the advice, and he sent one of his courtiers to the little tailor to offer him, after he woke up, a military position. The envoy remained standing near the sleeper until the tailor stretched his limbs and opened his eyes. Then the courtier made him the proposal.

'That's exactly why I've come here,' answered the little tailor. 'I am prepared to enter the king's service.'

So he was honourably received and given special living quarters. However, the soldiers were jealous of the little tailor and wished him a thousand miles away.

'What will come of all this?' they began saying among themselves. 'If we quarrel with him and he starts swinging, seven of us will fall with one blow. None of us can stand up to him.'

Once they had reached a decision, they all went to the king and asked for their discharge. 'We can't hold our own with a man who can slay seven with one blow,' they said.

The king was sad to lose all his faithful servants on account of one man, and he wished he had never laid eyes on him. He actually wanted to get rid of him, but he dared not dismiss him for fear that the tailor might kill him and all his people and take over the royal throne. The king thought about this for a long time, going back and forth in his mind until he hit upon a plan. Then he sent a message to the little tailor that contained a proposal for him—since he was such a great warrior. There were two giants living in a forest in the king's country, and they were causing great damage by robbing, murdering, ravaging, and burning. Anyone who came near the giants would be placing his life in danger. However, if the tailor could conquer these two giants and kill them, he would receive the king's only daughter for his wife and half the kingdom as dowry. Moreover, one hundred knights were to accompany him and lend him assistance.

That would be just right for a man like you! thought the little tailor. It's not every day somebody offers you a princess and half a kingdom. So he answered, 'Yes, indeed, I'll soon tame the giants, but I won't need the hundred knights. A man who's already slain seven with one blow does not need to be afraid of two.'

The little tailor set out, followed by the hundred knights. When he came to the edge of the forest, he said to his escorts, 'Just stay right here. I'll take care of the giants all by myself.'

After he scampered into the forest, he looked to the right and to the left. Soon he caught sight of the two giants, who were lying asleep under a tree and snoring so hard that the branches bobbed up and down. Since the little tailor was no slouch, he filled his pockets full of stones and carried them up a tree. When he got halfway up the tree, he slid out on a branch until he was perched right over the sleepers. Then he dropped one stone after another on the chest of one of the giants. It took some time before the giant felt anything. However, he finally woke up, shoved his companion, and said, 'Why are you hitting me?'

'You're dreaming,' the other said. 'I haven't been hitting you.'

They lay down to sleep again, and the tailor threw a stone at the other giant.

'What's the meaning of that?' the second giant cried out. 'Why are you throwing things at me?'

'I'm not throwing things at you,' the first one replied and growled.

They quarrelled for a while, but since they were tired, they let it pass, and their eyes closed again. Now the little tailor began his game anew. He took out his largest stone and threw it with all his might at the chest of the first giant.

'That does it!' he screamed, jumping up like a madman, and he slammed his companion against the tree so hard that it shook. The other giant paid him back in kind, and they both became so furious that they tore up trees and beat each other for some time until together they fell down dead. Then the little tailor jumped down from the tree.

'Lucky for me that they didn't tear up the tree I was sitting on,' he said. 'Otherwise, I'd have had to jump like a squirrel from one tree to another. Still, a man like me is always nimble.'

He drew his sword, gave the giants a few hearty blows on their chests, and went out of the forest to the knights.

'The work's done,' he said. 'I've put an end to the two of them. But the battle was a hard one. They became so desperate that they tore up trees to defend themselves. Yet, there's nothing anyone can do against a man like me who can slay seven with one blow.'

'Didn't they wound you?' the knights asked.

'It'll take more than two giants before that happens,' he answered. 'They couldn't even touch the hair on my head.'

The knights would not believe him and rode into the forest, where they found the giants swimming in their own blood, with uprooted trees lying all around them. Meanwhile, the little tailor went and demanded the reward promised by the king, but the king regretted his promise and thought up a new way to get rid of the hero.

'Before you can have my daughter and half the

kingdom,' he said to the tailor, 'you must put your heroism on display again and perform one more deed. There's a unicorn running around and causing great damage in the forest, and I want you to capture it.'

'Do you expect me to be afraid of a unicorn after facing two giants?' the tailor asked. 'Seven with one blow is more my style.'

He took some rope and an axe with him, went to the forest, and ordered his escorts once again to remain outside. He did not have to search long, for the unicorn did not keep him waiting: it charged right at him with its horn lowered, as if it meant to gore him without much ado.

'Easy does it, easy does it!' the tailor said. 'You won't get anywhere by doing things too hastily.'

The little tailor stood still and waited until the unicorn was very close. Then he jumped nimbly behind a tree, while the animal ran with all its might into the tree, thrusting its horn into the trunk so hard that it did not have the strength to pull it out again. This was the way the unicorn was caught.

'Now I've got the little bird,' the tailor said, and he came out from behind the tree, put the rope around the unicorn's neck, and chopped the horn free of the tree with the axe. When everything was all set, he led the unicorn away and took it to the king.

The king, however, still refused to give him the promised reward and made a third demand. Before the wedding could take place, the tailor was to capture a wild boar that was causing great damage in the forest, and the king's huntsmen were to lend him assistance.

'Gladly,' said the tailor. 'This is child's play.'

He did not take the huntsmen with him into the forest, and they were pleased, for the wild boar had already given them such rough treatment that they had no desire to chase it. When the boar caught sight of the tailor, it charged at him, foaming at the mouth and gnashing its teeth. The beast tried to trample him to the ground, but the nimble hero ducked into a nearby chapel and jumped right out again through one of the windows. The boar followed him inside, while the tailor ran around on the outside to shut the front door. Thus the raging beast was trapped, because it was much too heavy and clumsy to jump out the window. The little tailor called the huntsmen to see the prisoner with their own eyes, while the hero went to the king, who had to keep his promise this time, whether he liked it or not. So he gave the tailor his daughter and half the kingdom. If he had known that he had been dealing with a mere tailor and not a hero from the wars, the entire affair would have caused him even more grief than it did. As it was, the wedding was celebrated with great splendour but little joy, and a king was made out of a tailor.

After some time had passed, the young queen heard her husband talking in his sleep one night. 'Boy, finish that jerkin and mend the trousers fast, or else I'll give you a whack on your head with my yardstick!'

Now she knew the young lord was of humble origins, and the next morning she went to her father to complain and begged him to help her get rid of this husband who was nothing but a tailor. The king comforted her and said, 'Leave the door of your bedroom open tonight. My servants shall be waiting outside, and when he's asleep, they'll go inside, tie him up, and take him aboard a ship that will carry him out into the wide world.'

The king's daughter was content with this plan. But the king's armour-bearer had overheard everything, and since he was kindly disposed toward the young king, he told him all about the plot.

'I'm going to have to throttle their plans,' said the little tailor.

That evening he went to bed with his wife at the usual time. When she thought he had fallen asleep, she got up, opened the door, and returned to the bed. The little tailor, who was only pretending to be asleep, began to cry out in a clear voice, 'Boy, finish that jerkin and mend the trousers fast, or else I'll give you a whack on your head with my yardstick! I've slain seven with one blow, killed two giants, captured a unicorn, and trapped a wild boar. Do you think those fellows waiting outside my door could ever scare me?'

When the men heard the tailor talking like that, they were petrified and ran off as if the wild host of hell were after them, and none of them ever dared to do anything to him after this. Thus the tailor reigned as king and remained king for the rest of his life.

8
Cinderella

THE wife of a rich man fell ill, and as she felt her end approaching, she called her only daughter to her bedside and said, 'Dear child, be good and pious. Then the dear Lord shall always assist you, and I shall look down from heaven and take care of you.' She then closed her eyes and departed.

After her mother's death the maiden went every day to visit her grave and weep, and she remained good and pious. When winter came, snow covered the grave like a little white blanket, and by the time the sun had taken it off again in the spring, the rich man had a second wife, who brought along her two daughters. They had beautiful and fair features but nasty and wicked hearts. As a result a difficult time was ahead for the poor stepsister.

'Why should the stupid goose be allowed to sit in the parlour with us?' they said. 'Whoever wants to eat bread must earn it. Out with this kitchen maid!'

They took away her beautiful clothes, dressed her in an old grey smock, and gave her wooden shoes.

'Just look at the proud princess and how decked out she is!' they exclaimed with laughter, and led her into the kitchen.

They expected her to work hard there from morning till night. She had to get up before dawn, carry the water into the house, make the fire, cook, and wash. Besides this, her sisters did everything imaginable to cause her grief and make her look ridiculous. For instance, they poured peas and lentils into the hearth ashes so she had to sit there and pick them out. In the evening, when she was exhausted from working, they took away her bed, and she had to lie next to the hearth in the ashes. This is why she always looked so dusty and dirty and why they all called her Cinderella.

One day it happened that her father was going to the fair and asked his two stepdaughters what he could bring them.

'Beautiful dresses,' said one.

'Pearls and jewels,' said the other.

'And you, Cinderella?' he asked. 'What do you want?'

'Father,' she said, 'just break off the first twig that brushes against your hat on your way home and bring it to me.'

So he bought beautiful dresses, pearls, and jewels for the two stepsisters, and as he was riding through some green bushes on his return journey, a hazel twig brushed against him and knocked off his hat. So he broke off that twig and took it with him. When he arrived home, he gave his stepdaughters what they had requested, and Cinderella received the twig from the hazel bush. She thanked him, went to her mother's grave, planted the twig on it, and wept so hard that the tears fell on the twig and watered it. Soon the twig grew and quickly became a beautiful tree. Three times every day Cinderella would go and sit beneath it and weep and pray, and each time, a little white bird would also come to the tree. Whenever Cinderella expressed a wish, the bird would throw her whatever she had requested.

In the meantime, the king had decided to sponsor a three-day festival, and all the beautiful young girls in the country were invited so that his son could choose a bride. When the two stepsisters learned that they too had been summoned to make an appearance, they were in good spirits and called Cinderella.

'Comb our hair, brush our shoes, and fasten our

buckles!' they said. 'We're going to the wedding at the king's castle.'

Cinderella obeyed but wept, because she too would have liked to go to the ball with them, and so she asked her step-mother for permission to go.

'You, Cinderella!' she said. 'You're all dusty and dirty, and yet you want to go to the wedding? How can you go dancing when you've got no clothes or shoes?'

When Cinderella kept pleading, her stepmother finally said, 'I've emptied a bowlful of lentils into the ashes. If you can pick out all the lentils in two hours, you may have my permission to go.'

The maiden went through the back door into the garden and cried out, 'Oh, you tame pigeons, you turtledoves, and all you birds under heaven, come and help me pick

> the good ones for the little pot,
> the bad ones for your little crop.'

Two white pigeons came flying to the kitchen window, followed by the turtledoves. Eventually, all the birds under heaven swooped down, swarmed into the kitchen, and settled around the ashes. The pigeons bobbed their heads and began to peck, peck, peck, peck, and all the other birds also began to peck, peck, peck, peck, and they put all the good lentils into the bowl. It did not take longer than an hour for the birds to finish the work, whereupon they flew away. Happy, because she thought she would now be allowed to go to the wedding, the maiden brought the bowl to her stepmother. But her stepmother said, 'No, Cinderella. You don't have any clothes, nor do you know how to dance. Everyone would only laugh at you.'

When Cinderella started crying, the stepmother said, 'If you can pick two bowlfuls of lentils out of the ashes in one hour, I'll let you come along.' But she thought, She'll never be able to do it.

Then the stepmother dumped two bowlfuls of lentils into the ashes, and the maiden went through the back door into the garden and cried out, 'Oh, you tame pigeons, you turtledoves, and all you birds under heaven, come and help me pick

the good ones for the little pot,
the bad ones for your little crop.'

Two white pigeons came flying to the kitchen window, followed by the turtledoves. Eventually, all the birds under heaven swooped down, swarmed into the kitchen, and settled around the ashes. The pigeons bobbed their heads and began to peck, peck, peck, peck, and all the other birds also began to peck, peck, peck, peck, and they put all the good lentils into the bowl. Before half an hour had passed, they finished their work and flew away. Happy, because she thought she would now be allowed to go to the wedding, the maiden carried the bowls to her stepmother. But her stepmother said, 'Nothing can help you. I can't let you come with us because you don't have any clothes to wear and you don't know how to dance. We'd only be ashamed of you!'

Then she turned her back on Cinderella and hurried off with her two haughty daughters. When they had all departed, Cinderella went to her mother's grave beneath the hazel tree and cried out:

'Shake and wobble, little tree!
Let gold and silver fall all over me.'

The bird responded by throwing her a gold and silver dress and silk slippers embroidered with silver. She hastily slipped into the dress and went to the wedding. She looked so beautiful in her golden dress that her sisters and stepmother did not recognize her and thought she must be a foreign princess. They never imagined it could be Cinderella; they thought she was sitting at home in the dirt picking lentils out of the ashes.

Now, the prince approached Cinderella, took her by

the hand, and danced with her. Indeed, he would not dance with anyone else and would not let go of her hand. Whenever someone came and asked her to dance, he said, 'She's my partner.'

She danced well into the night, and when she wanted to go home, the prince said, 'I'll go along and escort you,' for he wanted to see whose daughter the beautiful maiden was. But she managed to slip away from him and got into her father's dovecote. Now the prince waited until her father came, and he told him that the unknown maiden had escaped into his dovecote. The old man thought, Could that be Cinderella? And he had an axe and pick brought to him so he could chop it down. However, no one was inside, and when they went into the house, Cinderella was lying in the ashes in her dirty clothes, and a dim little oil lamp was burning on the mantel of the chimney. Cinderella had swiftly jumped out the back of the dovecote and run to the hazel tree. There she had taken off the beautiful clothes and laid them on the grave. After the bird had taken them away, she had made her way into the kitchen, where she had seated herself in the grey ashes wearing her grey smock.

The next day when the festival had begun again and her parents and sisters had departed, Cinderella went to the hazel tree and cried out:

'Shake and wobble, little tree!
Let gold and silver fall all over me.'

The bird responded by throwing her a dress that was even more splendid than the one before. And when she appeared at the wedding in this dress, everyone was amazed by her beauty. The prince had been waiting for her, and when she came, he took her hand right away and danced with no one but her. When others went up to her and asked her to dance, he said, 'She's my partner.'

When evening came and she wished to leave, the prince followed her, wanting to see which house she went into, but she ran away from him and disappeared into the garden behind the house. There she went to a beautiful tall tree covered with the most wonderful pears, and she climbed up into the branches as nimbly as a squirrel. The prince did not know where she had gone, so he waited until her father came and said, 'The unknown maiden has slipped away from me, and I think she climbed the pear tree.'

The father thought, Can that be Cinderella? And he had an axe brought to him and chopped the tree down, but there was no one in it. When they went into the kitchen, Cinderella was lying in the ashes as usual, for she had jumped down on the other side of the tree, brought the beautiful clothes back to the bird, and put on her grey smock.

On the third day, when her parents and sisters had departed, Cinderella went to her mother's grave again and cried out to the tree:

> 'Shake and wobble, little tree!
> Let gold and silver fall all over me.'

The bird responded by throwing her a dress that was more magnificent and radiant than all the others she had received, and the slippers were pure gold. When she appeared at the wedding in this dress, the people were so astounded they did not know what to say. The prince danced with no one but her, and whenever someone asked her to dance, he said, 'She's my partner.'

When it was evening and Cinderella wished to leave, the prince wanted to escort her, but she slipped away from him so swiftly that he could not follow her. However, the prince had prepared for this with a trick: he had all the stairs coated with pitch, and when Cinderella went running down the stairs, her left slipper got stuck there. After the prince picked it up, he saw it was small and dainty and made of pure gold.

Next morning he carried it to Cinderella's father and

said, 'No one else shall be my wife but the maiden whose foot fits this golden shoe.'

The two sisters were glad to hear this because they had beautiful feet. The oldest took the shoe into a room to try it on, and her mother stood by her side. However, the shoe was too small for her, and she could not get her big toe into it. So her mother handed her a knife and said, 'Cut your toe off. Once you become queen, you won't have to walk anymore.'

The maiden cut her toe off, forced her foot into the shoe, swallowed the pain, and went out to the prince. He took her on his horse as his bride and rode off. But they had to pass the grave where the two pigeons were sitting on the hazel tree, and they cried out:

'Looky, look, look at the shoe that she took.
There's blood all over, and the shoe's too small.
She's not the bride you met at the ball.'

He looked down at her foot and saw the blood oozing out. So he turned his horse around, brought the false bride home again, and said that she was definitely not the right one and the other sister should try on the shoe. Then the second sister went into a room and was fortunate enough to get all her toes in, but her heel was too large. So her mother handed her a knife and said,

'Cut off a piece of your heel. Once you become queen, you won't have to walk anymore.'

The maiden cut off a piece of her heel, forced her foot into the shoe, swallowed the pain, and went out to the prince. He took her on his horse as his bride, and rode off with her. As they passed the hazel tree the two pigeons were sitting there, and they cried out:

'Looky, look, look at the shoe that she took.
There's blood all over, and the shoe's too small.
She's not the bride you met at the ball.'

He looked down at her foot and saw the blood oozing out of the shoe and staining her white stockings all red. Then he turned his horse around and brought the false bride home again.

'She isn't the right one either,' he said. 'Don't you have any other daughters?'

'No,' said the man. 'There's only little Cinderella, my dead wife's daughter, who's deformed, but she can't possibly be the bride.'

The prince told him to send the girl to him, but the mother responded, 'Oh, she's much too dirty and really shouldn't be seen.'

However, the prince demanded to see her, and Cinderella had to be called. First she washed her hands and face until they were clean, and then she went and curtsied before the prince, who handed her the golden shoe. She sat down on a stool, took her foot out of the heavy wooden shoe, and put it into the slipper that fit her perfectly. After she stood up and the prince looked her straight in the face, he recognized the beautiful maiden who had danced with him.

'This is my true bride!' he exclaimed.

The stepmother and the two sisters were horrified and turned pale with rage. However, the prince took Cinderella on his horse and rode away with her. As they passed the hazel tree the two white pigeons cried out:

'Looky, look, look
at the shoe that she took.
The shoe's just right, and there's no blood at all.
She's truly the bride you met at the ball.'

After the pigeons had made this known, they both came flying down and landed on Cinderella's shoulders, one on the right, the other on the left, and there they stayed.

On the day that the wedding with the prince was to take place, the two false sisters came to ingratiate themselves and to share in Cinderella's good fortune. When the bridal couple set out for the church, the oldest sister was on the right, the younger on the left. Suddenly the pigeons pecked out one eye from each of them. And as they came back from the church later on the oldest was on the left and the youngest on the right, and the pigeons pecked out the other eye from each sister. Thus they were punished with blindness for the rest of their lives due to their wickedness and malice.

9

The Mouse, the Bird, and the Sausage

ONCE upon a time a mouse, a bird, and a sausage came together and set up house. For a long time they lived together in peace and happiness, and they managed to increase their possessions by a considerable amount. The bird's job was to fly into the forest every day and bring back wood. The mouse had to carry water, light the fire, and set the table, while the sausage did the cooking.

Yet, those who lead the good life are always looking for ways to make it even better. And, one day, as the bird was flying about, he met another bird and boasted about how wonderful his life was. But the other bird called him a poor sap because he had to do all the hard work, while his companions just enjoyed themselves at home. Indeed, after the mouse started the fire and carried the water into the house, she generally went to her little room and rested until she was called to set the table. The sausage always stayed by the pot and kept an eye on the cooking, and right before mealtime he usually slid through the stew or vegetables to make sure everything was salted and seasoned properly. And that was all he did. When the bird came home and laid down his load, they would sit down at the table, and after finishing the meal they would sleep soundly until the next morning. Such was their glorious life.

However, the bird had been disturbed by what the other bird had said, and next day he refused to fly into the forest. He told his companions that he had been their slave long enough, and that they must have taken him for a fool. He demanded that they try another arrangement. The mouse and the sausage argued against this, but the bird would not be denied, and he insisted that they try a new way. So they drew lots, and it fell upon the sausage to get the wood from then on, while the mouse became cook, and the bird was to fetch water.

What happened?

After the sausage went to fetch the wood, the bird started the fire, and the mouse put the kettle on the stove. Then they waited for the sausage to return with the wood for the next day. However, the sausage was gone so long that the other two had an uneasy feeling, and the bird flew out a little way to meet him. Not far from their home, however, he encountered a dog, and he learned that this dog had considered the sausage free game and had grabbed him and swallowed him down. The bird was furious and accused the dog of highway robbery, but it was of no use, for the dog maintained he had found forged letters on the sausage, and therefore the sausage had had to pay for this with his life.

Now the bird sadly picked up the wood and carried it back home. He told the mouse what he had seen and heard, and they were very distressed. Nevertheless, they agreed to do the best they could and stay together. Meanwhile, the bird set the table, and the mouse prepared the meal. She intended to put the finishing touches on it by seasoning it and sliding through the vegetables the way the sausage used to do, but before she even reached the middle, she got stuck and had to pay for it with her life.

When the bird came to serve the meal, there was no cook. He became so upset that he scattered wood all over the place, calling and searching for the mouse. But his cook was no longer to be found. Due to the bird's distraction the wood soon caught fire, and the house went up in flames. When the bird rushed to fetch some water, however, the bucket slipped and fell into the well, dragging the bird along. Since he could not get himself out, he was left to drown.

10

Mother Holle

A WIDOW had two daughters, one who was beautiful and industrious, the other ugly and lazy. But she was fonder of the ugly and lazy one because she was her own daughter. The other had to do all the housework and carry out the ashes like a cinderella. Every day the poor maiden had to sit near a well by the road and spin and spin until her fingers bled.

Now, one day it happened that the reel became quite bloody, and when the maiden leaned over the well to rinse it, it slipped out of her hand and fell to the bottom. She burst into tears, ran to her stepmother, and told her about the accident. But the stepmother gave her a terrible scolding and was very cruel. 'If you've let the reel fall in,' she said, 'then you'd better get it out again.'

The maiden went back to the well but did not know where to begin. She was so distraught that she jumped into the well to fetch the reel, but she lost consciousness. When she awoke and regained her senses, she was in a beautiful meadow where the sun was shining and thousands of flowers were growing. She walked across this meadow, and soon she came to a baker's oven full of bread, but the bread was yelling, 'Take me out! Take me out, or else I'll burn. I've been baking long enough!'

She went up to the oven and took out all the loaves one by one with the baker's peel. After that she moved on and came to a tree full of apples.

'Shake me! Shake me!' the tree exclaimed. 'My apples are all ripe.'

She shook the tree till the apples fell like raindrops, and she kept shaking until they had all come down. After she had gathered them and stacked them in a pile, she moved on. At last she came to a small cottage where an old woman was looking out of a window. She had such big teeth that the maiden was scared and wanted to run away. But the old woman cried after her, 'Why are you afraid, my dear child? Stay with me, and if you do all the housework properly, everything will turn out well for you. Only you must make my bed nicely and carefully and give it a good shaking so the feathers fly. Then it will snow on earth, for I am Mother Holle.'*

Since the old woman had spoken so kindly to her, the maiden plucked up her courage and agreed to enter her service. She took care of everything to the old woman's satisfaction and always shook the bed so hard that the feathers flew about like snowflakes. In return, the woman treated her well: she never said an unkind word to the maiden, and she gave her roasted or boiled meat every day. After the maiden had spent a long time with Mother Holle, she became sad. At first she did not know what was bothering her, but finally she realized she was homesick. Even though everything was a thousand times better there than at home, she still had a desire to return. At last she said to Mother Holle, 'I've got a tremendous longing to return home, and even though everything is wonderful down here, I've got to return to my people.'

'I'm pleased that you want to return home,' Mother Holle responded, 'and since you've served me so faithfully, I myself shall bring you up there again.'

She took the maiden by the hand and led her to a large door. When it was opened and the maiden was standing

---

*Whenever it snowed in olden days, people in Hessia used to say Mother Holle is making her bed.

right beneath the doorway, an enormous shower of gold came pouring down, and all the gold stuck to her so that she became completely covered with it.

'I want you to have this because you've been so industrious,' said Mother Holle, and she also gave her back the reel that had fallen into the well. Suddenly the door closed, and the maiden found herself back up on earth, not far from her mother's house. When she entered the yard, the cock was sitting on the well and crowed:

'*Cock-a-doodle-doo!*
My golden maiden, what's new with you?'

She went inside to her mother, and since she was covered with so much gold, her mother and sister gave her a warm welcome. Then she told them all about what had happened to her, and when her mother heard how she had obtained so much wealth, she wanted to arrange it so her ugly and lazy daughter could have the same good fortune. Therefore, her daughter had to sit near the well and spin, and she made the reel bloody by sticking her fingers into a thornbush and pricking them. After that she threw the reel down into the well and jumped in after it. Just like her sister, she reached the beautiful meadow and walked along the same path.

When she came to the oven, the bread cried out again, 'Take me out! Take me out, or else I'll burn! I've been baking long enough!'

But the lazy maiden answered, 'I've no desire to get myself dirty!'

She moved on, and soon she came to the apple tree that cried out, 'Shake me! Shake me! My apples are all ripe.'

However, the lazy maiden replied, 'Are you serious? One of the apples could fall and hit me on my head.'

Thus she went on, and when she came to Mother Holle's cottage, she was not afraid because she had already heard of the old woman's big teeth, and she hired herself out to her right away. On the first day she made an effort to work hard and obey Mother Holle when the old woman told her what to do, for the thought of gold was on her mind. On the second day she started loafing, and on the third day she loafed even more. Indeed, she did not want to get out of bed in the morning, nor did she make Mother Holle's bed as she should have, and she certainly did not shake it hard so the feathers flew. Soon Mother Holle became tired of this and dismissed the maiden from her service. The lazy maiden was quite happy to go and expected that now the shower of gold would come. Mother Holle led her to the door, but as the maiden was standing beneath the doorway, a big kettle of pitch came pouring down over her instead of gold.

'That's a reward for your services,' Mother Holle said, and shut the door. The lazy maiden went home covered with pitch, and when the cock on the well saw her, it crowed:

'*Cock-a-doodle-doo!*
My dirty maiden, what's new with you?'

The pitch did not come off the maiden and remained on her as long as she lived.

11

Little Red Cap

ONCE upon a time there was a sweet little maiden. Whoever laid eyes upon her could not help but love her. But it was her grandmother who loved her most. She could never give the child enough. One time she made her a present, a small, red velvet cap, and since it was so becoming and the maiden insisted on always wearing it, she was called Little Red Cap.

One day her mother said to her, 'Come, Little Red Cap, take this piece of cake and bottle of wine and bring them to your grandmother. She's sick and weak, and this will strengthen her. Get an early start, before it becomes hot, and when you're out in the woods, be nice and good and don't stray from the path, otherwise you'll fall and break the glass, and your grandmother will get nothing. And when you enter her room, don't forget to say good morning, and don't go peeping in all the corners.'

'I'll do just as you say,' Little Red Cap promised her mother. Well, the grandmother lived out in the forest, half an hour from the village, and as soon as Little Red Cap entered the forest, she encountered the wolf. However, Little Red Cap did not know what a wicked sort of an animal he was and was not afraid of him.

'Good day, Little Red Cap,' he said.

'Thank you kindly, wolf.'

'Where are you going so early, Little Red Cap?'

'To Grandmother's.'

'What are you carrying under your apron?'

'Cake and wine. My grandmother's sick and weak, and yesterday we baked this so it will help her get well.'

'Where does your grandmother live, Little Red Cap?'

'Another quarter of an hour from here in the forest. Her house is under the three big oak trees. You can tell it by the hazel bushes,' said Little Red Cap.

The wolf thought to himself, This tender young thing is a juicy morsel. She'll taste even better than the old woman. You've got to be real crafty if you want to catch them both. Then he walked next to Little Red Cap, and after a while he said, 'Little Red Cap, just look at the beautiful flowers that are growing all around you!

Why don't you look around? I believe you haven't even noticed how lovely the birds are singing. You march along as if you were going straight to school, and yet it's so delightful out here in the woods!'

Little Red Cap looked around and saw how the rays of the sun were dancing through the trees back and forth and how the woods were full of beautiful flowers. So she thought to herself, If I bring Grandmother a bunch of fresh flowers, she'd certainly like that. It's still early, and I'll arrive on time.

So she ran off the path and plunged into the woods to look for flowers. And each time she plucked one, she thought she saw another even prettier flower and ran after it, going deeper and deeper into the forest. But the wolf went straight to the grandmother's house and knocked at the door.

'Who's out there?'

'Little Red Cap. I've brought you some cake and wine. Open up.'

'Just lift the latch,' the grandmother called. 'I'm too weak and can't get up.'

The wolf lifted the latch, and the door sprang open. Then he went straight to the grandmother's bed without saying a word and gobbled her up. Next he put on her clothes and her nightcap, lay down in her bed, and drew the curtains.

Meanwhile, Little Red Cap had been running around and looking for flowers, and only when she had as many as she could carry did she remember her grandmother and continue on the way to her house again. She was puzzled when she found the door open, and as she entered the room, it seemed so strange inside that she thought, Oh, my God, how frightened I feel today, and usually I like to be at Grandmother's. She called out, 'Good morning!' But she received no answer. Next she went to the bed and drew back the curtains. There lay her grandmother with her cap pulled down over her face giving her a strange appearance.

'Oh, Grandmother, what big ears you have!'

'The better to hear you with.'

'Oh, Grandmother, what big hands you have!'

'The better to grab you with.'

'Oh, Grandmother, what a terribly big mouth you have!'

'The better to eat you with!'

No sooner did the wolf say that than he jumped out of bed and gobbled up poor Little Red Cap. After the wolf had satisfied his desires, he lay down in bed again, fell asleep, and began to snore very loudly. The huntsman happened to be passing by the house and thought to himself, The way the old woman's snoring, you'd better see if anything's wrong. He went into the room, and when he came to the bed, he saw the wolf lying in it.

'So I've found you at last, you old sinner,' said the huntsman. 'I've been looking for you for a long time.'

He took aim with his gun, and then it occurred to him that the wolf could have eaten the grandmother and that she could still be saved. So he did not shoot but took some scissors and started cutting open the sleeping wolf's belly. After he made a couple of cuts, he saw the little red cap shining forth, and after he made a few more cuts, the girl jumped out and exclaimed, 'Oh, how frightened I was! It was so dark in the wolf's body.'

Soon the grandmother came out. She was alive but could hardly breathe. Little Red Cap quickly fetched some large stones, and they filled the wolf's body with them. When he awoke and tried to run away, the stones were too heavy so he fell down at once and died.

All three were quite delighted. The huntsman skinned the fur from the wolf and went home with it. The grandmother ate the cake and drank the wine that Little Red Cap had brought, and soon she regained her health. Meanwhile, Little Red Cap thought to herself, Never again will you stray from the path by yourself and go into the forest when your mother has forbidden it.

*

There is also another tale about how Little Red Cap returned to her grandmother one day to bring some baked goods. Another wolf spoke to her and tried to entice her to leave the path, but this time Little Red Cap was on her guard. She went straight ahead and told her grandmother that she had seen the wolf, that he had wished her good day, but that he had had such a mean look in his eyes that 'he would have eaten me up if we hadn't been on the open road.'

'Come,' said the grandmother. 'We'll lock the door so he can't get in.'

Soon after, the wolf knocked and cried out, 'Open up, Grandmother. It's Little Red Cap, and I've brought you some baked goods.'

But they kept quiet and did not open the door. So Greyhead circled the house several times and finally jumped on the roof. He wanted to wait till evening when Little Red Cap would go home. He intended to sneak after her and eat her up in the darkness. But the grandmother realized what he had in mind. In front of the house was a big stone trough, and she said to the child, 'Fetch the bucket, Little Red Cap. I cooked sausages yesterday. Get the water they were boiled in and pour it into the trough.'

Little Red Cap kept carrying the water until she had filled the big, big trough. Then the smell of sausages reached the nose of the wolf. He sniffed and looked down. Finally, he stretched his neck so far that he could no longer keep his balance on the roof. He began to slip and fell right into the big trough and drowned. Then Little Red Cap went merrily on her way home, and no one harmed her.

12

The Bremen Town Musicians

AMAN had a donkey who had diligently carried sacks of grain to the mill for many years. However, the donkey's strength was reaching its end, and he was less and less fit for the work. His master thought it was time to dispense with him and save on food, but the donkey got wind of what was in store for him. So he ran away and set out for Bremen, where he thought he could become a town musician. After travelling some distance he came across a hunting dog lying on the roadside and panting as if he had run himself ragged.

'Why are you panting so hard, you old hound dog?' asked the donkey.

'Ah,' the dog said, 'because I'm old and getting weaker every day. Now I can't even hunt anymore, and my master wanted to kill me. Naturally, I cleared out, but how am I going to earn a living now?'

'You know what,' said the donkey, 'I'm going to Bremen to become a town musician, and you can come with me and also join the town band. I'll play the lute, and you, the drums.'

The dog agreed, and they continued on their way. Soon after, they encountered a cat sitting on the roadside, making a long and sorry face.

'Well, what's gone wrong with you, old whiskers?' asked the donkey.

'How can I be cheerful when my neck's in danger?' the cat replied. 'My mistress wanted to drown me because I'm getting on in years. Moreover, my teeth are dull, and I'd rather sit behind the stove and purr than chase after mice. Anyway, I managed to escape, but now I don't know what to do or where to go.'

'Why don't you come along with us to Bremen? You know a great deal about night serenades, and you can become a town musician.'

The cat thought that was a good idea and went along. Then the three fugitives passed a farmyard where a rooster was perched on the gate and crowing with all his might.

'Your crowing gives me the chills,' said the donkey. 'Why are you screaming like this?'

'I've predicted good weather for today,' said the rooster, 'because it's Our Lady's Day, when she washes the Christ Child's shirts and sets them out to dry. Still, my mistress has no mercy. Tomorrow's Sunday, and guests are coming. So she told the cook to cut off my head tonight because she wants to eat me in the soup tomorrow. Now you know why I'm screaming my lungs out, while there's still time to scream.'

'That's foolish, redhead!' said the donkey. 'You'd be smarter if you'd come along with us. We're off to Bremen. Why die when you can find a better life somewhere else? You've got a good voice, and if we make music together, it's sure to be a good thing.'

The rooster liked the proposal, and all four of them continued the journey together. However, they could not reach the town of Bremen in one day, and by evening they came to a forest, where they decided to spend the night. The donkey and the dog lay down under a big tree, while the cat and rooster climbed up and settled down in the branches. To be on the safe side, the rooster flew to the top. Before he went to sleep, he looked around in all directions, and it seemed to him he saw a light burning in the distance. He called to his companions and told them there must be a house nearby, since he could see something shining.

'Well, this place is not all that comfortable, so let's get moving,' said the donkey.

The dog thought some bones and meat would be just right for him, and they all set out toward the light. Soon it began to grow brighter, and it got even more so once they reached a brightly lit robbers' den. Since the donkey was the tallest, he went up to the window and looked inside.

'What do you see, grey steed?' the rooster asked.

'What do I see?' replied the donkey. 'I see a table covered with wonderful food and drinks and some robbers sitting there and enjoying themselves.'

'That would be just the thing for us!' said the rooster.

'You're right!' said the donkey. 'If only we could get in!'

Then the animals discussed what they would have to do to drive the robbers away. Finally they hit upon a plan. The donkey was to stand upright and place his forefeet on the windowsill. The dog was to jump on the donkey's back, and the cat was to climb upon the dog. When that was done, the rooster was to fly up and perch on the cat's head. After they put their plan into action, the signal was given, and they all started to make music together: the donkey brayed, the dog barked, the cat meowed, and the rooster crowed. Then they crashed into the room, shattering the window. Startled by the horrible cries, the robbers were convinced that a ghost had burst into the room, and they fled in great fright into the forest. Then the four companions sat down at the table, delightedly gathered up the leftovers, and ate as if there were no tomorrow.

When the four minstrels were finished, they put out the light and looked for a place to sleep, each according to his nature and custom. The donkey lay down on the dung heap in the yard, the dog behind the door, the cat on the hearth near the warm ashes, and the rooster on the beam of the roof. Since they were tired from their long journey, they soon fell asleep.

When it was past midnight and the robbers saw from the distance that there was no light in the house and everything seemed peaceful, the leader of the band said, 'We shouldn't have let ourselves be scared out of our wits.'

He ordered one of the robbers to return and check out the house. When he found everything quiet, the robber went into the kitchen to light a candle and mistook the cat's glowing fiery eyes for live coals. So he held a match to them to light a fire, but the cat did not appreciate the joke. He jumped into the robber's face, spitting and scratching, and the robber was so terribly frightened that he ran out the back door. However, the dog was lying there and bit him in the leg. When the robber raced across the yard, he passed the dung heap, and here the donkey gave him a solid kick with his hind foot. All this noise woke the rooster from his sleep, and he became lively again and crowed '*Cock-a-doodle-doo!*' from his beam.

The robber ran back to the leader as fast as he could and said, 'There's a gruesome witch in the house! She spat on me and scratched my face with her long claws. At the door there's a man with a knife, and he stabbed my leg. In the yard there's a black monster who beat me with a wooden club. And on top of the roof the judge was sitting and screaming "Bring me the rascal!" I got out of there as fast as I could!'

Since that time the robbers have never dared return to the house, but the four Bremen Town musicians liked the place so much that they stayed on forever.

And the last person who told this tale has still got warm lips.

13

The Devil With the Three Golden Hairs

ONCE upon a time there was a poor woman who gave birth to a little son, and since he was born with a caul, it was prophesied he would marry the king's daughter by the time he was fourteen. Soon after, the king happened to come to the village, but no one knew that he was the king. When he asked the people about the latest news, they answered, 'Just recently a child was born with a caul. Now fortune will shine on him in all his endeavours. Indeed, it's been prophesied that he'll marry the king's daughter by the time he's fourteen.'

Since the king had an evil heart and was disturbed by the prophecy, he went to the boy's parents and pretended to be friendly.

'I know that you're very poor people,' he said. 'So let me have your child, and I'll take good care of him.'

At first they refused, but when the stranger offered them a great deal of gold for him, they thought, Since he's fortune's favourite, it's bound to turn out well for him. Therefore, they finally agreed and gave the child to the stranger.

The king laid him in a box and rode away with him until he came to a deep river. Then he threw the box into the water and thought, Well, now I've rid my daughter of an undesirable suitor. But the box did not sink. Instead, it floated like a little boat, and not a single drop of water got into it. The box drifted to within two miles of the king's capital city, where it was blocked from going any further by a mill dam. Fortunately, the miller's apprentice was standing on the bank and saw it. Thinking he had found a great treasure, he used a hook to pull the box ashore. However, when he opened it, he discovered a lovely-looking boy who was alive and well. So he took the boy to the miller and his wife because they did not have any children. Indeed, they were delighted and said, 'God has blessed us with this gift.'

They took good care of the foundling and made sure that he was raised with all the best virtues. Now, one day the king happened to get caught in a thunderstorm and arrived at the mill. There he asked the miller and his wife whether the big boy was their son.

'No,' they answered. 'He's a foundling. Fourteen years ago he floated down to the mill dam, and our apprentice fished him out of the water.'

The king realized that it was no one else but fortune's favourite, whom he had thrown into the water.

'My good people,' he said, 'would it be possible for the young boy to carry a letter to the queen? I'll give him two gold coins as a reward.'

'As Your Majesty commands,' they answered and told the young boy to get ready. Then the king wrote a letter to the queen, which said, 'As soon as the boy arrives with this letter, he's to be killed and buried. All this is to be done before my return.'

The boy set out with this letter but lost his way, and at night he came to a great forest. When he saw a small light in the darkness, he began walking toward it and soon reached a little cottage. Upon entering, he discovered an old woman sitting all alone by the fire. She was startled by the sight of him and asked, 'Where did you come from and where are you going?'

'I'm coming from the mill,' he answered, 'and I'm on my way to deliver a letter to the queen. But since I've lost my way, I'd like to spend the night here.'

'You poor boy,' said the woman. 'You've stumbled on a robbers' den. When they come home, they'll kill you.'

'I don't care if they come,' the young boy said. 'I'm not afraid. Besides, I'm too tired to go any further.'

He stretched himself out on a bench and fell asleep. Soon after, the robbers arrived and angrily asked who the strange boy was that was lying there.

'Oh,' said the old woman, 'he's just an innocent child who's lost his way in the forest, and I've taken him in out of pity. He's carrying a letter to the queen.'

The robbers opened the letter and read it, and they discovered that the boy was to be killed immediately upon arrival. The hard-hearted robbers felt sorry for him, and the leader of the band tore up the letter and wrote another one, which said that the boy was to wed the king's daughter immediately upon arrival. They let him sleep peacefully on the bench until morning, and when he awoke, they showed him the right path out of the forest.

Once the queen received the letter and read it, she did as it said: she prepared a splendid wedding feast, and the king's daughter was married to fortune's favourite. Since the boy was handsome and friendly, she was quite happy and content to live with him. After some time passed, the king returned to the castle and saw that the prophecy had been fulfilled and that fortune's favourite had married his daughter.

'How did it happen?' he asked. 'I gave entirely different orders in my letter.'

The queen handed him the letter and told him to see what it said for himself. The king read the letter and realized right away that it had been switched for the one he wrote. He asked the young boy what had happened to the letter he had been entrusted to carry and why he had delivered another instead.

'I know nothing about it,' he answered. 'It must have been switched while I was asleep in the forest.'

'Well, you're not going to get things as easily as you think!' said the king in a rage. 'Whoever wants to have my daughter must first travel to hell and fetch three golden hairs from the devil's head. If you bring me what I want, you may keep my daughter.'

This way the king hoped to get rid of him forever, but fortune's favourite answered, 'You can count on me to fetch the golden hairs. I'm not afraid of the devil.'

He then took his leave and began the journey. His way led him to a big city, where the watchman at the gate asked him what kind of trade he practised and what he knew.

'I know everything,' fortune's favourite said.

'Then you can do us a favour,' the watchman responded, 'and tell us why the fountain at our marketplace, which used to gush with wine, has run dry and doesn't even provide us with water anymore.'

'Just wait until I return,' he answered, 'and you shall learn the reason why.'

He continued on his way, and when he came to another city, the watchman at the gate again asked him what trade he practised and what he knew.

'I know everything,' he said.

'Then you can do us a favour and tell us why a tree in our city that used to bear golden apples doesn't produce even leaves anymore.'

'Just wait until I return,' he answered, 'and you shall learn the reason why.'

He went further and came to a big river that he had to cross. The ferryman asked him what kind of trade he practised and what he knew.

'I know everything,' he said.

'Then you can do me a favour,' said the ferryman, 'and tell me why I must take people back and forth without relief.'

'Just wait until I return,' he answered, 'and you shall learn the reason why.'

When fortune's favourite reached the other side of the river, he found the entrance to hell. It was dark and sooty inside, and the devil was not at home. However, his grandmother was sitting in a large easy chair.

'What do you want?' she asked him, but she did not look very wicked.

'I'd like to have three golden hairs from the devil's head,' he replied, 'or else I won't be able to keep my wife.'

'That's a lot to ask,' she said. 'If the devil comes home and finds you, it will cost you your neck. But, since I feel sorry for you, I'll see if I can help.'

She changed him into an ant and said, 'Crawl into the folds of my skirt. You'll be safe there.'

'All right,' he answered. 'That's fine, but there are still three things I'd like to know: Why has a fountain that used to gush with wine become dry and why doesn't it produce even water now? Why does a tree that used to bear golden apples no longer bear even leaves anymore? And, why must a ferryman take people back and forth without relief?'

'Those are difficult questions,' she replied. 'But keep still and quiet, and pay attention to what the devil says when I pull out the three golden hairs.'

At nightfall the devil came home. No sooner did he enter the house than he noticed the air was not pure.

'I smell, I smell the flesh of a man,' he said. 'Something's wrong here.'

Then he looked in all the nooks and crannies and searched around but could not find anything. The grandmother scolded him. 'I've just swept,' she said, 'and put everything in order. Now you're messing it all up again. You're always smelling the flesh of men. Just sit down and eat your supper!'

After he had something to eat and drink, he was tired and laid his head in his grandmother's lap. Then he told her to pick the lice from his head for a while. Soon after, he fell asleep and began to snore and wheeze. Now the old woman grabbed hold of a golden hair, ripped it out, and put it down beside her.

'*Ouch!*' screamed the devil. 'What are you doing to me?'

'I had a bad dream,' the grandmother said, 'and grabbed hold of your hair.'

'What did you dream?' the devil asked.

'I dreamed there was a fountain at the marketplace that used to gush with wine, and it ran dry. It even stopped providing water. Why do you think that happened?'

'Ha!' the devil replied. 'If they only knew! There's a toad sitting underneath a stone in the fountain. If they kill it, the wine will flow again.'

The grandmother began lousing him again until he fell asleep and snored so loudly that the windows trembled. Then she tore out a second hair.

'*Hey!* What are you doing?' the devil screamed angrily.

'I didn't mean it,' she said. 'I did it in a dream.'

'What did you dream this time?' he asked.

'I dreamed that in a kingdom there was an apple tree that used to bear golden apples, and now it can't produce even leaves. Why do you think that happened?'

'Ha!' the devil replied. 'If they only knew! There's a mouse gnawing at the roots. When they kill the mouse, the tree will bear golden apples again. If it continues to gnaw much longer, the tree will wither completely away. Now leave me alone with your dreams! If you disturb me in my sleep one more time, I'll give you a good hard slap!'

The grandmother spoke softly to him and loused him again until he fell asleep and began snoring. Then she grabbed hold of the third golden hair and tore it out. The devil jumped up, screamed, and was about to teach her a lesson, but she calmed him down again and said, 'What can you do against dreams?'

'What did you dream?' he asked and was curious in spite of himself.

'I dreamed of a ferryman who complained that he had to take people back and forth without relief. Why do you think he's got to do this?'

'Ha! The fool!' the devil replied. 'He just has to put

the pole into the hand of someone who wants to get across, and this person will have to do the ferrying, and the ferryman will be free.'

Since the grandmother had now torn out the three golden hairs and the three questions had been answered, she let the old snake rest peacefully and sleep until daybreak. Thereupon the devil departed, and the old woman took the ant from the fold in her skirt and restored fortune's favourite to his human form.

'Here are the three golden hairs,' she said. 'You undoubtedly heard what the devil said to your three questions.'

'Yes,' he answered. 'I heard everything, and I'll certainly remember it all.'

'Then you have what you need,' she said, 'and now you can move on.'

He thanked the old woman for helping him out of his predicament and left hell in a happy mood, for he had achieved what he had set out to do. When he came to the ferryman, he was obliged to keep his promise.

'Take me across first,' said fortune's favourite, 'and I'll tell you how you can be relieved of your work.'

When he was on the other side, he gave him the devil's advice. 'When someone comes and wants to be taken across, just put the pole in his hands.'

Then fortune's favourite moved on, and when he came to the city where the barren tree stood, the watchman was also expecting his answer. So fortune's favourite told him what he had heard from the devil. 'Kill the mouse that's been gnawing on the roots, then the tree will bear apples again.'

The watchman thanked him and rewarded him with two donkeys laden with gold. Next fortune's favourite went to the city where the fountain had run dry and told the watchman what the devil had said. 'There's a toad in the fountain sitting underneath a stone. You must find it and kill it. Then the fountain will gush with plenty of wine again.'

The watchman thanked him and also gave him two donkeys laden with gold. Finally, fortune's favourite returned home to his wife, who was very happy to see him again and to hear how successful he had been. He brought the king what he had demanded, the three golden hairs, and when the king saw the four donkeys laden with gold, he was very pleased and said, 'Now all the conditions have been fulfilled, and you may keep my daughter. But, my dear son-in-law, tell me, where did you get all this gold? It's such a great treasure!'

'I found it on the ground and picked it up after I crossed a river,' he replied. 'The bank is completely covered with gold instead of sand.'

'Can I also get some?' asked the king, who was very greedy.

'As much as you like,' he answered. 'There's a ferryman at the river. Just let him take you across, and you'll be able to fill your sacks to the brim.'

The greedy king set out as fast as he could, and when he came to the river, he signalled the ferryman to take him across. The ferryman came and told him to get into the boat, and when they reached the other side, the ferryman put the pole into his hand and ran away. From then on the king was compelled to ferry people back and forth as punishment for his sins.

'Is he still ferrying?'

'Why, of course. Do you think someone's about to take the pole away from him?'

14
Thumbling

THERE was once a poor farmer who was sitting by the hearth one evening and poking the fire, while his wife was spinning nearby.

'How sad that we have no children!' he said. 'It's so quiet here, and other homes are full of noise and life.'

'Yes,' his wife responded with a sigh. 'If only we had a child, just one, even if it were tiny and no bigger than my thumb, I'd be quite satisfied. We'd surely love him with all our hearts.'

Now it happened that the wife fell sick, and after seven months she gave birth to a child that was indeed perfect in every way but no bigger than a thumb.

'It's just as we wished,' they said, 'and he shall be dear to our hearts.'

Because of his size they named him Thumbling. Although they fed him a great deal, the child did not grow any bigger but stayed exactly as he was at birth. Still, he had an intelligent look and soon revealed himself to be a clever and nimble fellow who succeeded in all his endeavours.

One day the farmer was getting ready to chop wood in the forest, and he said to himself, 'If only there were someone who could drive the wagon into the forest after me.'

'Oh, Father,' cried Thumbling, 'I'll take care of the wagon. You can count on me. It'll be in the forest whenever you want it.'

The man laughed and said, 'How're you going to manage that? You're much too small to handle the reins.'

'That's not important,' Thumbling said. 'I just need Mother to hitch the horse, and I'll sit down in his ear and tell him which way to go.'

'Well,' answered the father. 'Let's try it once.'

When the time came, the mother hitched up the horse and put Thumbling in his ear. Then the little fellow shouted commands. 'Giddyap! Whoa! Giddyap!' Everything went quite well, as if a master were at the reins, and the wagon drove the right way toward the forest. As it took a turn and the little fellow cried out

'Giddyap! Giddyap!' two strangers happened to come along.

'My word!' said one of them. 'What's that? There goes a wagon without a driver, and yet, I hear a voice calling to the horse.'

'There's something strange going on here,' said the other. 'Let's follow the wagon and see where it stops.'

The wagon drove right into the forest up to the spot where the wood was being chopped. When Thumbling saw his father, he called out to him, 'You see, Father, here I am with the wagon! Now just get me down.'

The father grabbed the horse with his left hand, and with his right he took his little son out of its ear. Then Thumbling plopped himself sprightly on a piece of straw. When the two men caught sight of him, they were so amazed that they could not open their mouths. One of the men took the other aside and said, 'Listen, that little fellow could make our fortune if we exhibit him in the big city for money. Let's buy him.'

They went to the farmer and said, 'Sell us the little man, and we'll see to it that he's treated well.'

'No,' answered the father, 'he's the apple of my eye, and I wouldn't sell him for all the gold in the world.'

But when Thumbling heard the offer, he crawled up the pleat of his father's coat, stood up on his shoulder, and whispered into his ear, 'Father, don't you worry. Just give me away. I'll manage to get back soon.'

So the father gave him to the two men for a tidy sum of money.

'Where do you want to sit?' they asked Thumbling.

'Oh, set me on the brim of your hat. Then I'll be able to walk back and forth and look at the countryside without any danger of falling off.'

They did as he requested, and after Thumbling took leave of his father, they set out on their way. They walked until dusk, and just then the little fellow said, 'Put me down. It's urgent.'

'Just stay up there,' said the man on whose head he was sitting. 'I don't mind. I'm used to the birds dropping something on me every now and then.'

'No,' said Thumbling. 'I know what's proper. Hurry up and put me down!'

The man took off his hat and set the little fellow on a field by the wayside. Then Thumbling jumped and crawled among the clods scattered here and there on the ground. Suddenly he slipped into a mousehole, which was what he had been looking for.

'Good-bye, gentlemen!' he cried out, laughing at them. 'Just go home without me.'

They ran over to the spot and stuck sticks into the mousehole, but their efforts were in vain. Thumbling kept retreating farther and farther into the hole. When it became pitch dark outside, the two men had to head back home, full of rage but with empty purses.

When Thumbling saw they were gone, he crawled out of the underground passage and said, 'It's so dangerous walking in the field after dark. You can easily break a neck or a leg.' Fortunately, he stumbled upon an empty snail shell. 'Thank goodness,' he said. 'I can spend the night here in safety.' After he got inside and was about to go to sleep, he heard two men walking by and talking.

'How are we going to manage to get the rich pastor's money and silver?' one of them asked.

'I can tell you how,' said Thumbling, interrupting them.

'What was that?' the other thief said in horror. 'I heard a voice!'

The two men remained standing there and listened. Then Thumbling spoke again. 'Take me with you, and I'll help you.'

'Where are you, then?'

'Just look on the ground and pay attention to where the voice is coming from,' he answered.

After a while the thieves found him and lifted him up in the air.

'You little tyke,' they said. 'How are you going to help us?'

'Look,' he answered, 'I'll crawl between the iron bars into the pastor's room, and I'll hand you whatever you want.'

'All right,' they said. 'Let's see what you can do.'

When they got to the pastor's house, Thumbling crawled into the room and immediately cried out with all his might, 'Do you want to have everything that's here?'

The thieves were alarmed and said, 'Speak softly so nobody wakes up.'

But Thumbling pretended not to understand and screamed once more, 'What do you want? Do you want everything that's here?'

The maid, who was sleeping in the room next door, heard the voices. She sat up in bed and listened. But the thieves had retreated some distance out of fright. Gradually they regained their courage and thought, The little fellow is just teasing us. So they came back and whispered to him, 'Now, be serious and hand us something.'

Once again Thumbling screamed as loud as he could, 'Sure, I'll give you all you want! Just reach in here with your hands!'

The maid was still listening and heard everything quite clearly. She jumped out of bed and stumbled into the room through the door. The thieves rushed away and ran as if a wild huntsman were after them. Since the maid could not see a thing, she went to light a candle. When she returned with it, Thumbling had left without being seen and headed into the barn. The maid searched the entire place, but after finding nothing, she went back to bed and thought she had only been seeing and hearing things in her dreams.

In the meantime, Thumbling climbed about in the hay and found himself a nice place to sleep. He intended to rest there until daybreak and then return home to his parents. However, life did not turn out the way he expected! Indeed, there is a great deal of sorrow and misery in this world! When the day dawned, the maid got out of bed to feed the cows. Her first round was in the barn where she picked up an armful of hay, and it was that very hay in which Thumbling was lying asleep. Indeed, he was sleeping so soundly that he did not notice a thing, nor did he wake up until he was in the jaws of a cow that picked him up with the hay.

'Oh, God!' he exclaimed. 'How did I get into this churning mill?'

But soon he realized where he was, and he had to be careful not to get caught between the cow's teeth or else he would be crushed. Soon he slipped down into the cow's stomach with the hay.

'Hey, they forgot to put windows in this room!' he

said. 'No sunshine possible here, and it seems they won't be bringing candles.'

He was not very pleased with the accommodations, and the worst of it was that the fresh hay kept coming through the door, and the space became cramped. At last his fright became so great that he cried out as loud as he could, 'No more fodder! No more fodder!'

The maid was milking the cow when she heard the voice without seeing anybody. She recognized it as the same voice she had heard during the night and became so frightened that she slipped off her stool and spilled the milk. She ran in haste to her master and exclaimed, 'Oh, God, Pastor! The cow just talked!'

'You're crazy,' responded the parson, but he decided to go into the barn himself to check on the matter. No sooner did he set foot in the barn than Thumbling cried out once again, 'No more fodder! No more fodder!'

Now even the parson became frightened, and he concluded that an evil spirit had got into the cow and ordered it to be killed. So the cow was slaughtered, and the stomach where Thumbling was stuck was thrown on the dung heap. Thumbling had great difficulty working his way through, but he managed to find a way out for himself. However, just as he was about to stick out his head, another misfortune occurred: a hungry wolf came running by and swallowed the whole stomach with one gulp. Yet, Thumbling did not lose courage. Perhaps, he thought, the wolf will listen to reason. So he called to him from his belly, 'Dear wolf, I happen to know where you can find a wonderful meal.'

'Tell me where,' said the wolf.

'It's in such and such a house. You have to crawl through the drain, and then you'll find all the cake, bacon, and sausages you want to eat.'

Thumbling gave him an exact description of his father's house, and the wolf did not have to be told twice. When night came, he squeezed his way through the drain into the pantry and ate to his heart's content. When he had eaten his fill, he wanted to go back outside. However, he had become so fat that he could not return the same way. Thumbling had counted on this and began making a racket in the wolf's belly. Indeed, he threw a fit and yelled as loud as he could.

'Will you be quiet!' said the wolf. 'You're waking everyone up.'

'So what!' said the little fellow. 'You've had your fill. Now I want to have some fun too.' And he kept screaming with all his might.

At last his father and mother woke up, ran to the pantry, and looked through a crack in the door. When they saw the wolf in there, they ran back. The man fetched an axe, and the woman, a scythe.

'Stay behind me,' said the man as they approached the pantry.

'If my blow doesn't kill him right away, then swing your scythe and cut his body to pieces.'

When Thumbling heard his father's voice, he cried out, 'Dear Father, I'm in here! I'm stuck in the wolf's body.'

'Thank God!' said his father, full of joy. 'Our dear son has come back to us.' And he told his wife to put down the scythe so Thumbling would not be hurt. Then he lifted his arm and gave the wolf such a blow on his head that he fell down dead. He and his wife fetched a pair of scissors and a knife, cut the wolf's body open, and pulled the little fellow out.

'Oh,' said the father, 'we've been worried to death about you!'

'Yes, Father, I've travelled about the world a great deal. Thank God that I can breathe fresh air again!'

'Where in heaven's name have you been?'

'Oh, Father, I was in a mousehole, a cow's stomach, and a wolf's belly. Now I'm going to stay with you.'

'And we shall never sell you again for all the riches in the world,' said his parents. They hugged and kissed their dear Thumbling. Then they gave him something to eat and drink and had some new clothes made for him because his old ones had been spoiled during his journey.

15

The Wedding of Mrs Fox

FIRST TALE

Once upon a time there was an old fox with nine tails who believed his wife was unfaithful to him and wanted to put her to the test. So he stretched himself out under the bench, kept perfectly still, and pretended to be dead as a doornail. Mrs Fox went up to her room and shut herself in, while her maid, Miss Cat, went to the hearth and started cooking. When it became known that the old fox had died, suitors began to present themselves. Now, the maid heard someone outside knocking at the door, and when she went and opened it, there was a young fox, who said:

'What are you doing now, Miss Cat?
Are you wide awake or asleep on the mat?'

She answered:

'I'm not asleep. I'm wide awake.
What do you think, for goodness sake!
I'm using butter to brew warm beer.
You can be my guest if you stay right here.'

'No, thank you, Miss Cat,' said the fox. 'But tell me,
what's Mrs Fox doing?'

'She's sitting in her room
and weeping in her gloom.
Her eyes are now quite red,
for old Mr Fox is dead.'

'Be so kind as to tell her, Miss Cat, that a young fox is
here who would very much like to court her.'
'Very well, my young man.'

The cat went up the stairs, *trip-trap*,
and knocked upon the door, *tap-tap*.
'Mrs Fox, are you in there?'
'Oh, yes, Kitty Cat, yes, my dear.'

'Well, a suitor's here to see you.'

'What's he like? I want a clue.'

'Does he have nine beautiful tails like my late Mr Fox?'

'Oh, no,' answered Miss Cat. 'He has only one.'

'Then he's not for me.'

Miss Cat went downstairs and sent the suitor away. Soon there again was a knock at the door, and there was another fox outside who wanted to court Mrs Fox. Since he had only two tails, he fared no better than the first one. After that, others came, each with one tail more than the previous one, and they were all rejected. At last a fox came who had nine tails like old Mr Fox. When the widow heard that, she spoke joyfully to the maid:

'It's time to open the gate and the door,
and sweep Mr Fox out over the floor.'

However, just as the wedding was being held, old Mr Fox stirred from under the bench, rose up, and gave the whole crowd a good beating. Then he drove everyone, including Mrs Fox, out of the house.

After old Mr Fox had died, the wolf came courting. When he knocked at the door, the cat who was Mrs Fox's maid opened it, and she was greeted by the wolf, who said:

'Good day, Mrs Cat of Sweeping-Pit.
Are you all alone with your bright wit?
I'm sure you're making something tasty right now.'

The cat answered:

'I'm crumbling bread into my milk right here.
Be my guest and pull up a chair.'

'No, thank you, Mrs Cat,' the wolf replied. 'Is Mrs Fox at home?'
The cat said:

'She's sitting in her room
and is weeping in her gloom.
Many are the tears she's shed,
for old Mr Fox is dead.'

The wolf answered:

'If she wants another husband who's very fair,
tell her that I'm right down here.'
The cat ran up without a sound
and let her tail just swish around
until she reached the parlour door,
where with five golden rings she knocked.
'Mrs Fox, are you there?' she called and knocked once
more.

'If you want another husband who's very fair,
I can tell you that he's right down there.'

Mrs Fox asked, 'Is the gentleman wearing red trousers,
and does he have a pointed mouth?'
'No,' said the cat.
'Then he's not for me.'
After the wolf was turned down, he was followed by a
dog, a stag, a hare, a bear, a lion, and all the animals of the
forest, one after the other. However, they all lacked one of
the distinguished qualities of old Mr Fox, and each time,
the cat had to send the suitor away. Finally, a young fox
appeared, and Mrs Fox asked, 'Is the gentleman wearing
red trousers, and does he have a pointed mouth?'
'Yes,' said the cat. 'That he does.'
'Then let him come up,' said Mrs Fox, and she ordered
the maid to prepare the wedding feast.

'It's time to open the windows
and make sure that old Mr Fox now goes.
Indeed, he brought back many mice,
but he ate them all alone
and never did he offer me one.'

Then young Mr Fox was married to Mrs Fox.
Afterward there was dancing and rejoicing, and if they
have not stopped dancing, then they are still at it even
now.

16

The Robber Bridegroom

ONCE upon a time there was a miller who had a beautiful daughter, and when she was grown-up, he wanted to see her well provided for and well married. If the right suitor comes along and asks to marry her, he thought, I shall give her to him.

It was not long before a suitor appeared who seemed to be very rich, and since the miller found nothing wrong with him, he promised him his daughter. The maiden, however, did not love him the way a bride-to-be should love her bridegroom, nor did she trust him. Whenever she looked at him or thought about him, her heart shuddered with dread.

One day he said to her, 'You're my bride-to-be, and yet, you've never visited me.'

'I don't know where your house is,' the maiden replied.

'My house is out in the dark forest,' said the bridegroom.

She tried to make excuses and told him she would not be able to find the way. But the bridegroom said, 'Next Sunday I want you to come out and visit me. I've already invited the guests, and I shall spread ashes on the ground so you can find the way.'

When Sunday arrived and the maiden was supposed to set out on her way, she became very anxious but could not explain to herself why she felt so. She filled both her pockets with peas and lentils to mark the path. At the entrance to the forest, she found that ashes had been spread, and she followed them while throwing peas right and left on the ground with each step she took. She walked nearly the whole day until she came to the middle of the forest. There she saw a solitary house, but she did not like the look of it because it was so dark and dreary. She went inside and found nobody at home. The place was deadly silent. Then suddenly a voice cried out:

'Turn back, turn back, young bride.
The den belongs to murderers,
Who'll soon be at your side!'

The maiden looked up and saw that the voice came from a bird in a cage hanging on the wall. Once again it cried out:

> 'Turn back, turn back, young bride.
> The den belongs to murderers,
> Who'll soon be at your side!'

The beautiful bride moved from one room to the next and explored the entire house, but it was completely empty. Not a soul could be found. Finally, she went down into the cellar, where she encountered a very, very old woman, whose head was constantly bobbing.

'Could you tell me whether my bridegroom lives here?' asked the bride.

'Oh, you poor child,' the old woman answered. 'Do you realize where you are? This is a murderers' den! You think you're a bride soon to be celebrating your wedding, but the only marriage you'll celebrate will be with death. Just look! They ordered me to put this big kettle of water on the fire to boil. When they have you in their power, they'll chop you to pieces without mercy. Then they'll cook you and eat you, because they're cannibals. If I don't take pity on you and save you, you'll be lost forever.'

The old woman then led her behind a large barrel, where nobody could see her.

'Be still as a mouse,' she said. 'Don't budge or move! Otherwise, it will be all over for you. Tonight when the robbers are asleep, we'll escape. I've been waiting a long time for this chance.'

No sooner was the maiden hidden than the godless crew came home, dragging another maiden with them. They were drunk and paid no attention to her screams and pleas. They gave her wine to drink, three full glasses, one white, one red, and one yellow, and soon her heart burst in two. Then they tore off her fine clothes, put her on a table, chopped her beautiful body to pieces, and sprinkled the pieces with salt. Behind the barrel, the poor bride shook and trembled, for she now realized what kind of fate the robbers had been planning for her. One of them noticed a ring on the murdered maiden's little finger, and since he could not slip it off easily, he took a hatchet and chopped the finger off. But the finger sprang into the air and over the barrel and fell right into the bride's lap. The robber took a candle and went looking for it, but he could not find it. Then another robber said, 'Have you already looked behind the barrel?'

Now the old woman called out, 'Come and eat! You can look for it tomorrow. The finger's not going to run away from you.'

'The old woman's right,' the robbers said, and they stopped looking and sat down to eat. The old woman put a sleeping potion into their wine, and soon they lay down in the cellar, fell asleep, and began snoring. When the bride heard that, she came out from behind the barrel and had to step over the sleeping bodies lying in rows on the ground. She feared she might wake them up, but she got safely through with the help of God. The old woman went upstairs with her and opened the door, and the two of them scampered out of the murderers' den as fast as they could. The wind had blown away the ashes, but the peas and lentils had sprouted and unfurled, pointing the way in the moonlight. They walked the whole night, and by morning they had reached the mill. Then the maiden told her father everything that had happened.

When the day of the wedding celebration came, the bridegroom appeared, as did all the relatives and friends that the miller had invited. As they were all sitting at the table, each person was asked to tell a story. The bride, though, remained still and did not utter a word. Finally, the bridegroom said, 'Well, my dear, can't you think of anything? Tell us a good story.'

'All right,' she said. 'I'll tell you a dream: I was walking alone through the forest and finally came to a house.

There wasn't a soul to be found in the place except for a bird in a cage on the wall that cried out:

"Turn back, turn back, young bride.
The den belongs to murderers,
Who'll soon be at your side!"

'Then the bird repeated the warning.

(My dear, it was only a dream.)

'After that I went through all the rooms, and they were empty, but there was something about them that gave me an eerie feeling. Finally, I went downstairs into the cellar, where I found a very, very old woman, who was bobbing her head. I asked her, "Does my bridegroom live in this house?" "Oh, you poor child," she responded, "you've stumbled on a murderers' den. Your bridegroom lives here, but he wants to chop you up and kill you, and then he wants to cook you and eat you."

(My dear, it was only a dream.)

'The old woman hid me behind a large barrel, and no sooner was I hidden than the robbers returned home, dragging a maiden with them. They gave her all sorts of

wine to drink, white, red, and yellow, and her heart burst
in two.

(My dear, it was only a dream.)

'One of the robbers saw that a gold ring was still on
her finger, and since he had trouble pulling it off, he took
a hatchet and chopped it off. The finger sprang into the
air, over the barrel, and right into my lap. And here's the
finger with the ring!'

With these words she produced the finger and showed
it to all those present.

The robber, who had turned white as a ghost while
hearing her story, jumped up and attempted to flee.
However, the guests seized him and turned him over
to the magistrate. Then he and his whole band were
executed for their shameful crimes.

17
The Juniper Tree

ALL this took place a long time ago, most likely some two thousand years ago. There was a rich man who had a beautiful and pious wife, and they loved each other very much. Though they did not have any children, they longed to have some. Day and night the wife prayed for a child, but still none came, and everything remained the same.

Now, in the front of the house there was a yard, and in the yard stood a juniper tree. One day during winter the wife was under the tree peeling an apple, and as she was peeling it, she cut her finger, and her blood dripped on the snow.

'Oh,' said the wife, and she heaved a great sigh. While she looked at the blood before her, she became quite sad. 'If only I had a child as red as blood and as white as snow!' Upon saying that, her mood changed, and she became very cheerful, for she felt something might come of it. Then she went home.

After a month the snow vanished. After two months everything turned green. After three months the flowers sprouted from the ground. After four months all the trees in the woods grew more solid, and the green branches became intertwined. The birds began to sing, and their song resounded throughout the forest as the blossoms fell from the trees. Soon the fifth month passed, and when the wife stood under the juniper tree, it smelled so sweetly that her heart leapt for joy. Indeed, she was so overcome by joy that she fell down on her knees. When the sixth month had passed, the fruit was large and firm, and she was quite still. In the seventh month she picked the juniper berries and ate them so avidly that she became sad and sick. After the eighth month passed, she called her husband to her and wept.

'If I die,' she said, 'bury me under the juniper tree.'

After that she was quite content and relieved until the ninth month had passed. Then she had a child as white as snow and as red as blood. When she saw the baby, she was so delighted that she died.

Her husband buried her under the juniper tree, and he began weeping a great deal. After some time he felt much better, but he still wept every now and then.

Eventually, he stopped, and after more time passed, he took another wife. With his second wife he had a daughter, while the child from the first wife was a little boy, who was as red as blood and as white as snow. Whenever the woman looked at her daughter, she felt great love for her, but whenever she looked at the little boy, her heart was cut to the quick. She could not forget that he would always stand in her way and prevent her daughter from inheriting everything, which was what the woman had in mind. Thus the devil took hold of her and influenced her feelings toward the boy until she became quite cruel toward him: she pushed him from one place to the next, slapped him here and cuffed him there, so that the poor child lived in constant fear. When he came home from school, he found no peace at all.

One time the woman went up to her room, and her little daughter followed her and said, 'Mother, give me an apple.'

'Yes, my child,' said the woman, and she gave her a beautiful apple from the chest that had a large heavy lid with a big, sharp iron lock.

'Mother,' said the little daughter, 'shouldn't brother get one too?'

The woman was irritated by that remark, but she said, 'Yes, as soon as he comes home from school.' And, when she looked out of the window and saw he was coming, the devil seemed to take possession of her, and she snatched the apple away from her daughter.

'You shan't have one before your brother,' she said and threw the apple into the chest and shut it.

The little boy came through the door, and the devil compelled her to be friendly to him and say, 'Would you like to have an apple, my son?' Yet, she gave him a fierce look.

'Mother,' said the little boy, 'how ferocious you look! Yes, give me an apple.'

Then she felt compelled to coax him.

'Come over here,' she said as she lifted the lid. 'Take out an apple for yourself.'

And as the little boy leaned over the chest, the devil prompted her, and *crash!* She slammed the lid so hard that his head flew off and fell among the apples. Then she was struck by fear and thought, How am I going to get out of this? She went up to her room and straight to her dresser, where she took out a white kerchief from a drawer. She put the boy's head back on his neck and tied the neckerchief around it so nothing could be seen. Then she set him on a chair in front of the door and put the apple in his hand.

Some time later little Marlene came into the kitchen and went up to her mother, who was standing by the fire in front of a pot of hot water, which she was constantly stirring.

'Mother,' said Marlene, 'brother's sitting by the door and looks very pale. He's got an apple in his hand, and I asked him to give me the apple, but he didn't answer, and I became very scared.'

'Go back to him,' said the mother, 'and if he doesn't answer you, give him a box on the ear.'

Little Marlene returned to him and said, 'Brother, give me the apple.'

But he would not respond. So she gave him a box on the ear, and his head fell off. The little girl was so frightened that she began to cry and howl. Then she ran to her mother and said, 'Oh, Mother, I've knocked my brother's head off!' And she wept and wept and could not be comforted.

'Marlene,' said the mother. 'What have you done! You're not to open your mouth about this. We don't want anyone to know, and besides there's nothing we can do about it now. So we'll make a stew out of him.'

The mother took the little boy and chopped him into pieces. Next she put them into a pot and let them stew. But Marlene stood nearby and wept until all her tears fell into the pot, so it did not need any salt.

When the father came home, he sat down at the table and asked, 'Where's my son?'

The mother served a huge portion of the stewed meat, and Marlene wept and could not stop.

'Where's my son?' the father asked again.

'Oh,' said the mother, 'he's gone off into the country to visit his mother's great-uncle. He intends to stay there awhile.'

'What's he going to do there? He didn't even say good-bye to me.'

'Well, he wanted to go very badly and asked me if he could stay there six weeks. They'll take good care of him.'

'Oh, that makes me sad,' said the man. 'It's not right. He should have said good-bye to me.' Then he began to eat and said, 'Marlene, what are you crying for? Your brother will come back soon.' Without pausing he said, 'Oh, wife, the food tastes great! Give me some more!' The more he ate, the more he wanted. 'Give me some more,' he said. 'I'm not going to share this with you. Somehow I feel as if it were all mine.'

As he ate and ate he threw the bones under the table until he was all done. Meanwhile, Marlene went to her dresser and took out her best silk neckerchief from the bottom drawer, gathered all the bones from beneath the table, tied them up in her silk kerchief, and carried them outside the door. There she wept bitter tears and laid the bones beneath the juniper tree. As she put them there, she suddenly felt relieved and stopped crying. Now the juniper tree began to move. The branches separated and came together again as though they were clapping their hands in joy. At the same time smoke came out of the tree, and in the middle of the smoke there was a flame that seemed to be burning. Then a beautiful bird flew out of the fire and began singing magnificently. He soared high in the air, and after he vanished, the juniper tree was as it was before. Yet, the silk kerchief was gone. Marlene was very happy and gay. It was as if her brother were still alive, and she went merrily back into the house, sat down at the table, and ate.

Meanwhile, the bird flew away, landed on a goldsmith's house, and began to sing:

> 'My mother, she killed me.
> My father, he ate me.
> My sister, Marlene, she made sure to see
> my bones were all gathered together,
> bound nicely in silk, as neat as can be,
> and laid beneath the juniper tree.
> *Tweet, tweet!* What a lovely bird I am!'

The goldsmith was sitting in his workshop making a golden chain. When he heard the bird singing on his roof, he thought it was very beautiful. Then he stood up, and as he walked across the threshold, he lost a slipper. Still, he kept on going, right into the middle of the street with only one sock and a slipper on. He was also wearing his apron, and in one of his hands he held the golden chain, in the other his tongs. The sun was shining brightly on the street as he walked, and then he stopped to get a look at the bird.

'Bird,' he said, 'how beautifully you sing! Sing me that song again.'

'No,' said the bird, 'I never sing twice for nothing. Give me the golden chain, and I'll sing it for you again.'

'All right,' said the goldsmith. 'Here's the golden chain. Now sing the song again.'

The bird swooped down, took the golden chain in his right claw, went up to the goldsmith, and began singing:

'My mother, she killed me.
My father, he ate me.
My sister, Marlene, she made sure to see
my bones were all gathered together,
bound nicely in silk, as neat as can be,
and laid beneath the juniper tree.
Tweet, tweet! What a lovely bird I am!'

Then the bird flew off to a shoemaker, landed on his roof, and sang:

'My mother, she killed me.
My father, he ate me.
My sister, Marlene, she made sure to see
my bones were gathered together,
bound nicely in silk, as neat as can be,
and laid beneath the juniper tree.
Tweet, tweet! What a lovely bird I am!'

When the shoemaker heard the song, he ran to the door in his shirt sleeves and looked up at the roof, keeping his hand over his eyes to protect them from the bright sun.

'Bird,' he said. 'How beautifully you sing!' Then he called into the house, 'Wife, come out here for a second! There's a bird up there. Just look. How beautifully he sings!' Then he called his daughter and her children, and the journeyman, apprentices, and maid. They all came running out into the street and looked at the bird and saw how beautiful he was. He had bright red and green feathers, and his neck appeared to glisten like pure gold, while his eyes sparkled in his head like stars.

'Bird,' said the shoemaker, 'now sing me that song again.'

'No,' said the bird. 'I never sing twice for nothing. You'll have to give me a present.'

'Wife,' said the man, 'go into the shop. There's a pair of red shoes on the top shelf. Get them for me.'

His wife went and fetched the shoes.

'There,' said the man. 'Now sing the song again.'

The bird swooped down, took the shoes in his left claw, flew back up on the roof, and sang:

> 'My mother, she killed me.
> My father, he ate me.
> My sister, Marlene, she made sure to see
> my bones were all gathered together,
> bound nicely in silk, as neat as can be,
> and laid beneath the juniper tree.
> *Tweet, tweet!* What a lovely bird I am!'

When the bird finished the song, he flew away. He had the chain in his right claw and the shoes in his left, and he flew far away to a mill. The mill went *clickety-clack, clickety-clack, clickety-clack*. The miller had twenty men sitting in the mill, and they were hewing a stone. Their chisels went *click-clack, click-clack, click-clack*. And the mill kept going *clickety-clack, clickety-clack, clickety-clack*. The bird swooped down and landed on a linden tree outside the mill and sang:

> 'My mother, she killed me.'

Then one of the men stopped working.

'My father, he ate me.'

Then two more stopped and listened.

'My sister, Marlene, she made sure to see.'

Then four more stopped.

'My bones were all gathered together,
bound nicely in silk, as neat as can be.'

Now only eight kept chiselling.

'And laid beneath . . .'

Now only five.

'. . . the juniper tree.'

Now only one.

'*Tweet, tweet!* What a lovely bird I am!'

Then the last one also stopped and listened to the final
words.

'Bird, how beautifully you sing! Let me hear that too. Sing your song again for me.'

'No,' said the bird. 'I never sing twice for nothing. Give me the millstone, and I'll sing the song again.'

'I would if I could,' he said. 'But the millstone doesn't belong to me alone.'

'If he sings again,' said the others, 'he can have it.'

Then the bird swooped down, and all twenty of the miller's men took beams to lift the stone. 'Heave-ho! Heave-ho! Heave-ho!' Then the bird stuck his neck through the hole, put the stone on like a collar, flew back to the tree, and sang:

> 'My mother, she killed me.
> My father, he ate me.
> My sister, Marlene, she made sure to see
> my bones were all gathered together,
> bound nicely in silk, as neat as can be,
> and laid beneath the juniper tree.
> *Tweet, tweet!* What a lovely bird I am!'

When the bird finished his song, he spread his wings, and in his right claw he had the chain, in his left the shoes, and around his neck the millstone. Then he flew away to his father's house.

The father, mother, and Marlene were sitting at the table in the parlour, and the father said, 'Oh, how happy I am! I just feel so wonderful!'

'Not me,' said the mother. 'I feel scared as if a storm were about to erupt.'

Meanwhile, Marlene just sat there and kept weeping. Then the bird flew up, and when he landed on the roof, the father said, 'Oh, I'm in such good spirits. The sun's shining so brightly outside, and I feel as though I were going to see an old friend again.'

'Not me,' said his wife. 'I'm so frightened that my teeth are chattering. I feel as if fire were running through my veins.'

She tore open her bodice, while Marlene sat in a corner and kept weeping. She had her handkerchief in front of her eyes and wept until it was completely soaked with her tears. The bird swooped down on the juniper tree, where he perched on a branch and began singing:

'My mother, she killed me.'

The mother stopped her ears, shut her eyes, and tried not to see or hear anything, but there was a roaring in her ears like a turbulent storm, and her eyes burned and flashed like lightning.

'My father, he ate me.'

'Oh, Mother,' said the man, 'listen to that beautiful bird singing so gloriously! The sun's so warm, and it smells like cinnamon.'

'My sister, Marlene, made sure to see.'

Then Marlene laid her head on her knees and wept and wept, but the man said, 'I'm going outside. I must see the bird close up.'
'Oh, don't go!' said the wife. 'I feel as if the whole house were shaking and about to go up in flames!'
Nevertheless, the man went out and looked at the bird.

'My bones were all gathered together,
bound nicely in silk, as neat as can be,
and laid beneath the juniper tree.
Tweet, tweet! What a lovely bird I am!'

After ending his song, the bird dropped the golden chain, and it fell around the man's neck just right, so that it fit him perfectly. Then he went inside and said, 'Just look how lovely that bird is! He gave me this beautiful golden chain, and he's as beautiful as well!'

But the woman was petrified and fell to the floor. Her cap slipped off her head, and the bird sang again:

> 'My mother, she killed me.'

'Oh, I wish I were a thousand feet beneath the earth so I wouldn't have to hear this!'

> 'My father, he ate me.'

Then the woman fell down again as if she were dead.

> 'My sister, Marlene, she made sure to see.'

'Oh,' said Marlene, 'I want to go outside too and see if the bird will give me something.' Then she went out.

> 'My bones were all gathered together,
> bound nicely in silk, as neat as can be.'

Then the bird threw her the shoes.

> 'And laid them beneath the juniper tree.
> *Tweet, tweet!* What a lovely bird I am!'

Marlene felt gay and happy. She put on the new red shoes and danced and skipped back into the house.

'Oh,' she said, 'I was so sad when I went out, and now I feel so cheerful. That certainly is a splendid bird. He gave me a pair of red shoes as a gift.'

'Not me,' said the wife, who jumped up, and her hair flared up like red-hot flames. 'I feel as if the world were coming to an end. Maybe I'd feel better if I went outside.'

As she went out the door, *crash!* the bird threw the millstone down on her head, and she was crushed to death. The father and Marlene heard the crash and went outside. Smoke, flames, and fire were rising from the spot, and when it was over, the little brother was standing there. He took his father and Marlene by the hand, and all three were very happy. Then they went into the house, sat down at the table, and ate.

18

Old Sultan

A FARMER had a faithful dog named Sultan, and when the dog had grown old and lost all his teeth, he could no longer grip things tightly. One day, as the farmer was standing by the front door with his wife, he said, 'I'm going to shoot old Sultan tomorrow. He's no longer of any use to us.'

His wife felt sorry for the faithful creature, and she replied, 'Couldn't we just keep him on and feed him? After all, he's served us so many years and has been loyal to us.'

'My God!' the husband exclaimed. 'Don't you have any sense? He doesn't have a tooth left in his head, and there's not a thief who'd be afraid of him. It's time for him to go. He served us well, but he was also fed well in return.'

The poor dog was basking nearby in the sun and overheard everything that was said. He was sad that the next day was to be his last. But he had a good friend, the wolf, and in the evening he sneaked out into the forest to see him and whine about his impending fate.

'Listen, cousin,' said the wolf. 'Keep your spirits up. You can depend on me to help you out of your dilemma. In fact, I've already thought of something. Early tomorrow morning your master will be going out with his wife to make hay, and they'll take their little child with them because nobody will be staying at home. They generally lay the child behind the hedge in the shade while they work. Now, I want you to lie down next to the child as if you wanted to guard him. I'll come out of the forest and steal the child. Then you've got to take to your heels as if you wanted to get the child away from me. I'll let him drop, and you bring him back to his parents, who'll believe that you rescued him. Then they'll be too grateful to think of harming you. On the contrary, they'll be completely indebted to you and give you anything you want.'

The dog liked the scheme, and he carried it out just as planned. When the wolf stole the child and began carrying him through the fields, the father screamed, and when old Sultan brought the child back, he was happy and patted the dog.

'Nobody's going to touch a hair on your head,' he said. 'You can stay here and eat your fill for as long as you live.' Then he turned to his wife and said, 'Go home right away and cook some bread mush. He won't need to chew that. Also, bring the pillow from my bed. I want to give him that as a gift to lie on.'

From then on old Sultan had it good, and he could not have wished for a better life. Soon after, the wolf visited him and was glad to learn that everything succeeded so well.

'Now, cousin,' he said, 'I hope you'll wink an eye when I steal a fat sheep from your master every now and then. Times are getting hard for all of us.'

'Don't count on that,' the dog answered. 'I intend to stay faithful to my master, and I can't let you do it.'

The wolf did not believe that the dog meant what he said. So during the night he crept into the yard to steal a sheep. However, the farmer, who had learned about the wolf's plan from the faithful Sultan, was waiting for him and gave him a good thrashing with a flail. The wolf was forced to scamper away, but he cried out at the dog, 'Just wait, you traitor! You'll pay for this!'

The next morning the wolf sent the boar as his second to challenge the dog to meet him out in the forest and settle their affair. Old Sultan could find no one who would be his second except for a three-legged cat. And, when they went out together, the poor cat limped and had to hold his tail erect because of the pain he was suffering. The wolf and his second were already at the spot. When they saw the opponent coming, they thought he was carrying a sabre with him because they mistook the cat's erect tail for a sabre. Moreover, on seeing the cat limping on three legs, they thought he was picking up stones to throw at them. The wolf and the boar became so frightened that the boar crept into some bushes and the wolf jumped up a tree. When the dog and cat arrived at the spot, they were puzzled to find no one there. However, the wild boar had not been able to conceal himself completely in the bushes. One of his ears was showing, and as the cat was looking cautiously about, the boar twitched his ear. The cat thought a mouse might be stirring in the bushes and jumped on it. She took a good hard bite, and the boar leapt with a loud cry and ran away.

'The guilty one's sitting up there in the tree!' he screamed.

The dog and the cat looked up and saw the wolf, who was so ashamed he had shown such cowardice that he accepted the dog's offer of peace.

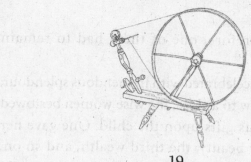

19

Brier Rose

IN TIMES of old there lived a king and queen, and every day they said, 'Oh, if only we had a child!' Yet, they never had one.

Then one day, as the queen went out bathing, a frog happened to crawl ashore and say to her, 'Your wish shall be fulfilled. Before the year is out, you shall give birth to a daughter.'

The frog's prediction came true, and the queen gave birth to a girl who was so beautiful that the king was overjoyed and decided to hold a great feast. Not only did he invite his relatives, friends, and acquaintances, but also the wise women, in the hope that they would be generous and kind to his daughter. There were thirteen wise women in his kingdom, but he had only twelve golden plates from which they could eat. Therefore, one of them had to remain home.

The feast was celebrated with tremendous splendour, and when it drew to a close, the wise women bestowed their miraculous gifts upon the child. One gave her virtue, another beauty, the third wealth, and so on, until they had given her nearly everything one could possibly wish for in the world. When eleven of them had offered their gifts, the thirteenth suddenly entered the hall. She wanted to get revenge for not having been invited, and without greeting anyone or looking around, she cried out with a loud voice, 'In her fifteenth year the princess shall prick herself with a spindle and fall down dead!'

That was all she said. Then she turned around and left the hall. Everyone was horrified, but the twelfth wise woman stepped forward. She still had her wish to make, and although she could not undo the evil spell, she could nevertheless soften it.

'The princess shall not die,' she said. 'Instead, she shall fall into a deep sleep for one hundred years.'

Since the king wanted to guard his dear child against such a catastrophe, he issued an order that all spindles in his kingdom were to be burned. Meanwhile, the gifts of the wise women fulfilled their promise in every way: the girl was so beautiful, polite, kind, and sensible that whoever encountered her could not help but adore her.

Now, on the day she turned fifteen, it happened that the king and queen were not at home, and she was left completely alone in the palace. So she wandered all over the place and explored as many rooms and chambers as she pleased. She eventually came to an old tower, climbed its narrow winding staircase, and came to a small door. A rusty key was stuck in the lock, and when she turned it, the door sprang open, and she saw an old woman in a little room sitting with a spindle and busily spinning flax.

'Good day, old granny,' said the princess. 'What are you doing there?'

'I'm spinning,' said the old woman, and she nodded her head.

'What's the thing that's bobbing about in such a funny way?' asked the maiden, who took the spindle and wanted to spin too, but just as she touched the spindle, the magic spell began working, and she pricked her finger with it.

The very moment she felt the prick, she fell down on the bed that was standing there, and she was overcome by a deep sleep. This sleep soon spread throughout the entire palace. The king and queen had just returned home, and when they entered the hall, they fell asleep, as did all the people of their court. They were followed by the horses in the stable, the dogs in the courtyard, the pigeons on the roof, and the flies on the wall. Even the fire flickering in the hearth became quiet and fell asleep. The roast stopped sizzling, and the cook, who was just about to pull the kitchen boy's hair because he had done something wrong, let him go and fell asleep. Finally, the wind died down so that not a single leaf stirred on the trees outside the castle.

Soon a brier hedge began to grow all around the castle, and it grew higher each year. Eventually, it surrounded and covered the entire castle, so that it was no longer visible. Not even the flag on the roof could be seen. The princess became known by the name Beautiful Sleeping Brier Rose, and a tale about her began circulating throughout the country. From time to time princes came and tried to break through the hedge and get to the castle. However, this was impossible because the thorns clung together tightly as though they had hands, and the young men got stuck there. Indeed, they could not pry themselves loose and died miserable deaths.

After many, many years had gone by, a prince came to this country once more and heard an old man talking about the brier hedge. Supposedly there was a castle standing behind the hedge, and in the castle was a remarkably beautiful princess named Brier Rose, who had been sleeping for a hundred years, along with the king and queen and their entire court. The old man also knew from his grandfather that many princes had come and had tried to break through the brier hedge, but they had got stuck and had died wretched deaths.

'I am not afraid,' said the young prince. 'I intend to go and see the beautiful Brier Rose.'

The good old man tried as best he could to dissuade him, but the prince would not heed his words.

Now the hundred years had just ended, and the day on which Brier Rose was to wake up again had arrived. When the prince approached the brier hedge, he found nothing but beautiful flowers that opened of their own accord, let him through, and then closed again like a hedge. In the castle courtyard he saw the horses and the spotted hunting dogs lying asleep. The pigeons were perched on the roof and had tucked their heads beneath their wings. When he entered the palace, the flies were sleeping on the wall, the cook in the kitchen was still holding his hand as if he wanted to grab the kitchen boy, and the maid was sitting in front of the black chicken that she was about to pluck. As the prince continued walking, he saw the entire court lying asleep in the hall with the king and queen by the throne. Then he moved on, and everything was so quiet that he could hear himself breathe.

Finally, he came to the tower and opened the door to the small room in which Brier Rose was asleep. There she lay, and her beauty was so marvellous that he could not take his eyes off her. Then he leaned over and gave her a kiss, and when his lips touched hers, Brier Rose opened her eyes, woke up, and looked at him fondly. After that they went downstairs together, and the king and queen woke up along with the entire court, and they all looked at each other in amazement. Soon the horses in the courtyard stood up and shook themselves. The hunting dogs jumped around and wagged their tails. The pigeons on the roof lifted their heads from under their wings, looked around, and flew off into the fields. The flies on the wall continued crawling. The fire in the kitchen flared up, flickered, and cooked the meat. The roast began to sizzle again, and the cook gave the kitchen boy such a box on the ear that he let out a cry, while the maid finished plucking the chicken.

The wedding of the prince with Brier Rose was celebrated in great splendour, and they lived happily to the end of their days.

20

King Thrushbeard

A KING had a daughter whose beauty was beyond comparison, but she was so proud and haughty that no suitor was good enough for her. Indeed, she rejected one after the other and ridiculed them as well. Once her father held a great feast and invited all the marriageable young men from far and wide to attend. They were all lined up according to their rank and class: first came the kings, then the dukes, princes, counts, and barons, and finally the gentry. The king's daughter was conducted down the line, and she found fault with each one of the suitors there. One was too fat for her. 'That wine barrel!' she said. Another was too tall. 'Tall and thin, he looks like a pin!' The third was too short. 'Short and fat, he's built like a vat!' The fourth was too pale. 'He resembles death!' The fifth was too red. 'What a rooster!' The sixth did not stand straight enough. 'Green wood, dried behind the stove!'

There was not a single man whom she did not criticize, but she made the most fun of a good king who stood at the head of the line and had a chin that was a bit crooked.

'My goodness!' she exclaimed, and laughed. 'He's got a chin like a thrush's beak!' From then on, everyone called him Thrushbeard.

When her father saw that she did nothing but ridicule people, and that she scorned all the suitors who were gathered there, he was furious and swore that she would have to marry the very first beggar who came to his door. A few days later a minstrel came and began singing beneath the windows to earn some money. When the king heard him, he said, 'Have him come up here.'

The minstrel, who was dressed in dirty, tattered clothes, entered the hall and sang in front of the king and his daughter. When he was finished, he asked for a modest reward.

'Your singing has pleased me so much,' the king said, 'that I shall give you my daughter for your wife.'

The king's daughter was horrified, but the king said, 'I swore I'd give you to the very first beggar who came along, and I intend to keep my word.'

All her objections were to no avail. The minister was fetched, and she was compelled to wed the minstrel. When that was done, the king said, 'It's not fitting for you to stay in my palace any longer since you're now a beggar woman. I want you to depart with your husband.'

The beggar took her by the hand, and she had to go with him on foot. When they came to a huge forest, she asked:

'Tell me, who might the owner of this forest be?'
'King Thrushbeard owns the forest and all you can see.
If you had taken him, it would belong to you.'
'Alas, poor me! What can I do?
I should have wed King Thrushbeard. If only I knew!'

Soon they crossed a meadow, and she asked again:

'Tell me, who might the owner of this meadow be?'
'King Thrushbeard owns the meadow and all you can see.
If you had taken him, it would belong to you.'
'Alas, poor me! What can I do?
I should have wed King Thrushbeard. If only I knew!'

Then they came to a large city, and she asked once more:

'Tell me, who might the owner of this city be?'
'King Thrushbeard owns the city and all you can see.
If you had taken him, it would belong to you.'
'Alas, poor me! What can I do?
I should have wed King Thrushbeard. If only I knew!'

'I'm not at all pleased by this,' said the minstrel. 'Why are you always wishing for another husband? Do you think I'm not good enough for you?'

Finally, they came to a tiny cottage, and she said:

'Oh, Lord! What a wretched tiny house!
It's not even fit for a mouse.'

The minstrel answered, 'This house is mine and yours, and we shall live here together.'

She had to stoop to get through the low doorway.

'Where are the servants?' the king's daughter asked.

'What servants?' answered the beggar. 'You must do everything yourself if you want something done. Now, make a fire at once and put the water on so you can cook me my meal. I'm very tired.'

However, the king's daughter knew nothing about making a fire or cooking, and the beggar had to lend a hand himself if he wanted anything done in a tolerable fashion. After they had eaten their meagre meal, they went to bed. But the next morning he got her up very early because she had to take care of the house. For a few days they lived like this and managed as best they could. When they had consumed all their provisions, the man said, 'Wife, we can't go on this way any longer. We've used everything up, and we're not earning a thing. You've got to weave baskets.'

He went out to cut some willows and brought them home, but the rough willows bruised her tender hands.

'I see that won't work,' said the man. 'Let's try spinning. Perhaps you'll be better at that.'

She sat down at the spinning wheel and tried to spin, but the hard thread soon cut her soft fingers, and blood began to flow.

'See now,' said the man. 'You're not fit for any kind of work. I made a bad bargain when I got you. But let's see how things go if I start a business with pots and earthenware. You're to sit in the marketplace and sell the wares.'

Oh, she thought, if some people from my father's kingdom come to the marketplace and see me selling wares, they'll surely make fun of me!

But there was no way to avoid it. She had to obey her husband if she did not want to die of hunger. The first time everything went well. People gladly bought her wares because she was beautiful, and they paid what she asked. Indeed, many gave her money and did not even bother to take the pots with them. So the couple lived off their earnings as long as they lasted. Then her husband bought a lot of new earthenware. His wife sat down with it at a corner in the marketplace, set her wares around her, and offered them for sale. Suddenly, a drunken hussar came galloping along and rode right over the pots so that they were all smashed to pieces. She began to weep and was paralyzed with fear.

'Oh, what's going to happen to me!' she exclaimed. 'What will my husband say?'

She ran home and told him about the accident, and he responded by saying, 'In heaven's name, who would ever sit down at a corner in the marketplace with earthenware? Now stop your weeping. I see full well that you're not fit for proper work. I've already been to the king's castle and have asked whether they could use a kitchen maid, and they've promised me to take you on. In return you'll get free meals.'

Now the king's daughter became a kitchen maid and had to assist the cook and do the lowest kind of work. She sewed two little jars inside her pockets and carried home the leftovers so they could have some food to live on. One day it happened that the king's oldest son was celebrating his wedding, and the poor woman went upstairs, stood outside the door of the large hall, and wanted to look inside. When the candles were lit, each guest entered, one more exquisitely dressed than the next, and everything was full of splendour. With a sad heart she thought about her fate and cursed her pride and arrogance for bringing about her humiliation and great poverty. Sometimes the servants threw her pieces of the delicious dishes they were carrying in and out of the hall, and she could also smell the aroma of the food. She put the pieces into her pockets and intended to carry them home.

Suddenly the king's son entered. He was dressed in velvet and silk and had a golden chain around his neck. And, when he saw the beautiful woman standing in the doorway, he grabbed her by the hand and wanted to dance with her, but she refused. Indeed, she was horrified because she saw it was King Thrushbeard, who had courted her and whom she had rejected with scorn. Although she struggled, it was to no avail, for he pulled her into the hall. Then the string that held her pockets together broke, and the jars fell out, causing the soup to spill and the scraps of food to scatter on the floor. When the people saw that, they laughed a good deal and poked fun at her. She was so ashamed that she wished she were a thousand fathoms under the earth. She ran out the door and tried to escape, but a man caught up with her on the stairs and brought her back. When she looked at him, she saw it was King Thrushbeard again, and he said to her in a friendly way, 'Don't be afraid. I and the minstrel who lived with you in the wretched cottage are one and the same person. I disguised myself out of love for you, and I was also the hussar who rode over your pots and smashed them to pieces. I did all that to humble your proud spirit and to punish you for the insolent way you behaved toward me.'

Then she shed bitter tears and said, 'I've done a great wrong and don't deserve to be your wife.'

However, he said, 'Console yourself. The bad days are over. Now we shall celebrate our wedding.'

The chambermaids came and dressed her in splendid clothes, and her father came along with his entire court, and they wished her happiness in her marriage with King Thrushbeard. Then the real rejoicing began, and I wish that you and I had been there too.

21

Snow White

ONCE upon a time, in the middle of winter, when snowflakes were falling like feathers from the sky, a queen was sitting and sewing at a window with a black ebony frame. And as she was sewing and looking out the window, she pricked her finger with the needle, and three drops of blood fell on the snow. The red looked so beautiful on the white snow that she thought to herself, If only I had a child as white as snow, as red as blood, and as black as the wood of the window frame!

Soon after she gave birth to a little daughter who was as white as snow, as red as blood, and her hair as black as ebony. Accordingly, the child was called Snow White, and right after she was born, the queen died. When a year had passed, the king married another woman, who was beautiful but proud and haughty, and she could not tolerate anyone else who might rival her beauty. She had a magic mirror and often she stood in front of it, looked at herself, and said:

> 'Mirror, mirror, on the wall,
> who in this realm is the fairest of all?'

Then the mirror would answer:

> 'You, my queen, are the fairest of all.'

That reply would make her content, for she knew the mirror always told the truth.

In the meantime, Snow White grew up and became more and more beautiful. By the time she was seven years old, she was as beautiful as the day is clear and more beautiful than the queen herself. One day when the queen asked her mirror:

> 'Mirror, mirror, on the wall,
> who in this realm is the fairest of all?'

The mirror answered:

> 'You, my queen, may have a beauty quite rare,
> but Snow White is a thousand times more fair.'

The queen shuddered and became yellow and green with envy. From that hour on, her hate for the girl was so great that her heart throbbed and turned in her breast each time she saw Snow White. Like weeds, the envy and arrogance grew so dense in her heart that she no longer had any peace, day or night. Finally, she summoned a huntsman and said, 'Take the child out into the forest. I never want to lay eyes on her again. You are to kill her and to bring me back her lungs and liver as proof of your deed.'

The huntsman obeyed and led Snow White out into the forest, but when he drew his hunting knife and was about to stab Snow White's innocent heart, she began to weep and said, 'Oh, dear huntsman, spare my life, and I'll run into the wild forest and never come home again.'

Since she was so beautiful, the huntsman took pity on her and said, 'You're free to go, my poor child!' Then he thought, The wild beasts will soon eat you up. Nevertheless, he felt as if a great weight had been lifted off his mind, because he did not have to kill her. Just then a young boar came dashing by, and the huntsman stabbed it to death. He took out the lungs and liver and brought them to the queen as proof that the child was dead. The cook was ordered to boil them in salt, and the wicked woman ate them and thought that she had eaten Snow White's lungs and liver.

Meanwhile, the poor child was all alone in the huge forest. When she looked at all the leaves on the trees, she was petrified and did not know what to do. Then she began to run, and she ran over sharp stones and through thornbushes. Wild beasts darted by her at times, but they did not harm her. She ran as long as her legs could carry her, and it was almost evening when she saw a little cottage and went inside to rest. Everything was tiny in the cottage and indescribably dainty and neat. There was a little table with a white tablecloth, and on it were seven little plates. Each plate had a tiny spoon next to it, and there were also seven tiny knives and forks and seven tiny cups. In a row against the wall stood seven little beds covered with sheets as white as snow. Since she was so hungry and thirsty, Snow White ate some vegetables and bread from each of the little plates and had a drop of wine to drink out of each of the tiny cups, for she did not want to take everything from just one place. After that she was tired and began trying out the beds, but none of them suited her at first: one was too long, another too short, but at last, she found that the seventh one was just right. So she stayed in that bed, said her prayers, and fell asleep.

When it was completely dark outside, the owners of the cottage returned. They were seven dwarfs who searched in the mountains for minerals with their picks and shovels. They lit their seven little candles, and when it became light in the house, they saw that someone had been there, for none of their things was in the exact same spot in which it had been left.

'Who's been sitting in my chair?' said the first dwarf.

'Who's been eating off my plate?' said the second.

'Who's been eating my bread?' said the third.

'Who's been eating my vegetables?' said the fourth.

'Who's been using my fork?' said the fifth.

'Who's been cutting with my knife?' said the sixth.

'Who's been drinking from my cup?' said the seventh.

Then the first dwarf looked around and noticed that his bed had been wrinkled and said, 'Who's been sleeping in my bed?'

The others ran over to their beds and cried out, 'Someone's been sleeping in my bed too!'

But when the seventh dwarf looked at his bed, he saw Snow White lying there asleep. So he called the others over to him, and when they came, they were so astounded that they fetched their seven little candles to allow more light to shine on Snow White.

'Oh, my Lord! Oh, my Lord!' they exclaimed. 'What a beautiful child!'

They were so delirious with joy that they did not wake her up. Instead, they let her sleep in the bed, while the seventh dwarf spent an hour in each one of his companions' beds until the night had passed. In the morning Snow White awoke, and when she saw the seven dwarfs, she was frightened. But they were friendly and asked, 'What's your name?'

'My name's Snow White,' she replied.

'What's brought you to our house?' the dwarfs continued.

She told them how her stepmother had ordered her to be killed, how the huntsman had spared her life, and how she had run all day until she had eventually discovered their cottage.

Then the dwarfs said, 'If you'll keep house for us, cook, make the beds, wash, sew, and knit, and if you'll keep everything neat and orderly, you can stay with us, and we'll provide you with everything you need.'

'Yes,' agreed Snow White, 'with all my heart.'

So she stayed with them and kept their house in order. In the morning they went to the mountains to search for minerals and gold. In the evening they returned, and their dinner had to be ready. During the day Snow White was alone, and the good dwarfs made sure to caution her.

'Beware of your stepmother,' they said. 'She'll soon know that you're here. Don't let anybody in!'

Since the queen believed she had eaten Snow White's liver and lungs, she was totally convinced that she was again the most beautiful woman in the realm. And when she went to her mirror, she said:

'Mirror, mirror, on the wall,
who in this realm is the fairest of all?'

The mirror answered:

'You, my queen, may have a beauty quite rare,
but beyond the mountains, where the seven dwarfs
dwell,
Snow White is thriving, and this I must tell:
Within this realm she's still a thousand times more
fair.'

The queen was horrified, for she knew that the mirror never lied, which meant that the huntsman had deceived her and Snow White was still alive. Once more she began plotting ways to kill her. As long as Snow White was the fairest in the realm, the queen's envy would leave her no peace. Finally, she thought up a plan. She painted her face and dressed as an old peddler woman so that nobody could recognize her. Then she crossed the seven mountains in this disguise and arrived at the cottage of the seven dwarfs, where she knocked at the door and cried out, 'Pretty wares for sale! Pretty wares!'

Snow White looked out of the window and called out, 'Good day, dear woman, what do you have for sale?'

'Nice and pretty things! Staylaces in all kinds of colours!' she replied and took out a lace woven from silk of many different colours.

I can certainly let this honest woman inside, Snow White thought. She unbolted the door and bought the pretty lace.

'My goodness, child! What a sight you are!' said the old woman. 'Come, I'll lace you up properly for once.'

Snow White did not suspect anything, so she stood in front of the old woman and let herself be laced with the new staylace. However, the old woman laced her so quickly and so tightly that Snow White lost her breath and fell down as if dead.

'Well, you used to be the fairest in the realm, but not now!' the old woman said and rushed off.

Not long after, at dinnertime, the dwarfs came home, and when they saw their dear Snow White lying on the ground, they were horrified. She neither stirred nor moved and seemed to be dead. They lifted her up, and when they saw that she was laced too tightly, they cut the staylace in two. At once she began to breathe a little, and after a while she had fully revived. When the dwarfs heard what had happened, they said, 'The old peddler woman was none other than the wicked queen! Beware, don't let anyone in when we're not with you!'

When the evil woman returned home, she went to her mirror and asked:

'Mirror, mirror, on the wall,
who in this realm is the fairest of all?'

Then the mirror answered as usual:

'You, my queen, may have a beauty quite rare,
but beyond the mountains, where the seven dwarfs dwell,
Snow White is thriving, and this I must tell:
Within this realm she's still a thousand times more fair.'

When the queen heard that, she was so upset that all her blood rushed to her heart, for she realized that Snow White had recovered.

'This time I'm going to think of something that will destroy her,' she said, and by using all the witchcraft at her command, she made a poison comb. Then she again disguised herself as an old woman and crossed the seven mountains to the cottage of the seven dwarfs, where she knocked at the door and cried out, 'Pretty wares for sale! Pretty wares!'

Snow White looked out the window and said, 'Go away! I'm not allowed to let anyone in.'

'But surely you're allowed to look,' said the old woman, and she took out the poison comb and held it up in the air. The comb pleased the girl so much that she let herself be carried away and opened the door. After they agreed on the price, the old woman said, 'Now I'll give your hair a proper combing for once.'

Poor Snow White did not give this a second thought and let the old woman do as she wished. But no sooner did the comb touch her hair than the poison began to take effect, and the maiden fell to the ground and lay there unconscious.

'You paragon of beauty!' said the wicked woman. 'Now you're finished!' And she went away.

Fortunately, it was nearly evening, the time when the seven dwarfs began heading home. And, when they arrived and saw Snow White lying on the ground as if she were dead, they immediately suspected the stepmother and began looking around. As soon as they found the poison comb, they took it out, and Snow White instantly regained consciousness. She told them what had happened, and they warned her again to be on her guard and not to open the door for anyone.

In the meantime, the queen returned home, went to the mirror, and said:

> 'Mirror, mirror, on the wall,
> who in this realm is the fairest of all?'

Then the mirror answered as before:

> 'You, my queen, may have a beauty quite rare,
> but beyond the mountains, where the seven dwarfs
> dwell,
> Snow White is thriving, and this I must tell:
> Within this realm she's still a thousand times more
> fair.'

When she heard the mirror's words, she trembled and shook with rage.

'Snow White shall die!' she exclaimed. 'Even if it costs me my own life!'

Then she went into a secret and solitary chamber where no one else ever went. Once inside she made a deadly poisonous apple. On the outside it looked beautiful—white with red cheeks. Anyone who saw it would be enticed, but whoever took a bite was bound to die. When the apple was ready, the queen painted her face and dressed herself up as a peasant woman and crossed the seven mountains to the cottage of the seven dwarfs. When she knocked at the door, Snow White stuck her head out of the window and said, 'I'm not allowed to let anyone inside. The seven dwarfs have forbidden me.'

'That's all right with me,' answered the peasant woman. 'I'll surely get rid of my apples in time. But let me give you one as a gift.'

'No,' said Snow White. 'I'm not allowed to take anything.'

'Are you afraid that it might be poisoned?' said the old woman. 'Look, I'll cut the apple in two. You eat the red part, and I'll eat the white.'

However, the apple had been made with such cunning that only the red part was poisoned. Snow White was eager to eat the beautiful apple, and when she saw the peasant woman eating her half, she could no longer resist, stretched out her hand, and took the poisoned half. No sooner did she take a bite than she fell to the ground dead. The queen stared at her with a cruel look, then burst out laughing and said, 'White as snow, red as blood, black as ebony! This time the dwarfs won't be able to bring you back to life!'

When she got home, she asked the mirror:

'Mirror, mirror, on the wall,
who in this realm is the fairest of all?'

Then the mirror finally answered, 'You, my queen, are now the fairest of all.' So her jealous heart was satisfied as much as a jealous heart can be satisfied.

When the dwarfs came home that evening, they found Snow White lying on the ground. There was no breath coming from her lips, and she was dead. They lifted her up and looked to see if they could find something poisonous. They unlaced her, combed her hair, washed her with water and wine, but it was to no avail. The dear child was dead and remained dead. They laid her on a bier, and all seven of them sat down beside it and mourned over her. They wept for three whole days, and then they intended to bury her, but she looked so alive and still had such pretty red cheeks that they said, 'We can't possibly bury her in the dingy ground.'

Instead, they made a transparent glass coffin so that she could be seen from all sides. Then they put her in it, wrote her name on it in gold letters, and added that she was a princess. They carried the coffin to the top of the mountain, and from then on one of them always stayed beside it and guarded it. Some animals came also and wept for Snow White. There was an owl, then a raven, and finally a dove. Snow White lay in the coffin for many, many years and did not decay. Indeed, she seemed to be sleeping, for she was still as white as snow, as red as blood, and her hair as black as ebony.

Now it happened that a prince came to the forest one day, and when he arrived at the dwarfs' cottage, he decided to spend the night. Then he went to the mountain and saw the coffin with beautiful Snow White inside. After he read what was written on the coffin in gold letters, he said to the dwarfs, 'Let me have the coffin, and I'll pay you whatever you want.'

But the dwarfs answered, 'We won't give it up for all the gold in the world.'

'Then give it to me as a gift,' he said, 'for I can't go on living without being able to see Snow White. I'll honour her and cherish her as my dearly beloved.'

Since he spoke with such fervour, the good dwarfs took pity on him and gave him the coffin. The prince ordered his servants to carry the coffin on their shoulders, but they stumbled over some shrubs, and the jolt caused the poisoned piece of apple that Snow White had bitten off to be released from her throat. It was not long before she opened her eyes, lifted up the lid of the coffin, sat up, and was alive again.

'Oh, Lord! Where am I?' she exclaimed.

The prince rejoiced and said, 'You're with me,' and he told her what had happened. Then he added, 'I love you more than anything else in the world. Come with me to my father's castle. I want you to be my wife.'

Snow White felt that he was sincere, so she went with

him, and their wedding was celebrated with great pomp and splendour.

Now, Snow White's stepmother had also been invited to the wedding celebration, and after she had dressed herself in beautiful clothes, she went to the mirror and said:

> 'Mirror, mirror, on the wall,
> who in this realm is the fairest of all?'

The mirror answered:

> 'You, my queen, may have a beauty quite rare,
> but Snow White is a thousand times more fair.'

The evil woman uttered a loud curse and became so terribly afraid that she did not know what to do. At first she did not want to go to the wedding celebration. But, she could not calm herself until she saw the young queen. When she entered the hall, she recognized Snow White. The evil queen was so petrified with fright that she could not budge. Iron slippers had already been heated over a fire, and they were brought over to her with tongs. Finally, she had to put on the red-hot slippers and dance until she fell down dead.

22

Rumpelstiltskin

ONCE upon a time there was a miller who was poor, but he had a beautiful daughter. Now it happened that he was talking with the king one time, and in order to make himself seem important, he said to the king, 'I have a daughter who can spin straw into gold.'

'That is an art that pleases me!' the king replied. 'If your daughter is as talented as you say, then bring her to my castle tomorrow, and I'll put her to a test.'

When the maiden was brought to him, he led her into a room that was filled with straw. There he gave her a spinning wheel and spindle and said, 'Now get to work! If you don't spin this straw into gold by morning, then you must die.' Then he locked the door himself, and she remained inside all alone.

The miller's poor daughter sat there feeling close to her wits' end, for she knew nothing about spinning straw into gold, and her fear grew greater and greater. When she began to weep, the door suddenly opened, and a little man entered.

'Good evening, mistress miller, why are you weeping so?'

'Oh,' answered the maiden, 'I'm supposed to spin straw into gold, and I don't know how.'

The little man then asked, 'What will you give me if I spin it for you?'

'My necklace,' the maiden said.

The little man took the necklace and sat down at the wheel, and *whizz, whizz, whizz*, three times round, the spool was full. Then he inserted another one, and *whizz, whizz, whizz*, the second was full. And so it went until morning, when all the straw was spun, and all the spools were filled with gold. The king appeared right at sunrise, and when he saw the gold, he was surprised and pleased, but his heart grew even greedier. He locked the miller's daughter in another room that was even larger than the first and ordered her to spin all the straw into gold if she valued her life. The maiden did not know what to do and began to weep. Once again the door opened, and the little man appeared and asked, 'What will you give me if I spin the straw into gold for you?'

'The ring from my finger,' answered the maiden.

The little man took the ring, began to work away at the wheel again, and by morning he had spun all the straw into shining gold. The king was extremely pleased by the sight, but his lust for gold was still not satisfied. So he had the miller's daughter brought into an even larger room filled with straw and said to her, 'You must spin all this into gold tonight. If you succeed, you shall become my wife.' To himself he thought, Even though she's just a miller's daughter, I'll never find a richer woman anywhere in the world.

When the maiden was alone, the little man came again for a third time and asked, 'What will you give me if I spin the straw into gold once more?'

'I have nothing left to give,' answered the maiden.

'Then promise me your first child when you become queen.'

Who knows whether it will ever come to that? thought the miller's daughter. And since she knew of no other way out of her predicament, she promised the little man what he had demanded. In return the little man spun the straw into gold once again. When the king came in the morning and found everything as he had wished, he married her, and the beautiful miller's daughter became a queen.

After a year she gave birth to a beautiful child. The little man had disappeared from her mind, but now he suddenly appeared in her room and said, 'Now give me what you promised.'

The queen was horrified and offered the little man all the treasures of the kingdom if he would let her keep her child, but the little man replied, 'No, something living is more important to me than all the treasures in the world.'

Then the queen began to grieve and weep so much that the little man felt sorry for her. 'I'll give you three days' time,' he said. 'If you can guess my name by the third day, you shall keep your child.'

The queen spent the entire night trying to recall all the names she had ever heard. She also sent a messenger out into the country to inquire high and low what other names there were. On the following day, when the little man appeared, she began with Kaspar, Melchior, Balzer, and then repeated all the names she knew, one after the other. But to all of them, the little man said, 'That's not my name.'

The second day she had her servants ask around in the neighbouring area what names people used, and she came up with the most unusual and strangest names when the little man appeared.

'Is your name Ribsofbeef or Muttonchops or Lacedleg?'

But he always replied, 'That's not my name.'

On the third day the messenger returned and reported,

'I couldn't find a single new name, but as I was climbing a high mountain at the edge of the forest, where the fox and the hare say good night to each other, I saw a small cottage, and in front of the cottage was a fire, and around the fire danced a ridiculous little man who was hopping on one leg and screeching:

"Today I'll brew, tomorrow I'll bake.
Soon I'll have the queen's namesake.
Oh, how hard it is to play my game,
for Rumpelstiltskin is my name!"'

You can imagine how happy the queen was when she heard the name. And as soon as the little man entered and asked 'What's my name, Your Highness?' she responded first by guessing.

'Is your name Kunz?'

'No.'

'Is your name Heinz?'

'No.'

'Can your name be Rumpelstiltskin?'

'The devil told you! The devil told you!' the little man screamed, and he stamped so ferociously with his right foot that his leg went deep into the ground up to his waist. Then he grabbed the other foot angrily with both hands and ripped himself in two.

23

The Golden Bird

IN DAYS of old there was a king who had a beautiful pleasure garden behind his castle, and in this garden there was a tree that bore golden apples. After the apples became ripe, they were counted, but on the very next morning one was missing. This was reported to the king, and he ordered the tree to be guarded every night.

Now, the king had three sons, and at nightfall he sent the oldest to the garden. When midnight came, however, he could not prevent himself from sleeping, and the next morning another apple was missing. The following night the second son had to keep watch, but he did not fare any better. When the clock struck twelve, he fell asleep, and in the morning another apple was missing. Then it was the third son's turn to keep watch. He was also ready, but the king did not trust him and thought he would do even worse than his brothers. Finally, he gave him permission, and the young prince lay down under the tree, kept watch, and fought off sleep. When the clock struck twelve, there was a rustling above him, and in the moonlight he saw a bird flying through the air. The bird's feathers were made of pure gold and glistened as it descended onto the tree. When the bird pecked off an apple, the young prince shot an arrow at it. The bird flew off, but the arrow clipped one of the golden feathers, and it dropped to the ground. The young prince picked up the feather, brought it to the king the next morning, and told him what had happened during the night. The king assembled his councillors and everyone declared that a feather like this was worth more than the entire kingdom.

'If the feather is so precious,' the king announced, 'then one alone won't do for me. I must have, and intend to have, the whole bird.'

So the oldest son set out; he believed he would certainly find the bird because he was so clever. After he had gone a short way, he saw a fox sitting at the edge of a forest, took aim with his gun, and was about to fire when the fox cried out, 'Don't shoot! I'll give you some good advice if you hold your fire. You're on the right way to the golden bird, and tonight you'll come to a village where you'll see two inns facing each other. One will be brightly lit with a great deal of merrymaking inside. Be sure you keep away from that place. Instead, you should go into the other inn, even though it looks dismal.'

How can such a foolish beast give sensible advice? thought the prince, and he pulled the trigger. However, his shot missed the fox, who stretched out his tail and dashed quickly into the forest. Then the prince continued his journey, and by evening he arrived at the village where the two inns were standing: in one of them there was singing and dancing, while the other appeared rather dismal and shabby.

I'd certainly be a fool, he thought, if I were to stay at that dismal-looking inn instead of staying at this fine one here. So he went into the cheerful inn, lived to the hilt like a king, and forgot the bird, his father, and all the good lessons he had ever learned.

After some time had passed, it became clear that the oldest son would not return. Therefore, the second son set out to look for the golden bird. Like the oldest son, he too met the fox, who gave him good advice that he did not heed. He came to the two inns and saw his brother at the window of the inn in which there were sounds of carousing. When his brother called out to him, he could not resist; he went inside and began living only to satisfy his lust.

Some more time passed, and now the youngest prince wanted to set out and try his luck. But his father would not let him.

'It's no use,' the king said. 'He'll have less of a chance of finding the golden bird than his brothers. And, if he has a mishap, he won't know how to fend for himself. He's not the smartest person in the world.'

However, the prince kept insisting, and the king finally gave him permission to set out. Once again the fox was sitting at the edge of the forest, pleaded for his life, and gave good advice. Since the young prince was good-natured, he said, 'Don't worry, little fox, I won't harm you.'

'You won't regret it,' answered the fox. 'Now climb on my tail, and I'll help you get there more quickly.'

No sooner did the prince sit down on the fox's tail than the fox began to run. And he went up hill and down dale so swiftly that the wind whistled through the prince's hair. When they came to the village, the prince got off the tail, followed the fox's good advice, and, without looking around, entered the shabbier inn. After spending a pleasant night there, he went out to the field the next morning and found the fox already sitting on the ground.

'I'm going to tell you what else you've got to do,' said the fox. 'If you go straight ahead, you'll eventually come to a castle. In front of this castle there's a whole troop of soldiers lying on the ground, but don't pay any attention to them, for they'll all be snoring and sleeping. Go right through the middle of their ranks and straight into the castle. Next, you're to go through all the rooms until you come to a chamber where the golden bird is hanging in a wooden cage. Nearby you'll also find a golden cage hanging just for decoration. But be careful not to take the bird out of its plain cage and put it into the splendid one. Otherwise, you'll be in for trouble.'

Upon saying these words, the fox stretched out his tail again, and the prince sat down on it. The fox raced up hill and down dale so swiftly that the wind whistled through the prince's hair. When the prince arrived at the castle, he found everything just as the fox had said it would be. Upon entering the last room, he saw the golden bird sitting in its wooden cage and also a golden cage beside it. The three golden apples were lying about the room as well. The prince thought it would be ridiculous to leave the beautiful bird in the plain, ugly cage. So he opened the door, grabbed hold of the bird, and put it into the golden cage. At that very moment the bird uttered a piercing cry that caused the soldiers to wake up; they rushed inside and took him off to prison. The next morning he was brought before the court, and after he confessed to everything, he was sentenced to death. However, the king said he would spare his life under one condition: the prince had to promise to bring him the golden horse that ran faster than the wind; if he did, he would receive the golden bird as his reward.

The prince set out, but he sighed and grew sad, for he did not know where to find the golden horse. Suddenly, he saw his old friend the fox again, sitting by the roadside.

'You see,' said the fox, 'all this happened because you didn't listen to me. However, keep your spirits up. I'm here to assist you, and I'll tell you how to get the golden horse. First, you must go straight ahead until you come to a castle where the horse is standing in the stable. There will be grooms lying on the ground in front of the stable, but they'll be snoring and sleeping, and you'll be able to lead the golden horse out of its stall with ease. But make sure you put the plain wooden and leather saddle on the horse and not the golden one that's hanging nearby. Otherwise, you'll be in for trouble.'

Then the fox stretched out its tail, and the prince sat down on it. The fox raced up hill and down dale so swiftly that the wind whistled through the prince's hair. Shortly after, everything happened as the fox said it would. The prince entered the stable where the golden horse was standing. However, when he was about to put the saddle on the horse, he thought, I'd be putting this beautiful horse to shame if I didn't give it the fine saddle that it deserves! Yet, no sooner did the golden saddle touch the horse than it began to neigh loudly, which caused the grooms to wake up; they seized the prince and threw him into prison. The next morning he was sentenced to death by the court. However, the king promised to spare his life and grant him the golden horse, as well, if the prince would fetch him the beautiful princess from the golden castle.

Now, the prince set out with a heavy heart, but fortunately for him he soon encountered the faithful fox.

'I really should leave you to your bad luck,' said the fox, 'but I feel sorry for you and want to help you out of your difficulty. This path leads directly to the golden castle. You'll arrive there in the evening, and at night, when everything's quiet, the beautiful princess will go to the bathhouse to bathe herself. When she goes there, you're to run up to her and give her a kiss. Then she'll follow you, and you can take her with you. But don't allow her to take leave of her parents. Otherwise, you'll be in for trouble.'

The fox stretched out his tail, and the prince sat down on it. The fox raced up hill and down dale so swiftly that the wind whistled through the prince's hair. When he arrived at the golden castle, it was just as the fox had said it would be. The prince waited until midnight, when everyone lay in a deep sleep and the beautiful maiden went to the bathhouse. Then he ran up to her and gave her a kiss. She said she would gladly go with him, but she implored him with tears to let her say farewell to her parents. At first he resisted her pleas, but when she kept on weeping and fell at his feet, he finally gave in. But no sooner did the maiden approach her father's bed than he and everyone else in the castle woke up, and the prince was seized and put in prison. The next morning the king said to him, 'Your life is worth nothing, and you'll be pardoned only if you take away the mountain that's lying in front of my window and blocking my view. If you successfully perform this task within eight days, you shall have my daughter as reward.'

The prince began to dig and shovel without stopping, but when he saw how little he had accomplished after seven days, that all his work amounted to nothing, he gave up all hope and became very depressed. However, on the evening of the seventh day, the fox appeared and said, 'You don't deserve my assistance, but just go and get some sleep. I'll do the job for you.'

The next morning, when the prince awoke and looked out the window, the mountain had vanished. His heart filled with joy, and he rushed to the king and reported that he had completed his task. Whether the king liked it or not, he had to keep his word and give him his daughter.

The prince and the king's daughter now set out together, and it did not take long before the faithful fox joined them.

'Nothing could be better than what you have now,' said the fox, 'but the golden horse goes along with the princess from the golden castle.'

'How am I to get it?' asked the prince.

'I'll tell you,' answered the fox. 'First you must bring the beautiful maiden to the king who sent you to the golden castle. There will be enormous rejoicing, and they'll gladly give you the golden horse. When they lead it out, mount it right away and shake hands with everyone and say good-bye. Make sure that the beautiful maiden is the last person, and when you have clasped her hand, swing her up to you in one motion and gallop away. Nobody can possibly catch you, for the horse runs faster than the wind.'

Everything went as planned, and the prince carried off the beautiful maiden on the golden horse. The fox followed them, and then he said to the prince, 'Now I'll help you get the golden bird. As you begin approaching the castle where the golden bird's being kept, let the maiden get down from the horse, and I'll look after her. Then ride the golden horse into the castle courtyard.

There will be great rejoicing at the sight of the golden horse, and they'll carry out the golden bird. As soon as you have the cage in your hand, race away and fetch the princess.'

After this plan had also been successfully carried out and the prince was about to ride home with his treasures, the fox said, 'Now I want you to reward me for my help.'

'What would you like?' asked the prince.

'When we come to the forest, I want you to shoot me dead and cut off my head and paws.'

'What kind of gratitude is that?' said the prince. 'I can't possibly do what you wish.'

'If you won't do it, I'll have to leave you. But before I depart, I want to give you one last piece of advice. Beware of two things: don't buy flesh that's bound for the gallows, and don't sit on the edge of a well.' Upon saying that, the fox ran into the forest.

What a strange animal! the prince thought. He's got all kinds of weird notions. Who would want to buy flesh bound for the gallows? And I've never had any desire to sit on the edge of a well.

He continued his journey with the beautiful maiden, and his way led again through the village where his two brothers had remained. Upon noticing that there was a great commotion and uproar, he asked what was going on and was told that two men were about to be hanged. When he came closer to the scene, he saw that the men were his brothers, who had committed all sorts of terrible acts and had squandered all their possessions. He asked whether they could be pardoned in some way.

'If you're willing to buy their freedom,' the people answered. 'But why would you want to waste your money on such evil criminals and set them free?'

However, he did not think twice about it and purchased their freedom. When they were released, he continued the journey in the company of his brothers. After some time they came to the forest where they had first met the fox, and since it was cool and lovely there and the sun was very hot, the two brothers said, 'Let's go over to the well and rest awhile. We could also eat and drink.'

He agreed, and during their conversation he forgot the fox's warning and sat down on the edge of the well, not suspecting anything evil. But the two brothers pushed him backward into the well, took the maiden, the horse, and the bird, and went home to their father.

'Not only have we brought you the golden bird,' they said to the king, 'but we've also got the golden horse and the maiden from the golden castle.'

There was a great celebration, but the horse refused to eat, the bird did not sing, and the maiden sat and wept.

Meanwhile, the youngest brother managed to survive. Fortunately, the well had been dry, and he fell on soft moss without harming himself. For a while he could not get out, but his faithful fox stood by his side even then and helped him out of his dilemma. He jumped down the well and scolded the prince for not listening to his advice.

'But I won't abandon you,' the fox said. 'You'll soon see the light of day.'

The fox told him to grab his tail and hold it tightly. Then he pulled him up to the top.

'You're still not completely out of danger,' the fox said. 'Your brothers were not positive that you had died. So they've ordered that the forest be surrounded by guards who are to shoot you on sight.'

Along the way the prince came across a poor man, with whom he exchanged clothes. That was how the prince succeeded in reaching the king's court without being recognized. However, the bird began to sing, the horse began to eat, and the beautiful maiden stopped weeping. The king was astonished and asked, 'What does all this mean?'

'I don't know,' said the beautiful maiden, 'but I was sad, and now I'm very cheerful. I feel as if my true bridegroom had come.'

She told the king what had happened, even though

the two older brothers had threatened to kill her if she revealed anything. The king ordered everyone in the castle to gather around him, and the young prince appeared also, as a poor man in rags. But the princess recognized him at once and embraced him. The godless brothers were seized and executed, while the youngest married the beautiful princess and was designated heir to the king.

But what happened to the poor fox? Well, many years later the prince went walking through the forest again and encountered the fox, who said, 'Now you have everything you desired, but there's been no end to my misfortune, even though it's been within your power to free me.'

Once again the fox implored him to shoot him dead and cut off his head and paws. This time the prince did it, and no sooner was it done than the fox turned into none other than the brother of the beautiful princess, who was finally released from a magic spell that had been cast over him. Now nothing more was missing from their happiness as long as they lived.

24
The Dog and the Sparrow

THERE once was a sheepdog whose master was cruel and let him starve. When he could no longer stand it, he departed sadly. Along the road he met a sparrow who said, 'Brother dog, why are you so sad?'

'I'm hungry and have nothing to eat,' the dog answered.

'Dear brother,' responded the sparrow, 'come with me to the city, and I'll see that you get plenty to eat.'

So they went into the city together, and when they came to a butcher shop, the sparrow said to the dog, 'Stay here. I'm going to peck off a piece of meat, and it will drop down for you.'

The bird flew to a counter and looked around to make sure that nobody had noticed him. Then he pecked, pulled, and tugged until a piece of meat lying near the edge of the counter slipped down to the ground. The dog grabbed it at once, ran into a corner, and devoured it.

'Now come with me to another shop,' said the sparrow. 'I'll get you one more piece so you'll be full.'

When the dog had eaten the second piece, the sparrow asked, 'Brother dog, have you had enough?'

'Yes, I've had enough meat,' he answered. 'But I still haven't had any bread.'

'You'll get that too,' said the sparrow. 'Just come along with me.'

So he led him to a baker's shop and pecked at some rolls until they tumbled down, and when the dog desired even more, the sparrow led him to another shop and fetched more bread for him. After that had been consumed, the sparrow said, 'Brother dog, have you had enough now?'

'Yes,' he answered. 'Let's take a little walk outside the city.'

Then the two of them went strolling down the highway, but the weather was so warm that, after they had gone a little way, the dog said, 'I'm tired and would very much like to sleep.'

'All right, just go to sleep,' answered the sparrow. 'In the meantime I'll sit down on a branch.'

The dog lay down on the road and fell soundly asleep.

While he lay there and slept, a wagoner came along with his wagon loaded with two barrels of wine and drawn by three horses. The sparrow realized that the wagon was heading straight down the lane in which the dog was lying and that it was not going to swerve.

'Wagoner, don't do that, or I'll make you a poor man!' the sparrow cried out.

'You won't make me poor!' the wagoner bellowed as he whipped the horses and drove the wagon over the dog, killing him with the wheels.

'You've run over my brother dog and killed him! That will cost you your wagon and horses!' exclaimed the sparrow.

'Don't make me laugh! My horses and wagon!' said the wagoner. 'You can't do anything to harm me.'

He drove on, but the sparrow crawled under the canvas and pecked at one of the bungholes of a barrel until a bung came out. Then all the wine ran out without the wagoner noticing it. Only after he turned around at one point did he realize that the wagon was dripping. So he examined the barrels and found that one was empty.

'Oh, poor me!' the wagoner cried out.

'Not poor enough yet,' said the sparrow, and he flew down onto the head of one of the horses and pecked its eyes out. When the wagoner saw that, he pulled out his axe and tried to hit the sparrow with it. But the bird flew into the air, and the wagoner instead struck his horse on the head and it fell down dead.

'Oh, poor me!' the wagoner cried out.

'Not poor enough yet,' said the sparrow, and when the wagoner drove away with two horses, the sparrow crawled under the canvas again and pecked out the bung of the second barrel so that all the wine flowed out. When the wagoner became aware of that, he cried out once more, 'Oh, poor me!'

But the sparrow answered, 'Not poor enough yet.' He flew down and landed on the head of the second horse and pecked its eyes out. The wagoner ran over and took out his axe, but the sparrow flew up into the air and thus caused the wagoner to strike his second horse dead.

'Oh, poor me!'

'Not poor enough yet,' said the sparrow, who landed on the head of the third horse and pecked its eyes out. The wagoner swung his axe at the sparrow in rage without bothering to look around. However, he missed the bird and struck his third horse dead.

'Oh, poor me!' he cried out.

'Not poor enough yet,' answered the sparrow. 'Now I'm going to make you poor at your own home.' And he flew off.

The wagoner had to leave the wagon standing there and walked home highly annoyed and furious. 'Oh,' he said to his wife, 'you can't imagine the bad luck I've had! The wine ran out, and all three horses are dead.'

'Oh, husband!' she answered. 'A wicked bird has flown into our house! It's brought all the birds in the whole world together, and they've descended on our wheat in the loft and are eating it up.'

The wagoner climbed up to the loft, and there he saw thousands of birds on the floor eating the wheat, and the sparrow was sitting in the middle.

'Oh, poor me!' the wagoner cried out.

'Not poor enough yet,' answered the sparrow. 'Wagoner, it's going to cost you your life!' And the sparrow flew off.

With all his property gone, the wagoner now went downstairs and sat by the stove, feeling angry and bitter. Then the sparrow landed outside his window and called out, 'Wagoner, it's going to cost you your life.'

The wagoner grabbed his axe and threw it at the sparrow. But it missed the bird and merely broke the windowpane in two. The sparrow hopped inside the house, sat down on the stove, and called out, 'Wagoner, it's going to cost you your life!'

Now the wagoner was furious and blind with rage. He chopped the stove in two and continued to chop all the furniture—the mirror, the benches, the table—and finally the walls of the house, all in an effort to hit the sparrow, who flew from spot to spot. At last the wagoner caught the bird with his hand.

'Do you want me to kill it?' his wife asked.

'No!' he yelled. 'That would be too merciful. I want it to die a more cruel death. I'm going to swallow it.'

Then he took the bird and swallowed him whole. However, the sparrow began to flutter inside his body and fluttered back up again into the man's mouth. Once there he stuck out his head and cried, 'Wagoner, it's going to cost you your life!'

The wagoner handed the axe to his wife and said, 'Wife, kill the bird in my mouth!'

His wife swung the axe, but she missed and hit the wagoner right on the head, and he fell down dead. But the sparrow flew up and away.

25
Freddy and Katy

ONCE there was a man named Freddy and a woman named Katy who got married and began living together in wedlock. One day Freddy said, 'I'm going to the field, Katy. When I return, I want some roast meat on the table to take care of my hunger and a cool drink for my thirst.'

'Just run along, Freddy,' Katy answered. 'Just go. I'll have everything ready the way you want it.'

When noontime drew near, she got a sausage from the chimney, put it in a frying pan, added butter, and set it on the fire. The sausage began to fry and sizzle, and while Katy was standing there and holding the handle of the pan, she began thinking, and it occurred to her, You could go down into the cellar and draw the beer before the sausage is done. She fixed the pan so it would not tip, took a tankard, and went down into the cellar, where she began to draw the beer. As the beer was flowing into the tankard and Katy was gazing at it, she suddenly recalled, Hey, the dog's upstairs, and since he's not tied up, he could get the sausage from the pan. Oh, it's a lucky thing I thought of that!

She ran up the cellar stairs in a jiffy, but her spitz had already grabbed the sausage with his jaws and was dragging it along the ground. Still, Katy was quick to act: she ran after him and chased him a long way over the fields, but the dog was faster and clasped the sausage tightly as he dashed off with it beyond her reach.

'What's gone is gone,' said Katy, who turned back home. Since she was tired from running, she walked very slowly and cooled herself off. In the meantime, the beer continued to flow from the keg, for Katy had forgotten to shut the tap. When the tankard became full and there was no more room in it, the beer flowed over onto the cellar floor until the whole keg was empty. As soon as Katy reached the top of the stairs, she saw the accident and cried out, 'Heavens! How are you going to keep Freddy from noticing it?'

She thought for a while until she finally remembered a sack with fine wheat flour that was still up in the loft. It had been bought at the last fair, and she thought it would be a good idea to fetch it and sprinkle it over the beer. 'Yes,' she said, 'a stitch in time saves nine.' She climbed up to the loft, brought down the sack and threw it right on the tankard full of beer, causing it to topple. Now even Freddy's drink swam about in the cellar. 'That's quite all right,' said Katy. 'They all belong in the same boat together.' Then she scattered the flour all over the cellar. When she was finished, she was tremendously pleased with her work and said, 'How clean and neat everything looks here!'

At noon Freddy came home and said, 'Well, wife, what have you made for me?'

'Oh, Freddy,' she answered, 'I wanted to fry a sausage for you, but while I was drawing the beer in the cellar, the dog came and made off with the pan. Then, while I was chasing the dog, the beer ran over, and as I went to dry up the beer with the wheat flour, I knocked over the tankard. But don't get upset, the cellar is all dry again.'

'Katy, Katy!' he said. 'You shouldn't have done that! Just think! You let the sausage be carried off, you let the beer run out of the keg, and on top of it, you squandered our fine flour!'

'Well, Freddy, I didn't know that. You should have told me.'

If that's the way your wife is, Freddy thought, then you'd better take precautions. Now, Freddy had saved up a nice sum in talers that he finally changed into gold, and he went to Katy and said, 'Look, these here are yellow chips, and I'm going to put them into a pot and bury them in the stable under the cow's manger. Make sure you keep away from them, or I'll teach you a lesson!'

'Don't worry, Freddy,' she said. 'I promise not to touch them.'

Soon after, while Freddy was away, some peddlers came to the village selling clay pots and bowls, and they asked the young woman whether she wanted to trade with them.

'Oh, you're so kind,' she said. 'I don't have any money and can't buy anything. But if you can use yellow chips, I'll make a trade with you.'

'Yellow chips? Why not? But we'd like to have a look first.'

'Well, just go into the barn and dig under the cow's manger and you'll find the yellow chips. I'm not allowed to go there.'

The scoundrels went there, dug up the ground, and found pure gold. Then they put it into their pack and ran off, leaving the pots and bowls behind in the house. Katy thought she should make use of her new kitchenware, but since there was already so much of it in the kitchen, she knocked the bottoms out of all the new pots and hung them as ornaments on the fence poles all

213

around the house. When Freddy came and saw the new ornaments, he asked, 'Katy, what have you done?'

'Well, Freddy, I bought them with the yellow chips that were buried under the cow's manger. I didn't go near them myself. I made the peddlers dig them up.'

'Oh, wife!' said Freddy. 'What have you done? They weren't yellow chips. They were pure gold, our entire fortune! You shouldn't have done that.'

'Well, Freddy,' she said. 'I didn't know that. You should have told me before.'

Katy stood there awhile and tried to think of something. Finally, she said, 'Listen, Freddy, we can get the gold back. Let's run after the thieves.'

'All right,' said Freddy. 'Let's try it, but take some butter and cheese so that we have something to eat along the way.'

'Yes, Freddy, I'll take some along.'

They set out on foot, and since Freddy was faster, Katy trailed after him. It's to my advantage, she thought. If we turn back, then I'll have a head start. Now she came to a hill where there were deep wagon ruts on both sides of the road. 'Just look!' said Katy. 'They've trampled and torn apart the poor earth, so that it's all beaten up! It will never get well again as long as it lives.' Out of the kindness of her heart, she took out the butter and smeared the ruts on the right and left so they would not be hurt so much by the wheels. While she was performing this charitable work and was bending over, a cheese rolled out of her pocket and down the hill.

'I've already climbed up the hill once,' said Katy, 'and I'm not going down again. Let some other cheese run down and fetch it back.'

So she took another cheese and rolled it down the hill. However, this cheese did not come back either, so she sent a third one after it and thought, Perhaps they don't like to walk alone and are waiting for company. When all three of them failed to return, she said, 'I'm not sure what all this means, but it's possible that the third one didn't find the way and has gone astray. I'll just send a fourth to call them all back.'

The fourth did not do the job any better than the third. Then Katy became so annoyed that she threw the fifth and sixth down the hill too, and they were the last she had. For a while she stood and waited for them to come back, but when they did not return, she said, 'Oh, you're just the right ones to send in search of death because you really drag your feet. Do you think I'm going to wait for you any longer? I'm moving on, and you can catch up with me. You've got younger legs than mine.'

Katy went on and found Freddy, who had stopped to wait for her because he wanted something to eat.

'Now let's have some of the food you brought along.'

She handed him the dry bread.

'Where's the butter and cheese?' her husband asked.

'Oh, Freddy,' said Katy, 'I smeared the ruts with the butter, and the cheese will soon be here. One got away from me, and so I sent the others after it.'

'You shouldn't have done that, Katy,' said Freddy. 'Just think! You smeared the butter on the road, and you let the cheese roll down the hill!'

'Well, Freddy, you should have told me.'

They ate the dry bread together, and Freddy said, 'Katy, did you lock up the house before you left?'

'No, Freddy, you should have told me before.'

'Well, then go home and lock it up before we continue on our way. Also, bring something else to eat with you. I'll wait for you here.'

As Katy began walking back, she began thinking, Freddy obviously wants something else to eat. Since he doesn't like butter and cheese, I'll bring him some dried pears in a handkerchief and a jug full of vinegar to drink.

When she was about to leave the house again, she bolted the upper half of the door and took the lower half off the hinges. Then she carried it on her back because she thought the house would be safer if she kept the door with her. Then she took her time walking back since she thought to herself, Freddy will have all the more time to rest himself.

Once she reached her husband again, Katy said, 'There, Freddy, now you have the house door, and you'll be able to keep the house safe yourself.'

'Oh, God!' he said. 'What a clever wife I've got! She takes off the lower half of the door so that anyone can walk in, and she bolts the upper half. Now it's too late to go home again, but since you brought the door here, you'll carry it the rest of the way yourself.'

'I don't mind carrying the door, Freddy, but the dried pears and the jug of vinegar are too heavy for me. I'll hang them on the door and let the door carry them.'

Now they went into the forest to look for the thieves, but they did not find them. When it finally became dark, they climbed up into a tree to spend the night. No sooner were they sitting up high than some men came along who tend to carry off things that do not want to be carried away and who tend to find things before they are lost. They camped out right beneath the tree in which Freddy and Katy were sitting. They made a fire and began to divide their loot. Freddy climbed down the other side of the tree and gathered some stones, after which he climbed back. He wanted to throw the stones at the thieves to kill them. However, he missed, and the thieves cried out, 'Soon it will be morning, and the wind's knocking down the pinecones.'

Katy was still carrying the door on her back, and since it was so heavy and weighing her down, she thought the dried pears were to blame and said, 'Freddy, I've got to throw the dried pears down.'

'No, Katy, not now,' he answered. 'They could give us away.'

'Oh, Freddy, I've got to! They're too heavy for me.'

'Well then, do it, for all I care!'

She rolled the pears down between the branches, and the thieves said, 'Here come some bird droppings.'

Shortly afterward, since the door was still very heavy on her back, Katy said, 'Oh, Freddy, I've got to pour out the vinegar.'

'No, Katy, you mustn't do that. It could give us away.'

'Oh, Freddy, I've got to! It's too heavy for me.'

'Well then, do it, for all I care!'

So she poured out the vinegar, and it splattered all over the thieves.

'The dew's already falling,' the men said to one another.

Finally, Katy thought, Could it be the door that's been weighing me down? And she said, 'Freddy, I've got to throw the door down.'

'No, Katy, that could give us away.'

'Oh, Freddy, I've got to. It's too heavy for me.'

'No, Katy, hold on to it tight.'

'Oh, Freddy, I'm going to let it drop.'

'All right!' Freddy answered irritably. 'Let it drop for all I care!'

Then the door fell down with a great crash, and the thieves below cried out, 'The devil's coming down the tree!'

They cleared out and left everything behind. Early the next morning, when Freddy and Katy came down the tree, they found all their gold again and carried it home.

When they were home once more, Freddy said, 'Katy, you've got to be industrious and work hard now.'

'Yes, Freddy, of course I will. I'll go into the field and cut down the fruit.'

When Katy went into the field, she said to herself, 'Should I eat before I cut, or should I sleep before I cut. I think I'll eat!' So Katy ate and became tired from eating. When she started to cut some fruit, she began daydreaming and cut all her clothes to pieces—her apron, her dress, and her blouse. Upon snapping out of her dream, she stood there half naked and said to herself, 'Is that me, or is it someone else? Oh, that's not me!'

Meanwhile, it was already night, and Katy ran into the village and knocked on her husband's window.

'Freddy!' she called out.

'What is it?'

'I'd like to know if Katy's inside.'

'Yes, yes,' answered Freddy. 'She's probably lying down asleep.'

'Good,' she said. 'Then I'm clearly at home already,' and she ran off.

Outside the village Katy came across some thieves who were planning a theft. She went up to them and said, 'I want to help you steal.'

The thieves thought she knew her way around the region and agreed to let her join them. Then Katy went in front of the houses and called out, 'Folks, do you have anything you want stolen?'

This won't do! thought the thieves, and they wished they could get rid of Katy.

'There's a turnip patch owned by the parson outside the village,' they said to her. 'We want you to go there and pull up some of the turnips for us.'

Katy went to the patch and began to pull up some turnips, but she was so lazy that she remained in a crouched position. Soon a man came by, stopped, watched her, and thought the devil was tearing up all the turnips in the patch. So he ran to the parson in the village and said, 'Parson, the devil's in your turnip patch, and he's tearing up all your turnips.'

'Oh, God!' exclaimed the parson. 'I've got a lame foot and can't run out to banish him.'

'I'll carry you on my back,' said the man, and he carried him out to the field. When they got to the turnip patch, Katy straightened herself up.

'Oh, it's really the devil!' the parson cried, and they both rushed off. Indeed, since his fright was so great, the parson was able to run faster with his lame foot than the man who had carried him with his two sound legs.

26

The Queen Bee

ONCE two princes went forth in search of adventure, and after they fell into a wild, decadent way of life, they never returned home again. Their youngest brother, who was called Simpleton, went out to look for them, but when he finally found them, they ridiculed him for thinking that he, as naive as he was, could make his way in the world when they, who were much more clever, had not been able to succeed.

At length the three of them travelled together and came to an anthill. The two oldest wanted to smash it and watch small ants crawl around in fright and carry away their eggs, but Simpleton said, 'Leave the little creatures in peace. I won't let you disturb them.'

They continued on their way and came to a lake where a great many ducks were swimming. The two brothers wanted to catch a few and roast them, but Simpleton would not let them.

'Leave the creatures in peace,' he said. 'I won't let you kill them.'

Next they came to a beehive, and there was so much honey in the hive that it had dripped down the tree trunk. The two older brothers wanted to build a fire underneath it and suffocate the bees to get at the honey. However, Simpleton prevented them again and said, 'Leave the creatures in peace. I won't let you burn them.'

Finally, the three brothers came to a castle, and they saw nothing but stone horses standing in the stables. Not a living soul could be seen. They went through all the halls until they reached the end, where there was a door with three locks hanging on it. In the middle of the door there was a peephole through which one could look into the room. In there they saw a grey dwarf sitting at a table. They called to him once, then twice, but he did not hear them. Finally, they called a third time, and he got up, opened the locks, and came out. However, he did not say a word. Instead, he just led them to a richly spread table, and after they had something to eat and drink, he brought each one to his own bedroom.

The next morning the grey dwarf went to the oldest brother, beckoned to him, and conducted him to a stone tablet on which were inscribed three tasks that had to be performed if the castle was to be disenchanted. The first task involved gathering one thousand pearls that were lying in the moss of the forest. They belonged to the king's daughter and had to be collected from the moss before sundown. If one single pearl was missing, the seeker would be turned to stone.

The oldest brother went to the moss and searched the entire day, but when the day drew to a close, he had found only one hundred. Consequently, he was turned into stone as was ordained by the tablet. The next day the second brother undertook the adventure, but he did not fare much better than the oldest: he found only two hundred pearls and was turned into stone. Finally, it was Simpleton's turn to search for the pearls in the moss. However, because it was so difficult to find them and everything went so slowly, he sat down on a stone and began to weep. While he was sitting on the stone and weeping, the king of the ants whose life he had once saved came along with five thousand ants, and it did not take long before the little creatures had gathered the pearls together and stacked them in a pile.

Now, the second task was to fetch the key to the bedroom of the king's daughter from the lake. When Simpleton came to the lake, the ducks whose lives he had once saved came swimming toward him and then dived down to fetch the key from the depths.

Next came the third task, which was the hardest. The king had three daughters who lay asleep, and Simpleton had to pick out the youngest and the loveliest. However, they all looked exactly alike, and the only difference between them was that they each had eaten a different kind of sweet before falling asleep: the oldest had eaten a piece of sugar, the second a little syrup, the youngest a spoonful of honey. Just then the queen bee whom Simpleton had protected from the fire came along and tested the lips of all three princesses. At last she settled on the mouth of the princess who had eaten honey, and thus the prince was able to recognize the right daughter. Now the magic spell was broken, and everyone was set free from the deep sleep. All those who had been turned into stone regained their human form. Simpleton married the youngest and loveliest daughter and became king after her father's death, while his two brothers were married to the other two sisters.

27
The Golden Goose

THERE was once a man who had three sons, and the youngest, who was called Simpleton, was constantly mocked, disdained, and slighted. Now, one day it happened that the oldest brother decided to go into the forest to chop wood, and before he went, his mother gave him a nice, fine pancake and a bottle of wine so that he would not have to suffer from hunger or thirst. When he reached the forest, he met a grey old dwarf, who wished him good day and said, 'Give me a piece of the pancake from your pocket, and let me have a drink of wine. I'm very hungry and thirsty.'

However, the clever son answered, 'If I give you my pancake and my wine, then I won't have anything for myself. So get out of my way,' and he left the dwarf standing there and went farther into the forest. When he began chopping down a tree, it did not take long for him to make a slip and cut himself in the arm. So he had to return home and have his arm bandaged. All this happened because of the grey dwarf.

Shortly thereafter, the second son went into the forest, and the mother gave him a pancake and a bottle of wine, just as she had given the oldest. The second son too met the grey old dwarf, who asked him for a piece of the pancake and a drink of wine. But the second son also spoke quite sensibly. 'Whatever I give you, I'll be taking from myself. So get out of my way.' Then he left the dwarf standing there and went farther into the forest. Soon his punishment came as well. After he had whacked a tree a few times, he struck himself in the leg. Consequently, he had to be carried home.

Then Simpleton said, 'Father, let me go now and chop some wood.'

'Your brothers hurt themselves doing that,' said the father. 'So I want you to steer clear of the woods, especially since you know nothing about chopping down trees.'

However, Simpleton kept insisting until his father finally said, 'Go ahead. Perhaps you'll learn something after you've hurt yourself.'

The mother gave him a pancake made out of water and ashes along with a bottle of sour beer. When he went into the forest, he too met the grey old dwarf, who greeted him and said, 'Give me a piece of your pancake and a drink out of your bottle. I'm very hungry and thirsty.'

'I have only a pancake made of ashes and some sour beer,' answered Simpleton. 'If that's all right with you, let's sit down and eat.'

So they sat down, and when Simpleton took out his cake made of ashes, it turned out to be a fine pancake, and the sour beer was good wine. After they had eaten and drunk, the dwarf said, 'Since you have such a good heart and gladly share what you have, I'm going to grant you some good luck. There's an old tree over there. Just go and chop it down, and you'll find something among the roots.' Then the dwarf took leave of him.

Simpleton went over and chopped down the tree. When it fell, he saw a goose with feathers of pure gold lying among the roots. He lifted the goose up and carried it with him to an inn, where he intended to spend the night. Now, the innkeeper had three daughters, and when they saw the goose, they were curious to know what kind of strange bird it was. Moreover, they each wanted to have one of its golden feathers. The oldest thought, I'll surely find an opportunity to pluck one of its feathers.

At one point Simpleton went out, and she seized the goose by its wing, but her hand and fingers remained stuck to it. Soon afterward the second sister came and also intended to pluck a golden feather. However, no sooner did she touch her sister than she became stuck to her. Finally, the third sister came with the same intention, but the other two screamed, 'Keep away! For heaven's sake, keep away!'

But she did not comprehend why she should keep away and thought, If they're there, I see no reason why I can't be. So she ran over, and when she touched her sister, she became stuck to her, and all three had to spend the night with the goose.

The next morning Simpleton took the goose in his arm, set out, and did not bother himself about the three sisters who were stuck to the goose. They were compelled to run after him constantly, left and right, wherever his legs took him. In the middle of a field they came across the parson, and when he saw the procession, he said, 'Shame on you, you naughty girls! Is that the right way to behave?'

Upon saying that, he grabbed the youngest sister by the hand and attempted to pull her away, but when he touched her, he also got stuck and had to run along behind them. Shortly afterward the sexton came by and saw the parson trailing the three girls on their heels. In his amazement he called out, 'Hey, Parson, where are you off to in such a hurry? Don't forget that we have a christening today!'

The sexton ran up to the parson, and as soon as he touched his sleeve, he became stuck like the others. Now the five of them had to trot after Simpleton, one stuck to the other, and they approached two farmers who were coming from the fields with their hoes. The parson called out to them to set them loose. However, as soon as they touched the sexton, they got stuck, and now there were seven of them trailing Simpleton and his goose.

After some time Simpleton came to a city ruled by a king who had a daughter that was so serious, she never laughed. Consequently, the king issued a decree that whoever could make her laugh would have her for his wife. When Simpleton heard that, he went before the king's daughter with his goose and its followers, and when she saw the seven people all attached to one another and running along, she burst out laughing, and it appeared as if she would never stop. So Simpleton demanded the princess as his bride, but the king had no desire to have him for a son-in-law and raised all kinds of objections. Eventually, he said that first Simpleton would have to produce a man capable of drinking the contents of a cellar full of wine before he could wed his daughter.

Now, Simpleton quickly remembered the grey dwarf, for he thought that he might help him. Therefore, he went out into the forest, right to the spot where he had chopped down the tree. There he saw a man with a sad face sitting and moping. Simpleton asked what was bothering him so much, and he answered, 'I'm terribly thirsty and don't seem to be able to quench my thirst. I can't stand cold water, and just now I emptied a barrel of wine, but that was like a drop on a hot stone.'

'Well, I can help you,' said Simpleton. 'Just come with me, and you'll be able to drink your fill.'

He led him to the king's cellar, and the man rushed over to the large barrels and set to work: he drank so much that his sides began to hurt, but before the day was over, he had emptied the entire cellar. So once again Simpleton demanded his bride, but the king was perturbed that such a common fellow, whom everyone called Simpleton, was to have his daughter. Therefore, he set a new condition: now Simpleton had to produce a man who could eat a mountain of bread.

Simpleton immediately reacted by going directly into the forest. There, on the same spot as before, he saw a man sitting who was pulling in a belt around his waist. The man made an awful face and said, 'I've eaten an oven full of coarse bread, but what good is that when

I'm as hungry as a lion. My stomach's still empty, and I have to pull in my belt if I don't want to die of hunger.'

Simpleton was glad to hear that and said, 'Get up and come with me. You shall eat your fill.'

He led him to the king's courtyard, where the king had gathered all the flour of the entire kingdom and had had it baked into a tremendous mountain. However, the man from the forest stepped up to it, began eating, and consumed the whole mountain in one day. Now for the third time, Simpleton claimed his bride, but the king found another way out and demanded a ship that could sail on land and water.

'As soon as you come sailing back in it,' he said, 'you shall have my daughter for your wife.'

Simpleton went straight into the forest and encountered the grey old dwarf to whom he had given his cake.

'I've drunk and eaten for you,' said the dwarf. 'Now I'll also give you the ship. I'm doing all this because you treated me so kindly.'

Then he gave him the ship, and when the king saw it, he could no longer prevent him from marrying his daughter. The wedding was celebrated, and after the king's death, Simpleton inherited the kingdom and lived happily ever after with his wife.

28
All Fur

ONCE upon a time there was a king whose wife had golden hair and was so beautiful that her equal could not be found anywhere on earth. Now, it happened that she became sick, and when she felt she was about to die, she called the king to her and said, 'If you desire to marry again after my death, I'd like you to take someone who is as beautiful as I am and who has golden hair like mine. Promise me that you will do this.'

After the king had promised her that, she closed her eyes and died. For a long time the king could not be consoled and did not think about remarrying. Finally, his councillors said, 'This cannot continue. The king must marry again so that we may have a queen.'

Messengers were sent far and wide to search for a

bride who might equal the beauty of the dead queen. Yet, they could not find anyone like her in the world, and even had they found such a woman, she certainly would not have had such golden hair. So the messengers returned with their mission unaccomplished.

Now, the king had a daughter who was just as beautiful as her dead mother, and she also had the same golden hair. When she was grown-up, the king looked at her one day and realized that her features were exactly the same as those of his dead wife. Suddenly he fell passionately in love with her and said to his councillors, 'I'm going to marry my daughter, for she is the living image of my dead wife.'

When the councillors heard that, they were horrified and said, 'God has forbidden a father to marry his daughter. Nothing good can come from such a sin, and the kingdom will be brought to ruin.'

When she heard of her father's decision, the daughter was even more horrified, but she still hoped to dissuade him from carrying out his plan. Therefore, she said to him, 'Before I fulfil your wish, I must have three dresses, one as golden as the sun, one as silvery as the moon, and one as bright as the stars. Furthermore, I want a cloak made up of a thousand kinds of pelts and furs, and each animal in your kingdom must contribute a piece of its skin to it.' She thought, He'll never be able to obtain all those furs, and by demanding this, I shall divert my father from his evil intentions.

The king, however, persisted, and the most skilful women in his realm were assembled to weave the three dresses, one as golden as the sun, one as silvery as the moon, and one as bright as the stars. His huntsmen had to catch all the animals in his entire kingdom and take a piece of their skin. Thus a cloak was made from a thousand kinds of fur. At last, when everything was finished, the king ordered the cloak to be brought and spread out before her. Then he announced, 'The wedding will be tomorrow.'

When the king's daughter saw that there was no hope whatsoever of changing her father's inclinations, she decided to run away. That night, while everyone was asleep, she got up and took three of her precious possessions: a golden ring, a tiny golden spinning wheel, and a little golden reel. She packed the dresses of the sun, the moon, and the stars into a nutshell, put on the cloak of all kinds of fur, and blackened her face and hands with soot. Then she commended herself to God and departed. She walked the whole night until she reached a great forest, and since she was tired, she climbed into a hollow tree and fell asleep.

When the sun rose, she continued to sleep and sleep until it became broad daylight. Meanwhile, it happened that the king who was the lord of this forest was out hunting in it, and when his dogs came to the tree, they started to sniff and run around it and bark.

'Go see what kind of beast has hidden itself there,' the king said to his huntsmen.

The huntsmen obeyed the king's command, and when they returned to him, they said, 'There's a strange animal lying in the hollow tree. We've never seen anything like it. Its skin is made up of a thousand different kinds of fur, and it's lying there asleep.'

'See if you can catch it alive,' said the king. 'Then tie it to the wagon, and we'll take it with us.'

When the huntsmen seized the maiden, she woke up in a fright and cried to them, 'I'm just a poor girl, forsaken by my father and mother! Please have pity on me and take me with you.'

'You'll be perfect for the kitchen, *All Fur*,' they said. 'Come with us, and you can sweep up the ashes there.'

So they put her into the wagon and drove back to the royal castle. There they showed her to a little closet beneath the stairs that was never exposed to daylight.

'Well, you furry creature,' they said, 'you can live and sleep here.'

Then she was sent to the kitchen, where she carried wood and water, kept the fires going, plucked the fowls, sorted the vegetables, swept up the ashes, and did all the dirty work. All Fur lived there for a long time in dire poverty. Ah, my beautiful princess, what shall become of you?

At one time a ball was being held in the castle, and All Fur asked the cook, 'May I go upstairs and watch for a while? I'll just stand outside the door.'

'Yes,' said the cook. 'Go ahead, but be back in half an hour. You've got to sweep up the ashes.'

All Fur took her little oil lamp, went to her closet, took off her fur cloak, and washed the soot from her face and hands so that her full beauty came to light again. Then she opened the nut and took out the dress that shone like the sun. When that was done, she went upstairs to the ball, and everyone made way for her, for they had no idea who she was and believed that she was nothing less than a royal princess. The king approached her, offered her his hand, and led her forth to dance. In his heart he thought, Never in my life have my eyes beheld anyone so beautiful! When the dance was over, she curtsied, and as the king was looking around she disappeared, and nobody knew where she had gone. The guards who were standing in front of the castle were summoned and questioned, but no one had seen her.

In the meantime, the princess had run back to her closet and had undressed quickly. Then she blackened her face and hands, put on the fur cloak, and became

All Fur once more. When she went back to the kitchen, she resumed her work and began sweeping up the ashes.

'Let that be until tomorrow,' said the cook. 'I want you to make a soup for the king. While you're doing that, I'm going upstairs to watch a little. You'd better not let a single hair drop into the soup or else you'll get nothing more to eat in the future!'

The cook went away, and All Fur made the soup for the king by brewing a bread soup as best she could. When she was finished, she fetched her golden ring from the closet and put it into the bowl in which she had prepared the soup. When the ball was over, the king ordered the soup to be brought to him, and as he ate it, he was convinced that he had never eaten a soup that had tasted as good. However, he found a ring lying at the bottom of the bowl when he had finished eating, and he could not imagine how it could have got there. He ordered the cook to appear before him, and the cook became terrified on learning that the king wanted to see him.

'You must have let a hair drop into the soup,' he said to All Fur. 'If that's true, you can expect a good beating!'

When he went before the king, he was asked who had made the soup.

'I did,' answered the cook.

However, the king said, 'That's not true, for it was much different from your usual soup and much better cooked.'

'I must confess,' responded the cook. 'I didn't cook it. The furry creature did.'

'Go and fetch her here,' said the king.

When All Fur appeared, the king asked, 'Who are you?'

'I'm just a poor girl that no longer has a mother or father.'

'Why are you in my castle?' the king continued.

'I'm good for nothing but to have boots thrown at my head,' she replied.

'Where did you get the ring that was in the soup?' he asked again.

'I don't know anything about the ring,' she answered. So the king could not find out anything and had to send her away.

Some months later there was another ball, and like the previous time, All Fur asked the cook's permission to go and watch.

'Yes,' he answered. 'But come back in half an hour and cook the king the bread soup that he likes so much.'

She ran to the little closet, washed herself quickly, took the dress as silvery as the moon out of the nut, and put it on. When she appeared upstairs, she looked like a royal princess. The king approached her again and was delighted to see her. Since the dance had just begun, they danced together, and when the dance was over, she again disappeared so quickly that the king was unable to see where she went. In the meantime, she returned to the little closet, made herself into the furry creature again, and returned to the kitchen to make the bread soup. While the cook was still upstairs, she fetched the tiny golden spinning wheel, put it into the bowl, and covered it with the soup. Then the soup was brought to the king, and he ate it and enjoyed it as much as he had the previous time. Afterward he summoned the cook, who again had to admit that All Fur had made the soup. Now All Fur had to appear before the king once more, but she merely repeated that she was good for nothing but to have boots thrown at her and that she knew nothing about the tiny golden spinning wheel.

When the king held a ball for the third time, everything happened just as it had before. To be sure, the cook now asserted, 'Furry creature, I know you're a witch. You always put something in the soup to make it taste good and to make the king like it better than anything I can cook.'

However, since she pleaded so intensely, he let her go upstairs at a given time. Thereupon she put on the dress as bright as the stars and entered the ballroom wearing it. Once again the king danced with the beautiful maiden and thought that she had never been more beautiful. While he danced with her, he put a golden ring on her finger without her noticing it. He had also ordered the dance to last a very long time, and when it was over, he tried to hold on to her hands, but she tore herself away and quickly ran into the crowd, vanishing from his sight. However, she had stayed upstairs too long, more than half an hour, and she could not take off her beautiful dress but had to throw her fur cloak over it. Moreover, she was in such a hurry, she could not make herself completely black, and one of her fingers was left white. Then All Fur ran into the kitchen and cooked the soup for the king. While the cook was away, she put the golden reel into the bowl. So, when the king found the reel at the bottom of the bowl, he summoned All Fur and saw the ring that he had put on her finger during the dance. Then he seized her hand and held it tight, and when she tried to free herself and run away, the fur cloak opened a bit, and the dress of bright stars was unveiled. The king grabbed the cloak and tore it off her. Suddenly her golden hair toppled down, and she stood there in all her splendour unable to conceal herself any longer. After she had wiped the soot and ashes from her face, she was more beautiful than anyone who had ever been glimpsed on earth.

'You shall be my dear bride,' the king said, 'and we shall never part from each other!'

Thereupon the wedding was celebrated, and they lived happily together until their death.

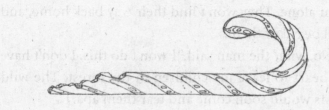

29

Hansel and Gretel

A POOR woodcutter lived with his wife and his two children on the edge of a large forest. The boy was called Hansel and the girl Gretel. The woodcutter did not have much food around the house, and when a great famine devastated the entire country, he could no longer provide enough for his family's daily meals. One night, as he was lying in bed and thinking about his worries, he began tossing and turning. Then he sighed and said to his wife, 'What's to become of us? How can we feed our poor children when we don't even have enough for ourselves?'

'I'll tell you what,' answered his wife. 'Early tomorrow morning we'll take the children out into the forest where it's most dense. We'll build a fire and give them each a piece of bread. Then we'll go about our work and leave them alone. They won't find their way back home, and we'll be rid of them.'

'No, wife,' the man said. 'I won't do this. I don't have the heart to leave my children in the forest. The wild beasts would soon come and tear them apart.'

'Oh, you fool!' she said. 'Then all four of us will have to starve to death. You'd better start planing the boards for our coffins!' She continued to harp on this until he finally agreed to do what she suggested.

'But still, I feel sorry for the poor children,' he said.

The two children had not been able to fall asleep that night either. Their hunger kept them awake, and when they heard what their stepmother said to their father, Gretel wept bitter tears and said to Hansel, 'Now it's all over for us.'

'Be quiet, Gretel,' Hansel said. 'Don't get upset. I'll soon find a way to help us.'

When their parents had fallen asleep, Hansel put on his little jacket, opened the bottom half of the door, and crept outside. The moon was shining very brightly, and the white pebbles glittered in front of the house like pure silver coins. Hansel stooped down to the ground and stuffed his pocket with as many pebbles as he could fit in. Then he went back and said to Gretel, 'Don't worry, my dear little sister. Just sleep in peace. God will not forsake us.' And he lay down again in his bed.

At dawn, even before the sun began to rise, the woman came and woke the two children: 'Get up, you lazybones! We're going into the forest to fetch some wood.' Then she gave each one of them a piece of bread and said, 'Now you have something for your noonday meal, but don't eat it before then because you're not getting anything else.'

Gretel put the bread under her apron because Hansel had the pebbles in his pocket. Then they all set out together toward the forest. After they had walked awhile, Hansel stopped and looked back at the house. He did this time and again until his father said, 'Hansel, what are you looking at there? Why are you dawdling? Pay attention, and don't forget how to use your legs!'

'Oh, Father,' said Hansel, 'I'm looking at my little white cat that's sitting up on the roof and wants to say good-bye to me.'

'You fool,' the mother said. 'That's not a cat. It's the morning sun shining on the chimney.'

But Hansel had not been looking at the cat. Instead, he had been taking the shiny pebbles from his pocket and constantly dropping them on the ground. When they reached the middle of the forest, the father said, 'Children, I want you to gather some wood. I'm going to make a fire so you won't get cold.'

Hansel and Gretel gathered together some brushwood and built quite a nice little pile. The brushwood was soon kindled, and when the fire was ablaze, the woman said, 'Now, children, lie down by the fire, and rest yourselves. We're going into the forest to chop wood. When we're finished, we'll come back and get you.'

Hansel and Gretel sat by the fire, and when noon came, they ate their pieces of bread. Since they heard the sounds of the axe, they thought their father was nearby. But it was not the axe. Rather, it was a branch that he had tied to a dead tree, and the wind was banging it back and forth. After they had been sitting there for a long time, they became so weary that their eyes closed, and they fell sound asleep. By the time they finally awoke, it was already pitch black, and Gretel began to cry and said, 'How are we going to get out of the forest?'

But Hansel comforted her by saying, 'Just wait awhile until the moon has risen. Then we'll find the way.'

And when the full moon had risen, Hansel took his little sister by the hand and followed the pebbles that glittered like newly minted silver coins and showed them the way. They walked the whole night long and arrived back at their father's house at break of day. They knocked at the door, and when the woman opened it and saw it was Hansel and Gretel, she said, 'You wicked children, why did you sleep so long in the forest? We thought you'd never come back again.'

But the father was delighted because he had been deeply troubled by the way he had abandoned them in the forest.

Not long after that the entire country was once again ravaged by famine, and one night the children heard their mother talking to their father in bed. 'Everything's been eaten up again. We only have half a loaf of bread, but after it's gone, that will be the end of our food. The children must leave. This time we'll take them even farther into the forest so they won't find their way back home again. Otherwise, there's no hope for us.'

All this saddened the father, and he thought, It'd be much better to share your last bite to eat with your children. But the woman would not listen to anything he said. She just scolded and reproached him. Once you've given a hand, people will take your arm, and since he had given in the first time, he also had to yield a second time.

However, the children were still awake and had overheard their conversation. When their parents had fallen asleep, Hansel got up, intending to go out and gather pebbles as he had done the time before, but the woman had locked the door, and Hansel could not get out. Nevertheless, he comforted his little sister and said,

'Don't cry, Gretel. Just sleep in peace. The dear Lord is bound to help us.'

Early the next morning the woman came and got the children out of bed. They each received little pieces of bread, but they were smaller than the last time. On the way into the forest Hansel crumbled the bread in his pocket and stopped as often as he could to throw the crumbs on the ground.

'Hansel, why are you always stopping and looking around?' asked the father. 'Keep going!'

'I'm looking at my little pigeon that's sitting on the roof and wants to say good-bye to me,' Hansel answered.

'Fool!' the woman said. 'That's not your little pigeon. It's the morning sun shining on the chimney.'

But little by little Hansel managed to scatter all the bread crumbs on the path. The woman led the children even deeper into the forest until they came to a spot they had never in their lives seen before. Once again a large fire was made, and the mother said, 'Just keep sitting here, children. If you get tired, you can sleep a little. We're going into the forest to chop wood, and in the evening, when we're done, we'll come and get you.'

When noon came, Gretel shared her bread with Hansel, who had scattered his along the way. Then they fell asleep, and evening passed, but no one came for the poor children. Only when it was pitch black did they finally wake up, and Hansel comforted his little sister by saying, 'Just wait until the moon has risen, Gretel. Then we'll see the little bread crumbs that I scattered. They'll show us the way back home.'

When the moon rose, they set out but could not find the crumbs, because the many thousands of birds that fly about in the forest and fields had devoured them.

'Don't worry, we'll find the way,' Hansel said to Gretel, but they could not find it. They walked the entire night and all the next day as well, from morning till night, but they did not get out of the forest. They were now also very hungry, for they had had nothing to eat except some berries that they had found growing on the ground. Eventually they became so tired that their legs would no longer carry them, and they lay down beneath a tree and fell asleep.

It was now the third morning since they had left their father's house. They began walking again, and they kept going deeper and deeper into the forest. If help did not arrive soon, they were bound to perish of hunger and exhaustion. At noon they saw a beautiful bird as white as snow sitting on a branch. It sang with such a lovely voice that the children stood still and listened to it. When the bird finished its song, it flapped its wings and flew ahead of them. They followed it until they came to a little house that was made of bread. Moreover, it had cake for a roof and pure sugar for windows.

'What a blessed meal!' said Hansel. 'Let's have a taste. I want to eat a piece of the roof. Gretel, you can have some of the window, since it's sweet.'

Hansel reached up high and broke off a piece of the roof to see how it tasted, and Gretel leaned against the windowpanes and nibbled on them. Then they heard a shrill voice cry out from inside:

'Nibble, nibble, I hear a mouse.
Who's that nibbling at my house?'

The children answered:

'The wind, the wind; it's very mild,
blowing like the Heavenly Child.'

And they did not bother to stop eating or let themselves be distracted. Since the roof tasted so good, Hansel ripped off a large piece and pulled it down, while Gretel pushed out a round piece of the windowpane, sat down, and ate it with great relish. Suddenly the door opened, and a very old woman leaning on a crutch came slinking out of the house. Hansel and Gretel were so tremendously frightened that they dropped what they had in their hands. But the old woman wagged her head and said, 'Well now, dear children, who brought you here? Just come inside and stay with me. Nobody's going to harm you.'

She took them both by the hand and led them into her house. Then she served them a good meal of milk and pancakes with sugar and apples and nuts. Afterward she made up two little beds with white sheets, whereupon Hansel and Gretel lay down in them and thought they were in heaven.

The old woman, however, had only pretended to be friendly. She was really a wicked witch on the lookout for children, and had built the house made of bread only to lure them to her. As soon as she had any children in her power, she would kill, cook, and eat them. It would be like a feast day for her. Now, witches have red eyes and cannot see very far, but they have a keen sense of smell, like animals, and can detect when human beings are near them. Therefore, when Hansel and Gretel had come into her vicinity, she had laughed wickedly and scoffed, 'They're mine! They'll never get away from me!'

Early the next morning, before the children were awake, she got up and looked at the two of them sleeping so sweetly with full rosy cheeks. Then she muttered to herself, 'They'll certainly make for a tasty meal!'

She seized Hansel with her scrawny hands and carried him into a small pen, where she locked him up behind a grilled door. No matter how much he screamed, it did not help. Then she went back to Gretel, shook her until she woke up, and yelled, 'Get up, you lazybones! I want you to fetch some water and cook your brother something nice. He's sitting outside in a pen, and we've got to fatten him up. Then, when he's fat enough, I'm going to eat him.'

Gretel began to weep bitter tears, but they were all in vain. She had to do what the wicked witch demanded. So the very best food was cooked for poor Hansel, while Gretel got nothing but crab shells. Every morning the old woman went slinking to the little pen and called out, 'Hansel, stick out your finger so I can feel how fat you are.'

However, Hansel stuck out a little bone, and since the old woman had poor eyesight, she thought the bone was Hansel's finger. She was puzzled that Hansel did not get any fatter, and when a month had gone by and Hansel still seemed to be thin, she was overcome by her impatience and decided not to wait any longer.

'Hey there, Gretel!' she called to the little girl. 'Get a move on and fetch some water! I don't care whether Hansel's fat or thin. He's going to be slaughtered tomorrow, and then I'll cook him.'

Oh, how the poor little sister wailed as she was carrying the water, and how the tears streamed down her cheeks!

'Dear God, help us!' she exclaimed. 'If only the wild beasts had eaten us in the forest, then we could have at least died together!'

Early the next morning Gretel had to go out, hang up a kettle full of water, and light the fire.

'First we'll bake,' the old woman said. 'I've already heated the oven and kneaded the dough.' She pushed poor Gretel out to the oven, where the flames were leaping from the fire. 'Crawl inside,' said the witch, 'and see if it's properly heated so we can slide the bread in.'

The witch intended to close the oven door once Gretel had climbed inside, for the witch wanted to bake her and eat her too. But Gretel sensed what she had in mind and said, 'I don't know how to do it. How do I get in?'

'You stupid goose,' the old woman said. 'The opening's large enough. Watch, even I can get in!'

She waddled up to the oven and stuck her head through the oven door. Then Gretel gave her a push that sent her flying inside and shut the iron door and bolted it. *Whew!* The witch began to howl dreadfully, but Gretel ran away, and the godless witch was miserably burned to death.

Meanwhile, Gretel ran straight to Hansel, opened the pen, and cried out, 'Hansel, we're saved! The old witch is dead!'

Then Hansel jumped out of the pen like a bird that hops out of a cage when the door is opened. My how happy they were! They hugged each other, danced around, and kissed. Since they no longer had anything to fear, they went into the witch's house, and there they found chests filled with pearls and jewels all over the place.

'They're certainly much better than pebbles,' said Hansel, and he put whatever he could fit into his pockets, and Gretel said, 'I'm going to carry some home too,' and she filled her apron full of jewels and pearls.

'We'd better be on our way now,' said Hansel, 'so we can get out of the witch's forest.'

When they had walked for a few hours, they reached a large river.

'We can't get across,' said Hansel. 'I don't see a bridge or any way over it.'

'There are no boats either,' Gretel responded, 'but there's a white duck swimming over there. It's bound to help us across if I ask it.' Then she cried out:

'Help us, help us, little duck!
We're Hansel and Gretel, out of luck.
We can't get over, try as we may.

Please take us across right away!'

The little duck came swimming up to them, and Hansel got on top of its back and told his sister to sit down beside him.

'No,' Gretel answered. 'That will be too heavy for the little duck. Let it carry us across one at a time.'

The kind little duck did just that, and when they were safely across and had walked on for some time, the forest became more and more familiar to them, and finally they caught sight of their father's house from afar. They began to run at once, and soon rushed into the house and threw themselves around their father's neck. The man had not had a single happy hour since he had abandoned his children in the forest, and in the meantime his wife had died. Gretel opened and shook out her apron so that the pearls and jewels bounced about the room, and Hansel added to this by throwing one handful after another from his pocket. Now all their troubles were over, and they lived together in utmost joy.

My tale is done. See the mouse run. Catch it, whoever can, and then you can make a great big cap out of its fur.

30

Jorinda and Joringel

ONCE upon a time there was an old castle in the middle of a great, dense forest. An old woman lived there all by herself, and she was a powerful sorceress. During the day she turned herself into a cat or a night owl, but in the evening she would return to her normal human form. She had the ability to lure game and birds, which she would slaughter and then cook or roast. If any man came within a hundred steps of the castle, she would cast a spell over him, so that he would not be able to move from the spot until she broke the spell. If an innocent maiden came within her magic circle, she would change her into a bird and stuff her into a wicker basket. Then she would carry the basket up to a room in her castle where she had well over seven thousand baskets with rare birds of this kind.

Now, once there was a maiden named Jorinda, who was more beautiful than any other maiden in the kingdom. She was betrothed to a handsome youth named Joringel. During the time before their marriage, they took great pleasure in being in each other's company. One day they went for a walk in the forest so they could be alone and talk intimately with one another.

'Be careful,' Joringel said, 'that you don't go too close to the castle.'

At dusk the sun shone brightly through the tree trunks and cast its light on the dark green of the forest. The turtledoves were singing mournfully in the old beech trees, and at times Jorinda wept. Then she sat down in the sunshine and sighed, and Joringel sighed too. They became very sad as if they were doomed to die, and when they looked around them, they became confused and did not know how to get home. The sun was still shining half above and half behind the mountains. When Joringel looked through the bushes and saw the wall of the old castle not very far away, he became so alarmed that he was nearly frightened to death, while Jorinda sang:

'Oh, my bird, with your ring of red,
sitting and singing your tale of woe!
You tell us now that the poor dove is dead.
You sing your tale of woe—*oh-oh, oh-oh!*'

Just then, as Joringel looked at Jorinda, she was turned into a nightingale singing 'oh-oh, oh-oh!' A night owl with glowing eyes flew around her three times, and each time it cried, 'To-whoo! To-whoo! To-whoo!'

Joringel could not budge. He stood there like a stone, unable to weep, to talk, or to move hand or foot. When the sun was about to set, the owl flew into a bush and then immediately returned as a haggard old woman, yellow and scrawny, with large red eyes and a crooked nose that almost touched her chin with its tip. She muttered something to herself, caught the nightingale, and carried it away in her hand. Joringel was still unable to speak, nor could he move from the spot. The nightingale was gone. Soon the woman came back and said with a muffled voice, 'Greetings, Zachiel. When the moon shines into the basket, let him loose, Zachiel, just at the right moment.'

Then Joringel was set free, and he fell on his knees before the woman and begged her to give Jorinda back to him, but she said he would never get her back again and went away. He shouted, he wept, he moaned, but it was all in vain. 'Oh, no, what's to become of me?'

Joringel went off and eventually came to an unfamiliar village, where he tended sheep for a long time. He often went round and round the castle and always kept his distance. Finally, he dreamed one night that he had found a flower as red as blood, and in the middle of it was a pearl. He plucked the flower and went with it to the castle: everything that he touched with the flower was set free from the magic spell. He also dreamed that he managed to regain his Jorinda with the flower.

When he awoke the next morning, he began searching all over the mountains and valleys for the flower of his dream. He searched for nine days, and early on the ninth day he found a flower as red as blood. In its middle was a large dewdrop as big as the finest pearl. He carried this flower day and night until he reached the castle. When he came to within a hundred steps of the castle, he was not spellbound but was able to get to the gate. Overjoyed by that, Joringel touched the gate with the flower, and it sprang open. So he entered, crossed the courtyard, and listened for the sound of birds. Finally, he heard them and went toward the room where the sorceress was feeding the birds in their seven thousand baskets. When she saw Joringel, she became angry, very angry. She began berating him and spitting poison and gall at him, but she could only come within two feet of him, and he paid no attention to her. Instead, he went and examined the baskets with the birds. Since there were hundreds of nightingales, he did not know how he would be able to find his Jorinda again. While he was examining the baskets, he noticed that the old woman had stealthily picked up one of the baskets and was heading toward the door. Quick as a flash he ran over and touched the basket with the flower and the old woman as well. Now she could no longer use her magic, and thus Jorinda appeared before him. She threw her arms around his neck and was just as beautiful as before. After Joringel had turned all the other birds into young women, he went home with his Jorinda, and they lived happily together for a long time.

31

The Three Sons of Fortune

A FATHER once called his three sons to him and gave the first a rooster, the second a scythe, and the third a cat.

'I'm already quite old,' he said, 'and my death is near. So I want to provide for you before my end. I have no money, and what I'm giving you now does not seem to be worth much. But everything depends on whether you use these gifts intelligently. Just search for a country where such things are still unknown, and your fortune will be made.'

After the father's death, the oldest son set out with his rooster, but wherever he went, the people already knew about roosters. As he approached the cities he saw roosters from afar perched on towers and turning with the wind. As he approached villages he heard several roosters crowing, and nobody found anything remarkable about his bird. It seemed as if the oldest son would not make his fortune with the rooster, but finally he landed on an island where the people knew nothing about roosters and did not even know how to regulate the time of their days. To be sure, they knew when it was morning and evening, but if they happened to wake during the night, then nobody knew how to determine what time it was.

'Just look at this noble creature!' he said. 'It's got a ruby red crown on its head and wears spurs like a knight. It will crow three times during the night at set hours, and when it crows the last time, you'll know that the sun is about to rise. But, if it crows during broad daylight, you'd better prepare yourself for a certain change in the weather.'

The people were extremely pleased by the rooster, and they did not sleep a wink the next night so that they could listen and enjoy the rooster, which crowed loudly and clearly at two, four, and six in the morning to announce the time. Then they asked him whether the rooster was for sale and how much he wanted for it.

'I want about as much gold as a donkey can carry,' he answered.

'So little for such a precious bird!' they all exclaimed

as if in a chorus, and they gladly gave him what he demanded.

When he returned home with his wealth, his brothers were astounded, and the second said, 'Well, it's time for me to set out and see whether I can make as much of a profit with my scythe as you did with your rooster.'

At first it did not seem he would, for everywhere he went he met farmers with scythes on their shoulders just as good as his. However, he eventually reached an island where the people knew nothing about scythes. When the grain was ripe there, they brought cannons to the fields and shot down the grain. That was a very uncertain way of doing things: some of the cannons would hit targets beyond the grain, while others would shoot off the ears instead of the stems. A great deal was destroyed in the process, and over and beyond that, the noise was unbearable. So the man went out to the fields and began to mow the grain so quietly and quickly that the people gaped in amazement. They were willing to give him anything he wanted for the scythe, and he received a horse loaded with as much gold as it could carry.

Now the third brother wanted to see if he could make something out of his cat, and he had the exact same experiences as his brothers. As long as he stayed on the mainland, he accomplished nothing: there were cats everywhere. Indeed, there were so many that the newborn kittens were generally thrown into the water to drown. Therefore, he sailed to an island, and fortunately for him, it happened that nobody there had ever seen a cat before. In fact, the mice had multiplied so much that they had gained the upper hand. They could dance all over the tables and benches whether the master was home or not. The people complained a great deal about this plague, and even the king in his castle did not know what to do about it: there were mice squeaking in every corner and gnawing whatever they could lay hold of with their teeth.

Once the cat began to hunt them, she was soon able to clear out several rooms in the castle. So the people begged the king to buy this miraculous creature for the kingdom. The king gladly gave the third brother what he demanded, and that was a mule loaded with gold, and he returned home with the greatest treasure of all.

The cat continued to have a great time hunting mice in the royal castle, and she killed so many that it was impossible to count them. Finally, she became hot from all that work and got thirsty. So she stopped in her tracks, turned her head, and cried out, 'Meow! Meow!'

Upon hearing these strange cries, the king and his entire court became so terrified that they all ran out of the castle in dread. When they were outside the castle, the king held a council meeting to determine what measures should be taken. At last it was decided to send a page to the cat to demand that she leave the castle or be removed by force. The councillors said, 'Since we're accustomed to the mice, it would be better to be plagued by them than to surrender our lives to such a monster.'

So the page went to the castle to ask the cat whether she would voluntarily evacuate the castle. But the cat, whose thirst had become even greater in the meantime, merely answered with '*Meow! Meow!*'

The page understood that to mean 'Not at all! Not at all!' and he brought the reply to the king.

'Well,' said the councillors. 'She shall have to yield to force.'

Cannons were brought before the castle, which was soon set on fire by a barrage of shots. When the fire reached the room where the cat was sitting, she jumped safely out of the window. However, the besiegers did not stop until the whole castle was levelled to the ground.

32
The Elves

FIRST TALE

There was once a shoemaker who, through no fault of his own, had become so poor that he had only enough leather left for a single pair of shoes. That evening he cut out the shoes, which he planned to work on the next morning, and since he had a clear conscience, he lay down quietly in his bed, commended himself to God, and fell asleep. In the morning, after he had said his prayers and was about to sit down to do his work, he saw the two shoes standing all finished on his workbench. He was so astounded by this that he did not know what to say. He took the shoes in his hand to examine them more closely and saw that the shoes were perfect. Not a single bad stitch could be found, and it was as if the shoes were intended to be masterpieces.

Shortly after, a customer entered the shop, and he liked the shoes so much he paid more than the usual price for them. The money enabled the shoemaker to purchase leather for two pairs of shoes. In the evening he cut them out and planned to begin work on them with renewed vigour the next morning. However, it was not necessary, for the shoes were already finished by the time he awoke. Once again he found customers for them, and they gave him enough money to purchase leather for four pairs of shoes. The following morning he found the four pairs of shoes already made, and so it went: whatever he cut out in the evening was finished by morning, and soon he had a decent income again and eventually became a well-to-do man.

Now one evening, not long before Christmas, it happened that the man had been cutting leather, and just before he went to bed, he said to his wife, 'What would you think about staying up tonight? If we do that, we might be able to see who's been lending us such a helping hand.'

His wife agreed and lit a candle. Then they hid themselves behind some clothes that were hanging in the corner of the room and watched closely. When it was midnight, two cute little naked elves scampered into the room, sat down at the shoemaker's workbench, took all the work that had been cut out, and began to stitch, sew, and hammer so skilfully and nimbly with their little fingers that the amazed shoemaker could not take his eyes off them. Indeed, they did not stop until everything was done and the shoes were left standing on the workbench. Then they quickly ran away.

The next morning the wife said, 'The little men have made us rich. We ought to show them that we're grateful for their help. Do you know what? Since they run around without any clothes on and must be freezing, I'm going to sew some shirts, coats, jackets, and trousers for them. I'll also knit a pair of stockings for each, and you can make them both a pair of shoes.'

'That's fine with me,' the husband said.

In the evening, after they had finished everything, they put the gifts on the workbench, instead of the cut-out leather, and hid themselves in order to see how the elves would react. At midnight the elves came scampering into the room and wanted to get right down to work, but they found the nice little clothes instead of the cut-out leather. At first they were puzzled, but then they were tremendously pleased. They put the clothes on quickly, smoothed them down, and said:

'Now we look so fine and dandy,
no more need to work and be so handy!'

Then they skipped, danced, and jumped over chairs and benches. Finally, they danced right out the door and were never seen again. But the shoemaker continued to be prosperous until the end of his life and succeeded in all his endeavours.

SECOND TALE

Once upon a time there was a poor servant girl who was industrious and neat. She swept the house every day and dumped the dirt on a large pile outside the door. One morning, when she was about to start work again, she found a letter on the pile, and since she could not read, she put the broom in the corner and took the letter to her employers. It was an invitation from the elves, who asked the girl to be godmother for one of their children at a christening. The maiden did not know what to do, but her employers finally persuaded her that it would not be wise to refuse the invitation, and she accepted.

Three elves came and led her to a hollow mountain where the little folk lived. Everything there was tiny and indescribably dainty and splendid. The mother was lying on a black ebony bed with pearl knobs. The covers were embroidered with gold. The cradle was ivory. The bathtub was made of gold. After the maiden performed her duties as godmother, she wanted to go back home, but the elves implored her earnestly to spend three days with them. She remained and had a pleasant and joyful time. The little folk did all they could to please her. Finally, when she insisted it was time for her to leave, they filled her pockets with gold and led her back out the mountain.

When she arrived home, she wanted to resume her work, so she took the broom that was standing in the corner and began sweeping. At that moment some strange people came out of the house and asked her who she was and what she was doing there. Indeed, she had not been gone for three days, as she had thought, but she had spent seven years in the mountains with the little folk. In the meantime, her former employers had died.

THIRD TALE

The elves had stolen a mother's child from the cradle and had replaced the baby with a changeling who had a fat head and glaring eyes and would do nothing but eat and drink. In her distress the mother went to her neighbour and asked for advice. The neighbour told her to carry the changeling into the kitchen, put him down on the hearth, start a fire, and boil water in two eggshells. That would make the changeling laugh, and when he laughed, he would lose his power. The woman did everything the neighbour said, and when she put the eggshells filled with water on the fire, the blockhead said:

'Now I'm as old
as the Westerwald,
and in all my life I've never seen
eggshells cooked as these have been.'

And the changeling began to laugh. As soon as he laughed, a bunch of elves appeared. They had brought the right child with them and put him down on the hearth and took the changeling away.

33

Clever Gretel

THERE was once a cook named Gretel, who wore shoes with red heels, and when she went out in them, she whirled this way and that way and was as happy as a lark. 'You really are quite pretty!' she would say to herself. And when she returned home, she would drink some wine out of sheer delight. Since the wine would whet her appetite, she would take the best things she was cooking and taste them until she was content. Then she would say, 'The cook must know what the food tastes like!'

One day her master happened to say to her, 'Gretel, tonight I'm having a guest for dinner. Prepare two chickens for me and make them as tasty as possible.'

'I'll take care of it, sir,' Gretel responded. So she killed two chickens, scalded them, plucked them, stuck them on a spit, and toward evening placed them over a fire to roast. The chickens began to turn brown and were almost ready, but the guest did not make his appearance. So Gretel called to her master, 'If the guest doesn't come soon, I'll have to take the chickens off the fire. It would be a great shame if they weren't eaten now, while they're still at their juiciest.'

'Then I'll run and fetch the guest myself,' said the master.

When the master had left the house, Gretel laid the spit with the chickens to one side and thought, If I keep standing by the fire, I'll just sweat and get thirsty. Who knows when they'll come? Meanwhile, I'll hop down into the cellar and take a drink.

She ran downstairs, filled a jug with wine, and said, 'May God bless it for you, Gretel!' and she took a healthy swig. 'The wine flows nicely,' she continued talking, 'and it's not good to interrupt the flow.' So she took another long swig. Then she went upstairs and placed the chickens back over the fire, basted them with butter, and merrily turned the spit. Since the roast chickens smelled so good, Gretel thought, Perhaps something's missing. I'd better taste them to see how they are. She touched one of them with her finger and said, 'Goodness! The chickens are really good! It's a crying shame not to eat them all at once!' She ran to the window to see if her master was on his way with the guest, but when she saw no one coming, she returned to the chickens and thought, That one wing is burning. I'd better eat it up.

So she cut it off, ate it, and enjoyed it. When she had finished, she thought, I'd better eat the other wing or else my master will notice that something's missing. After she had consumed the two wings, she returned to the window, looked for her master, but was unable to see him. Who knows, it suddenly occurred to her, Perhaps they've decided not to come and have stopped somewhere along the way. Then she said to herself, 'Hey, Gretel, cheer up! You've already taken a nice chunk. Have another drink and eat it all up! When it's gone, there'll be no reason for you to feel guilty. Why should God's good gifts go to waste?'

Once again she ran down into the cellar, took a good honest drink, and then went back to eat up the chicken with relish. When the one chicken had been eaten and her master still had not returned, Gretel looked at the other bird and said, 'Where one is, the other should be too. The two of them belong together: whatever's right for one is right for the other. I think if I have another drink, it won't do me any harm.' Therefore she took another healthy swig and let the second chicken run to join the other.

Just as she was in the midst of enjoying her meal, her

master came back and called, 'Hurry, Gretel, the guest will soon be here!'

'Yes, sir, I'll get everything ready,' answered Gretel.

Meanwhile, the master checked to see if the table was properly set and took out the large knife with which he wanted to carve the chickens and began sharpening it on the steps in the hallway. As he was doing that the guest came and knocked nicely and politely at the door. Gretel ran and looked to see who was there, and when she saw the guest, she put her finger to her lips and whispered, 'Shhh, be quiet! Get out of here as quick as you can! If my master catches you, you'll be done for. It's true he invited you to dinner, but he really wants to cut off both your ears. Listen to him sharpening his knife!'

The guest heard the sharpening and hurried back down the steps as fast as he could. Gretel wasted no time and ran screaming to her master. 'What kind of guest did you invite!' she cried.

'Goodness gracious, Gretel! Why do you ask? What do you mean?'

'Well,' she said, 'he snatched both chickens just as I was about to bring them to the table, and he's run away with them!'

'That's not at all a nice way to behave!' said her master, and he was disappointed by the loss of the fine chickens.

'At least he could have left me one of them so I'd have something to eat.'

He then shouted after the guest to stop running, but the guest pretended not to hear. So the master ran after him, with the knife still in his hand, and screamed, 'Just one, just one!' merely meaning that the guest should at least leave him one of the chickens and not take both. But the guest thought that his host was after just one of his ears, and to make sure that he would reach home safely with both his ears, he ran as if someone had lit a fire under his feet.

34
Lucky Hans

AFTER Hans had served his master for seven years, he said to him, 'Master, my time is up, and since I want to go back home to my mother now, I'd like to have my wages.'

'You've served me faithfully and honestly,' said the master, 'and I shall reward you in kind.'

So he gave Hans a gold nugget as big as his head, whereupon Hans pulled a kerchief out of his pocket, wrapped it around the nugget, lifted it to his shoulder, and set out for home. As he was meandering along, one foot following the other, he caught a glimpse of a rider trotting toward him on a lively horse. The man appeared to be very cheerful and vigorous.

'Ah!' said Hans very loudly. 'Riding is such a wonderful thing! All you have to do is sit there as if you were in a chair. You never have to worry about stumbling on stones. You can save on shoes and get wherever you want in a jiffy.'

Upon hearing Hans speak this way, the rider stopped his horse and cried out, 'If that's so, why in the world are you walking, Hans?'

'I have to,' he answered. 'I've got to carry this large nugget. Sure, it's gold, but it's so heavy that I can't keep my head straight, and my shoulder's been feeling the weight.'

'I'll tell you what,' said the horseman. 'Let's exchange. I'll give you my horse, and you give me your gold nugget.'

'Gladly,' said Hans. 'But let me warn you, it's a terribly heavy load to carry.'

The horseman dismounted, took the gold, and helped Hans get on the horse. The horseman put the reins firmly into his hands and said, 'If you want to go at a quick pace, you've got to click your tongue and shout "Giddyap! Giddyap!"'

Hans was in seventh heaven as he sat on the horse, and he began riding free and easy. After a while he thought he ought to be going faster. So he clicked his tongue and shouted, 'Giddyap! Giddyap!' whereupon the horse broke out into such a fast trot that Hans was thrown off and was soon lying in a ditch between the road and the fields. The horse would have run away too if it had not been stopped by a farmer who happened to be coming that way and driving a cow before him. Hans pulled himself together and got up on his feet, but he was very irritated and said to the farmer, 'Riding's no fun at all, especially when you wind up with a mare like this one that bucks and throws you off. I'm never getting on that horse again. Now, your cow's a different story. You can walk behind it at your ease. Not only that, you're sure of having milk, butter, and cheese every day. I'd give anything to have a cow like that!'

'Well,' said the farmer, 'if you really like my cow so much, then I'd be glad to trade the cow for the horse.'

Hans agreed with utmost joy. So the farmer swung himself onto the horse and rode off in a hurry. Now Hans drove the cow before him in a leisurely way and thought about his lucky deal. All I need now is a piece of bread—and I'm sure to get some bread—then I'll be able to eat my butter and cheese with it as often as I like. If I get thirsty, I'll just milk my cow and drink the milk. What more could my heart possibly ask for? When he reached a tavern, he stopped and ate up everything he had with great relish, both his lunch and supper, and he ordered a glass of beer with his last few hellers. Then he continued to drive his cow onward toward his mother's village. As midday approached and Hans was traipsing over a heath that would take at least another hour to cross, the heat became unbearable. Indeed, it became so hot that his tongue stuck to the roof of his mouth with thirst. There's a way to remedy this situation, thought Hans. I'll just milk my cow and refresh myself with the milk.

He tied the cow to a withered tree, and since he did not have a bucket, he put his leather cap underneath. However, no matter how much he tried, not one drop of milk came out. And since he was so clumsy in the attempt, the cow finally lost her patience and gave him such a kick in the head with one of her hind legs that he fell down. It took a long time for him to recover and regain a sense of where he was. Fortunately, a butcher happened to come his way at that moment. He was pushing a young pig in a wheelbarrow and called out to Hans, 'Somebody's been playing tricks on you!' He helped good old Hans to his feet, and then Hans proceeded to tell him what had happened. The butcher handed him his flask and said, 'Just take a drink, and you'll feel better. That cow of yours probably won't give you milk because it's too old. At best it's fit only for the plow or for the slaughterhouse.'

'No fooling,' said Hans, who stroked his hair. 'Who would ever have thought that? Naturally it's a good thing to have a beast around your home that you can slaughter. It'll sure make for a lot of meat! But I don't care for beef that much. It's not juicy enough for me. On the other hand, a young pig like yours has quite a different taste. And, just think of the sausages!'

'Listen, Hans,' said the butcher. 'I'd like to do you a personal favour, as a friend, and trade the pig for your cow.'

'May God reward your kindness!' said Hans, and he handed over the cow to the butcher, who, in turn, got the pig out of the wheelbarrow and gave Hans the rope to which the pig was tied so he could lead it away.

As Hans resumed his journey he thought to himself how everything was going just as he wished. Whenever anything disturbing happened, it was always set right immediately. Soon he met up with a boy carrying a white goose under his arm. They said good day to each other, and Hans began to tell him about his luck and how he always managed to make such advantageous trades. The boy responded and said he was carrying the goose to a christening feast. 'Just lift her,' he continued, and he grabbed the goose by her wings. 'See how heavy she is? They've been fattening her up for the last eight weeks. Anyone who takes a bite of her after she's been roasted will have to wipe the fat from both sides of his mouth.'

'I agree,' said Hans as he weighed the goose with one hand. 'She certainly is heavy enough, but my pig is no lightweight either.'

Meanwhile, the boy began looking around suspiciously in all directions and shaking his head. 'Listen,' he spoke again, 'there's something the matter here, and it concerns your pig. Somebody stole a pig from the mayor's sty in the village I just passed through. I fear, yes, I really fear that you've got the pig in your hands. They've sent some people out, and it would be terrible if they caught you with the pig. The very least they'd do to you would be to throw you into a dark dungeon.'

Good old Hans was horrified. 'Oh, God!' he said. 'Couldn't you help me out of this mess? You know your way around these parts better than I do. Take my pig there and give me your goose.'

'This means my taking a risk too,' responded the boy. 'But I don't want to be at fault for your getting into trouble.' So he took the rope in his hand and quickly moved off with the pig down a side road.

Now good old Hans felt free of his worries and continued his journey homeward with the goose under his arm. 'When I really think about it,' he said, 'I got the better of him in the deal. First there's the fine roast meat, then the large amount of fat that will drip out and supply me with enough goose fat for my bread for the next three months, and finally there are the beautiful white feathers. I'll have my pillow stuffed with them, and nobody will ever have to rock me to sleep again. I'm sure my mother will be delighted about that!'

As he was passing through the last village he came upon a scissors grinder standing next to his cart. His wheel was humming, and he was singing along:

> 'I sharpen scissors and grind away,
>   and let the wind guide me from day to day.'

Hans stopped and watched him. Finally, he went over to the man and said, 'You feel so well because you like what you're doing, don't you?'

'Yes,' said the scissors grinder. 'This business has got a solid foundation. A good scissors grinder is someone who always finds money whenever he digs into his pocket. But, tell me, where did you buy that beautiful goose?'

'I didn't buy it, I traded my pig for it.'

'And the pig?'

'That I got for a cow.'

'And the cow?'

'That I received for a horse.'

'And the horse?'

'That I got for a gold nugget that was as big as my head.'

'And the gold?'

'Oh, that made up my wages for seven years' service.'

'Say, you really know how to look out for your interests. Now, if only you could manage it so that you would hear money jingling in your pocket whenever you stood up, your luck would be made!'

'How can I manage that?' Hans asked.

'You've got to become a scissors grinder like me. All you really need for that is a grindstone. The rest takes care of itself. Now, I happen to have one here for you. It's a little damaged, but you won't have to give me anything for it except your goose. What about it?'

'How can you even ask?' Hans answered. 'You'll make me the luckiest man on earth. If I have money whenever I put my hand in my pocket, I won't have to worry about a thing anymore.' So he handed him the goose and took the grindstone in return.

'Now,' said the scissors grinder, as he picked up a plain, ordinary stone that was lying near him on the ground, 'I'm going to give you this solid stone as part of the bargain. You can hit as hard as you want on it and straighten out all your old nails. Just make sure that you take good care of it.'

Hans lifted the stones, put them on his back, and continued happily on his way. His eyes sparkled for joy. 'I must have been born under a lucky star!' he exclaimed. 'Everything I wish for comes true. It's as though the gods were looking after me.'

In the meantime, since he had been walking all day, he had become tired. In addition he was suffering from hunger because he had eaten up all his provisions to celebrate the great cow trade he had made. It was only with great difficulty that he managed to continue, and even then, he had to stop every other minute. The stones were weighing him down unmercifully, and he could not help thinking how nice it would be if he could get rid of them at that moment. Finally, he saw a well in a field, and as he crawled toward it he resembled a snail. He was hoping to rest and refresh himself with a cool drink of water, and he laid the rocks carefully on the edge of the well, right next to him, to avoid damaging them. After that he sat down and leaned over to drink. But he made a false move and nudged the stones just enough that they fell into the water. As Hans saw the stones sink to the bottom he jumped up for joy. He then knelt down and thanked God with tears in his eyes for showing him such mercy and for relieving him of the stones in such a gracious way. Indeed, those stones had become a great burden for him.

'Nobody under the sun is as lucky as I am!' exclaimed Hans, and with a light heart and free from all his burdens, he now ran all the way home until he reached his mother.

35
The Singing, Springing Lark

ONCE upon a time there was a man who was about to go on a long journey, and right before his departure he asked his three daughters what he should bring back to them. The oldest wanted pearls, the second, diamonds, but the third said, 'Dear Father, I'd like to have a singing, springing lark.'

'All right,' said the father. 'If I can get one, you shall have it.'

So he kissed all three daughters good-bye and went on his way. When the time came for his return journey, he had purchased pearls and diamonds for the two oldest, but even though he had looked all over, he had not been able to find the singing, springing lark for his youngest daughter. He was particularly sorry about that because she was his favourite. In the meantime, his way took him through a forest, in the middle of which he discovered a magnificent castle. Near the castle was a tree, and way on top of this tree he saw a lark singing and springing about.

'Well, you've come just at the right time,' he said, quite pleased, and he ordered his servant to climb the tree and catch the little bird. But when the servant went over to the tree, a lion jumped out from under it, shook himself, and roared so ferociously that the leaves on the trees trembled.

'If anyone tries to steal my singing, springing lark,' he cried, 'I'll eat him up.'

'I didn't know that the bird belonged to you,' said the man. 'I'll make up for my trespassing and give you a great deal of gold if only you'll spare my life.'

'Nothing can save you,' said the lion, 'unless you promise to give me the first thing you meet when you get home. If you agree, then I'll not only grant you your life, but I'll also give you the bird for your daughter.'

At first the man refused and said, 'That could be my youngest daughter. She loves me most of all and always runs to meet me when I return home.'

But the servant was very scared of the lion and said, 'It doesn't always have to be your daughter. Maybe it'll be a cat or dog.'

The man let himself be persuaded and took the

singing, springing lark. Then he promised the lion he would give him the first thing that met him when he got home.

Upon reaching his house, he walked inside, and the first thing that met him was none other than his youngest and dearest daughter: she came running up to him, threw her arms around him, and kissed him. When she saw that he had brought her a singing, springing lark, she was overcome with joy. But her father could not rejoice and began to cry.

'My dearest child,' he said. 'I've had to pay a high price for this bird. In exchange I was compelled to promise you to a wild lion, and when he gets you, he'll tear you to pieces and eat you up.' Then he went on to tell her exactly how everything had happened and begged her not to go there, no matter what the consequences might be. Yet, she consoled him and said, 'Dearest Father, if you've made a promise, you must keep it. I'll go there, and once I've made the lion nice and tame, I'll be back here safe and sound.'

The next morning she had her father show her the way. Then she took leave of him and walked calmly into the forest. Now, it turned out that the lion was actually an enchanted prince. During the day he and his men were lions, and during the night they assumed their true human form. When she arrived there, she was welcomed in a friendly way, and they conducted her to the castle. When night came, the lion became a handsome man, and the wedding was celebrated in splendour. They lived happily together by remaining awake at night and asleep during the day. One day he came to her and said, 'Tomorrow there will be a celebration at your father's house since your oldest sister is to be married. If you wish to attend, my lions will escort you there.'

She replied that, yes, she would very much like to see her father again, and she went there accompanied by the lions. There was great rejoicing when she arrived, for they all had believed that she had been torn to pieces by the lions and had long been dead. But she told them what a handsome husband she had and how well off she was. She stayed with them just as long as the wedding celebration lasted. Then she went back to the forest.

When the second daughter was about to be married, she was again invited to the wedding, but this time she said to the lion, 'I don't want to go without you.'

However, the lion said it would be too dangerous for him because he would be changed into a dove and have to fly about with the doves for seven years if the ray of a burning candle were to fall upon him.

'Please, come with me,' she said. 'I'll be sure to take good care of you and protect you from the light.'

So they went off together and took their small child with them. Once there she had a hall built for him, so strong and thick that not a single ray of light could penetrate it. That was the place where he was to sit when the wedding candles were lit. However, its door was made out of green wood, and it split and developed a crack that nobody saw. The wedding was celebrated in splendour, but when the wedding procession with all the candles and torches came back from church and passed by the hall, a ray about the width of a hair fell upon the prince, and he was instantly transformed. When his wife entered the hall to look for him, she could find only a white dove sitting there, and he said to her, 'For seven years I shall have to fly about the world, but for every seven steps you take I shall leave a drop of red blood and a little white feather to show you the way. And, if you follow the traces, you'll be able to set me free.'

Then the dove flew out the door, and she followed him. At every seventh step she took, a drop of blood and a little white feather would fall and show her the way. Thus she went farther and farther into the wide world and never looked about or stopped until the seven years were almost up. She was looking forward to that and thought they would soon be free. But, they were still quite far from their goal.

Once, as she was moving along, she failed to find any more feathers or drops of blood, and when she raised her head, the dove had also vanished. I won't be able to get help from a mortal, she thought, and so she climbed up to the sun and said to her, 'You shine into every nook and cranny. Is there any chance that you've seen a white dove flying around?'

'No,' said the sun, 'I haven't, but I'll give you a little casket. Just open it when your need is greatest.'

She thanked the sun and continued on her way until the moon came out to shine in the evening. 'You shine the whole night through and on all the fields and meadows. Is there any chance that you've seen a white dove flying around?'

'No,' said the moon, 'I haven't, but I'll give you an egg. Just crack it open when your need is greatest.'

She thanked the moon and went farther until the Night Wind stirred and started to blow at her. 'You blow over every tree and under every leaf. Is there any chance that you've seen a white dove flying around?'

'No,' said the Night Wind, 'I haven't, but I'll ask the three other winds. Perhaps they've seen one.'

The East Wind and the West Wind came and reported they had not seen a thing, but the South Wind said, 'I've seen the white dove. It's flown to the Red Sea and has become a lion again, for the seven years are over. The lion's now in the midst of a fight with a dragon that's really an enchanted princess.'

Then the Night Wind said to her, 'Here's what I would advise you to do: Go to the Red Sea, where you'll find some tall reeds growing along the shore. Then count them until you come to the eleventh one, which you're to cut off and use to strike the dragon. That done, the lion will be able to conquer the dragon, and both will regain their human form. After that, look around, and you'll see the griffin sitting by the Red Sea. Get on his back with your beloved, and the griffin will carry you home across the sea. Now, here's a nut for you. When you cross over the middle of the sea, let it drop. A nut tree will instantly sprout up out of the water, and the griffin will be able to rest on it. If he can't rest there, he won't be strong enough to carry you both across the sea. So if you forget to drop the nut into the sea, he'll let you fall into the water.'

She went there and found everything as the Night Wind had said. She counted the reeds by the sea, cut off the eleventh, and struck the dragon with it. Whereupon the lion conquered the dragon, and both immediately regained their human form. But when the princess, who had previously been a dragon, was set free from the magic spell, she picked the prince up in her arms, got on the griffin, and carried him off with her. So the poor maiden, who had journeyed so far, stood alone and forsaken again, and sat down to cry. Eventually, she took heart and said, 'I'll keep going as far as the wind blows and so long as the cock crows until I find him.' And off she went and wandered a long, long way until she came to the castle where the two were living together. Then she heard that their wedding celebration was soon to take place. 'God will still come to my aid,' she remarked as she opened the little casket that the sun had given her. There she found a dress as radiant as the sun itself. She took it out, put it on, and went up to the castle. Everyone at the court and the bride herself could not believe their eyes. The bride liked the dress so much she thought it would be nice to have for her wedding and asked if she could buy it.

'Not for money or property,' she answered, 'but for flesh and blood.'

The bride asked her what she meant by that, and she responded, 'Let me sleep one night in the bridegroom's room.'

The bride did not want to let her, but she also wanted the dress very much. Finally, she agreed, but the bridegroom's servant was obliged to give him a sleeping potion. That night when the prince was asleep, she was led into his room, sat down on his bed, and said, 'I've followed you for seven years. I went to the sun, the moon, and the four winds to find out where you were. I helped you conquer the dragon. Are you going to forget me forever?'

But the prince slept so soundly that it merely seemed to him as if the wind were whispering in the firs. When morning came, she was led out again and had to give up her golden dress.

Since her ploy had not been of much use, she was quite sad and went out to a meadow, where she sat down and wept. But as she was sitting there, she remembered the egg that the moon had given her. She cracked it open, and a hen with twelve chicks came out, all in gold. The peeping chicks scampered about and then crawled under the mother hen's wings. There was not a lovelier sight to see in the world. Shortly after that she stood up and drove them ahead of her over the meadow until they came within sight of the bride, who saw them from her window. She liked the little chicks so much that she came right down and asked if she could buy them.

'Not with money or possessions, but for flesh and blood. Let me sleep another night in the bridegroom's room.'

The bride agreed and wanted to trick her as she had done the night before. But when the prince went to bed, he asked his servant what had caused all the murmuring and rustling during the night, and the servant told him everything: that he had been compelled to give him a sleeping potion because a poor girl had secretly slept in his room, and that he was supposed to give him another one that night.

'Dump the drink by the side of my bed,' said the prince.

At night the maiden was led in again, and when she began to talk about her sad plight, he immediately recognized his dear wife by her voice, jumped up, and exclaimed, 'Now I'm really free from the spell! It was all like a dream. The strange princess had cast a spell over me and made me forget you, but God has delivered me from the spell just in time.'

That night they left the castle in secret, for they were afraid of the princess's father, who was a sorcerer. They got on the griffin, who carried them over the Red Sea, and when they were in the middle, she let the nut drop. Immediately a big nut tree sprouted, and the griffin was able to rest there. Then he carried them home, where they found their child, who had grown tall and handsome. From then on they lived happily until their death.

36

The Goose Girl

THERE once was an old queen whose husband had been dead for many years, and she had a beautiful daughter. When the daughter grew up, she was betrothed to a prince who lived far away. Soon the time came for her to be married, and the princess got ready to depart for the distant kingdom. So the old queen packed up a great many precious items and ornaments and goblets and jewels, all made with silver and gold. Indeed, she gave her everything that suited a royal dowry, for she loved her child with all her heart. She also gave her a chambermaid, who was to accompany her and deliver her safely into the hands of her bridegroom. Each received a horse for the journey, but the princess's horse was named Falada and could speak. When the hour of departure arrived, the old mother went into her bedroom, took a small knife, and cut her finger to make it bleed. Then she placed a white handkerchief underneath her finger, let three drops of blood fall on it, and gave it to her daughter.

'My dear child,' she said, 'take good care of these three drops, for they will help you on your journey when you're in need.'

After they had bid each other a sad farewell, the princess stuck the handkerchief into her bosom, mounted her horse, and began her journey to her bridegroom. After riding an hour, she felt very thirsty and said to her chambermaid, 'Get down and fetch some water from the brook with the golden cup you brought along for me. I'd like to have something to drink.'

'If you're thirsty,' said the chambermaid, 'get down yourself. Just lie down by the water and drink. I'm not going to be your servant.'

Since the princess was very thirsty, she dismounted, bent over the brook, and drank some water, but she was not allowed to drink out of the golden cup.

'Dear Lord!' she said.

Then the three drops of blood responded, 'Ah, if your mother knew, her heart would break in two!'

But the princess was humble. She said nothing and got back on her horse. They continued riding a few miles, but the day was warm, the sun was scorching hot, and soon she got thirsty again. When they came to a stream, she called to her chambermaid once more. 'Get down and bring me something to drink from my golden cup,' for she had long since forgotten her nasty words.

'If you want to drink,' the chambermaid said even more haughtily than before, 'drink by yourself. I'm not going to be your servant.'

Since she was very thirsty, the princess dismounted, lay down next to the running water, and wept.

'Dear Lord!' she said.

Once again the drops of blood responded, 'Ah, if your mother knew, her heart would break in two!'

As she was leaning over the bank and drinking the water, her handkerchief with the three drops of blood fell out of her bosom and floated downstream without her ever noticing it, so great was her fear. But the chambermaid had seen it and was pleased because she knew that now she could have power over the princess. Without the three drops of blood, the princess was weak and helpless. So, as she was about to get back on the horse named Falada, the chambermaid said, 'That's my horse. Yours is the nag!'

The princess had to put up with all that. Moreover, the chambermaid spoke rudely to her and ordered her to take off her royal garments and to put on the maid's shabby clothes. Finally, she had to swear under open skies that she would never tell a soul at the royal court what the chambermaid had done. If the princess had not given her word, she would have been killed on the spot. But Falada saw all this and took good note of it.

Now the chambermaid mounted Falada, and the true bride had to get on the wretched nag. Thus they continued their journey until they finally arrived at the royal castle. There was great rejoicing when they entered the courtyard, and the prince ran to meet them. He lifted the chambermaid from her horse, thinking that she was his bride. Then he led her up the stairs, while the princess was left standing below. Meanwhile, the old king peered out a window, and when he saw her standing in the courtyard, he was struck by her fine, delicate, and beautiful features. He went straight to the royal suite and asked the bride about the girl she had brought with her, the one standing below in the courtyard, and who she was.

'I picked her up along the way to keep me company. Just give her something to keep her busy.'

But the old king had no work for her and could only respond, 'I have a little boy who tends the geese. Perhaps she could help him.'

The boy's name was Conrad, and the true bride had to help him tend the geese.

Shortly after, the false bride said to the young king, 'Dearest husband, I'd like you to do me a favour.'

'I'd be glad to,' he answered.

'Well then, summon the knacker and have him cut off the head of the horse that carried me here. It gave me nothing but trouble along the way.'

However, the truth was that she was afraid the horse would reveal what she had done to the princess. When all the preparations had been made and faithful Falada was about to die, word reached the ears of the true princess, and she secretly promised the knacker a gold coin if he would render her a small service. There was a big dark gateway through which she had to pass every morning and evening with the geese, and she wanted him to nail Falada's head on the wall under the dark gateway, where she could always see it. The knacker promised to do it, and when he cut off the horse's head, he nailed it on hard to the wall under the dark gateway.

Early the next morning, when she and Conrad drove the geese out through the gateway, she said in passing:

'Oh, poor Falada, I see you hanging there.'

Then the head answered:

'Dear Queen, is that you really there?
Oh, if your mother knew,
her heart would break in two!'

She walked out of the city in silence, and they drove the geese into the fields. When she reached the meadow, she sat down and undid her hair, which was as pure as gold. Conrad liked the way her hair glistened so much that he tried to pull out a few strands. Then she said:

'Blow, wind, oh, blow with all your might!
Blow Conrad's cap right out of sight,
and make him chase it everywhere
until I've braided all my hair
and put it up all right.'

Then a gust of wind came and blew off Conrad's cap into the fields, and he had to run after it. By the time he returned with it, she had finished combing and putting her hair up, and he could not get a single strand of it. Conrad became so angry that he would not speak to her after that. Thus they tended the geese until evening, when they set out on their way home.

The next morning, when they drove the geese through the dark gateway, the maiden said:

'Oh, poor Falada, I see you hanging there.'

Then Falada responded:

> 'Dear Queen, is that you really there?
> Oh, if your mother knew,
> her heart would break in two!'

Once she and Conrad were out in the fields again, she sat down in the meadow and began to comb out her hair. Conrad ran up and tried to grab it, but she quickly said:

> 'Blow, wind, oh, blow with all your might!
> Blow Conrad's cap right out of sight,
> and make him chase it everywhere
> until I've braided all my hair
> and put it up all right.'

The wind blew and whisked the cap off his head and drove it far off so that Conrad had to run after it. When he came back, she had long since put up her hair, and he could not get a single strand. Thus they tended the geese until evening. However, upon returning that evening, Conrad went to the old king and said, 'I don't want to tend the geese with that girl anymore.'

'Why not?' asked the old king.

'Well, she tortures me the whole day long.'

The old king ordered him to tell him what she did, and Conrad said, 'In the morning, when we pass through the dark gateway, there's a horse's head on the wall, and she always says:

'Oh, poor Falada, I see you hanging there.'

'And the head answers:

"Dear Queen, is that you really there?
Oh, if your mother knew,
her heart would break in two!"'

And thus Conrad went on to tell the king what had happened out on the meadow, and how he had had to chase after his cap.

The old king ordered him to drive the geese out again the next day, and when morning came, the old king himself sneaked behind the dark gateway and heard her speak to Falada's head. Then he followed her into the fields and hid behind some bushes in the meadow. Soon he saw with his own eyes how the goose girl and the goose boy brought the geese to the meadow, and how she sat down after a while and undid her hair that glistened radiantly. Before long, she said:

> 'Blow, wind, oh, blow with all your might!
> Blow Conrad's cap right out of sight,
> and make him chase it everywhere
> until I've braided all my hair
> and put it up all right.'

Then a gust of wind came and carried Conrad's cap away, so that he had to run far, and the maiden calmly combed and braided her hair. All this was observed by the old king. He then went home unnoticed, and when the goose girl came back that evening, he called her aside and asked her why she did all those things.

'I'm not allowed to tell you, nor am I allowed to bemoan my plight to anyone. Such is the oath I swore under the open skies. Otherwise, I would have been killed.'

Although he kept on insisting and would give her no peace, she would not talk. Then he said, 'If you don't want to tell me anything, then let the iron stove over there listen to your sorrows.'

After the king departed, she crawled into the iron stove and began to lament and weep and pour her heart out.

'Here I sit now,' she said. 'Forsaken by the world, and yet I'm a king's daughter. A wicked chambermaid forced me to give her my royal garments, and then she took my place with my bridegroom. Now I must do menial work as a goose girl. Oh, if my mother knew, her heart would break in two!'

Meanwhile, the old king stood next to the stovepipe outside and listened to what she said. Afterward he went back into the room and ordered her to come out of the stove. He had her dressed in royal garments, and it was like a miracle to see how beautiful she really was. The old king called his son and revealed to him that he had the wrong bride, who was nothing but a chambermaid. The true bride, however, was standing there before him, the former goose girl. The young king was extremely pleased, for he saw how beautiful and virtuous she was.

Now a great feast was prepared, and all their friends and the entire court were invited to attend. At the head of the table sat the bridegroom, with the princess at one side and the chambermaid at the other, but the chambermaid was so distracted that she could no longer recognize the princess, who was dressed in such a dazzling manner. After they finished eating and drinking and were all in high spirits, the old king gave the chambermaid a riddle to solve: what punishment did a woman deserve who deceived her lord in such and such a way? Whereupon he told her the whole story and concluded by asking, 'How would you sentence her?'

'She deserves nothing better,' said the false bride, 'than to be stripped completely naked and put inside a barrel studded with sharp nails. Then two white horses should be harnessed to the barrel and made to drag her through the streets until she's dead.'

'You're the woman,' said the king, 'and you've pronounced your own sentence. All this shall happen to you.'

When the sentence had been carried out, the young king married his true bride, and they both reigned over their kingdom in peace and bliss.

37
The Young Giant

A FARMER had a son no bigger than the size of a thumb. After some years had passed, his son did not show the least sign of getting any bigger or even growing so much as a hair's breadth. One day, when the farmer was preparing to go out to the field to do some ploughing, the little fellow said, 'Father, I want to go with you.'

'You want to go with me?' asked the farmer. 'Well, I think you'd better stay here. You're of no use to me out there, and you could get lost.'

When he heard that, Thumbling began to cry, so his father stuck him in his pocket and took him along in order to have some peace and quiet. Once he was out in the field, he pulled his son out again and set him down in a freshly ploughed furrow. As the boy was sitting there a big giant came over the hill.

'Do you see the big bogeyman over there?' said the father, who just wanted to scare the little fellow so he would behave. 'He's coming to get you.'

It took the giant only a few steps with his long legs before he reached the furrow. Then he lifted Thumbling up carefully with two fingers, examined him, and carried him away without saying a word. The father stood there so petrified with fright that he could not utter a sound. He was certain his child was now lost to him and he would never set eyes on him again.

In the meantime, the giant took the boy home and let him suckle at his breast, and Thumbling grew and became big and strong like most giants. When two years had passed, the old giant took him into the woods to test him.

'Pull up a stick for yourself,' he said.

By now the boy had become so strong that he tore up a young tree right out of the ground, roots and all. But the giant thought, We must do better than that. So he took him home again and nursed him for two more years. When he tested him once more, the boy's strength had increased so much that he could tear an old tree out of the ground. Yet, it still was not enough for the giant, who nursed him another two years, and when he then took him into the woods, he said, 'Now, make sure you tear up a stick of decent size!'

The boy tore up the thickest possible oak tree right out of the ground so that it cracked in two, and this was mere child's play for him.

'That's enough now,' said the giant. 'You've learned all you need to know,' and he took him back to the field where he had found him. His father was ploughing there as the young giant came over to him and said, 'Look, Father, look what a fine man your son has grown up to be!'

The farmer was frightened and said, 'No, you're not my son. I don't want you. Go away!'

'Of course I'm your son! Let me do your work. I can plough just as well as you can, or even better.'

'No, no, you're not my son. I don't want you, and I don't want you to plough either. Go away!'

However, since the farmer was afraid of the big man, he let go of the plough, stepped aside, and sat down at the edge of the field. Then the young man grabbed the plough and merely pressed his hand on it, but his grip was so powerful that the plough sank deep into the earth. The farmer could not bear to watch all that, and so he called over to him. 'If you're so set on ploughing, then you've got to learn not to press down so hard. Otherwise, you'll ruin the field.'

Then the young man unharnessed the horses and began pulling the plough himself. 'Just go home, Father,' he said, 'and have Mother cook me a large dish of food. In the meantime, I'll plough the field for you.'

The farmer went home and told his wife to cook the food, and the young man ploughed the field, two whole acres, all by himself. After that he harnessed himself to the harrow and harrowed the field with two harrows at the same time. When he was finished, he went into the woods and pulled up two oak trees, put them on his shoulders, and attached a harrow at each end of a tree and a horse at each end of the other tree. Then he carried everything to his parents' house as if it were a bundle of straw. When he reached the barnyard, his mother did not recognize him and asked, 'Who's that horrible big man?'

'That's our son,' the farmer said.

'No,' she said, 'that can't be our son. We never had one that large. Our son was a tiny thing.' Then she yelled at him, 'Go away! We don't want you!'

The young man did not respond but led the horses into the stable and gave them oats and hay and whatever else they normally had. When he was finished, he went into the kitchen, sat down at a bench, and said, 'Mother, I'd like to eat now. Is supper almost ready?'

'Yes,' she replied, and brought him two tremendous bowls of food that would have lasted her and her husband a week. However, the young man finished everything by himself and then asked whether she could give him something more.

'No,' she said, 'that's all we have.'

'That was really just a nibble. I've got to have more.'

She did not dare contradict him. So she went out and put a large pig's trough full of food on the fire. When it was ready, she carried it in.

'At last, a few more crumbs of food to eat,' he said and gobbled up everything that was in it. But that was not enough to satisfy his hunger.

'Father,' he said, 'I can tell I'll never get enough to eat here. So, if you'll get me an iron staff strong enough that I won't break it across my knees, I'll make my way out into the world.'

The farmer was happy to hear that. He hitched two horses to his wagon and went to the blacksmith, who gave him a staff so big and thick that the two horses could barely pull it. The young man laid it across his knees, and *crack!* he broke it in two, as if it were a beanstalk, and threw it away. His father hitched four horses to his wagon and fetched another staff, one so large and thick that the four horses could barely pull it. Once again his son snapped it across his knees and threw it away. 'Father,' he said, 'this one's no use to me. You've got to harness some more horses and fetch a stronger staff.'

Then his father hitched up eight horses to his wagon and brought back a staff so large and thick that the eight horses could barely pull it. When his son took it in his hand, he immediately broke off a piece from the top and said, 'Father, I see that you can't get the kind of staff I need. So I won't stay around here any longer.'

The young man went away, and he began passing himself off as a journeyman blacksmith. Soon he came to a village that had a blacksmith among its inhabitants. He was a greedy man who never gave anyone a thing and kept everything for himself. The young man went to the smithy and asked him whether he could use a journeyman.

'Yes,' said the blacksmith, who looked him over and thought, That's a sturdy fellow. He'll certainly be good at hammering, and he's sure to earn his keep. Then he asked, 'How much wages do you want?'

'None at all,' he answered. 'But every two weeks when the other journeymen receive their wages, I shall give you two blows that you must be able to withstand.'

The miser voiced great satisfaction with the terms, because he thought he could save money this way. The next morning the strange journeyman was supposed to hammer first, and when the master brought out the red-hot bar and the journeyman dealt the blow, the iron flew all over in pieces, and the anvil sank so deep into the ground that they could not get it out again. The miser became furious and said, 'That's all! I can't use you anymore. You hammer much too roughly. What do I owe you for the one blow?'

'I'll give you just a tiny tap, that's all,' said the journeyman, and he lifted his foot and gave him such a kick that he flew over four stacks of hay. Then the journeyman picked out the thickest iron staff he could find in the smithy, used it as a walking stick, and went on his way. After he had been travelling for a while, he came to a large farming estate and asked the bailiff if he needed a foreman.

'Yes,' said the bailiff, 'I can use one. You look like a sturdy and able fellow. What would you like your wages to be for the year?'

Again he answered that he did not want to be paid, but that the bailiff would have to withstand three blows that he would give him at the end of every year. The bailiff was satisfied with that, for he too was a miser. The next morning the hired workers got up early because they were supposed to drive to the forest and cut wood, but the young man was still in bed. One of the workers called to him, 'Hey, it's time to get up! We're going to the forest, and you've got to come with us.'

'Not yet,' he replied in a rude and surly voice. 'You all go. I'll get there and back before the rest of you anyway.'

Then the workers went to the bailiff and told him that the foreman was still in bed and would not drive to the forest with them. The bailiff told them to wake him again and order him to hitch up the horses. But the foreman answered just as he had before, 'You all go. I'll get there and back before the rest of you anyway.'

So he remained in bed another two hours, and when he finally managed to get up, he fetched two bushels of peas from the loft, cooked himself a porridge, and took his own sweet time in eating it. After that was done, he went out and hitched up the horses and drove to the forest. Near the forest was a ravine through which he had to drive. When he drove through it, he stopped the horses, got out, walked behind the wagon, and took some trees and bushes to build a large barricade that would prevent horses from getting through the ravine. When he arrived at the forest, the others were just leaving with their loaded wagons and heading home.

'Drive on,' he said to them. 'I'll still get home before you.'

He did not drive very far into the forest, for as soon as he saw two of the biggest oak trees, he ripped them out of the ground, threw them into his wagon, and turned back. When he reached the barricade, the others were still standing around, since they had been prevented from getting through.

'You see,' he said. 'If you had stayed with me, you'd have made it home just as quickly, and you'd have had another hour's sleep.'

He wanted to drive on, but his horses could not work their way through the barricade. So he unharnessed them, set them on top of the wagon, took hold of the shafts, and whisked everything through as easily as if the wagon were loaded with feathers. Once he was on the other side, he said to the workers, 'You see, I got through faster than you.' And he drove on, while the others had to stay where they were. At the barnyard he grabbed hold of one of the trees, lifted it by his hand, showed it to the bailiff, and said, 'How do you like this nice cord of wood?'

The bailiff said to his wife, 'He's a good man, our foreman. Even if he does sleep long, he still makes it home sooner than the others.'

So the young man served the bailiff for a year, and when it was over and the other workers received their wages, it was time for him to collect his pay as well. However, the bailiff was afraid of the blows he had coming to him. He begged the foreman to forgo everything and said that, in return, he would make him bailiff and take over the job as foreman himself.

'No,' said the young man. 'I don't want to be bailiff. I'm foreman and want to stay foreman. And I intend to dole out what we agreed upon.'

The bailiff offered to give him whatever he wanted, but it did no good. The foreman rejected everything he proposed, and the bailiff did not know what to do except to ask him for a two-week period of grace. He needed time to think of a way out of his situation. The foreman granted him an extension, and now the bailiff summoned all his clerks together. He asked them to think up a way to help him and to advise him. After they had deliberated a long time, they finally said that nobody's life was safe from the foreman: he could kill a man as easily as he could a gnat. They advised the bailiff, therefore, to order the foreman to climb down into the well and clean it out; when he was down below, they would roll one of the millstones that were lying around there over to the well and heave it on his head. Then he would never see the light of day again.

The bailiff liked the idea, and the foreman was willing to climb down into the well. Once he was standing below, they rolled down the largest millstone they could find and were convinced they broke his skull with it. However, he called up to them, 'Chase the chickens away from the well! They're scratching around in the sand and throwing grains into my eyes so that I can't see.'

So the bailiff yelled, '*Shoo! Shoo!*' as if he were scaring the chickens away. When the foreman had finished his work, he climbed up and said, 'Just look at what a fine necklace I've got on now!' but he meant the millstone that he was wearing around his neck.

Now the foreman wanted to receive his pay, but the bailiff requested another two weeks' grace to think up a new plan. The clerks met again and advised him to send the foreman to the haunted mill to grind grain at night since nobody had ever emerged alive from it the next morning. The bailiff liked the proposal and called the foreman to him that very same evening. He ordered him to carry eight bushels of grain to the mill and grind it that night because they needed it right away. So the foreman went to the loft and put two bushels in his right pocket and two in his left. He carried the other four in a sack that he slung over his shoulder so that half was on his back and half on his chest. And off he went to the haunted mill.

The miller told him he could easily grind the grain during the day, but not at night, because the mill was haunted, and anyone who had gone in there at night had not been alive in the morning to return.

'Don't worry, I'll manage,' said the foreman. 'Why don't you go and get some sleep.' Then he went into the mill and poured the grain into the hopper. Toward eleven o'clock he went into the miller's room and sat down on a bench. After he had been sitting there awhile, the door suddenly opened, and an enormous table came in. Next he saw wine, roast meat, and all sorts of good food appear on the table by themselves, but nobody carried these things in. After that the chairs slid to the table, but nobody came. All at once he saw fingers handling knives and forks and putting food on the plates. Aside from that, he could not see a thing. Since he was hungry and saw all this food, he too sat down at the table, ate along with all those present, and enjoyed the meal. When he had eaten his fill and the others had also emptied their plates, he distinctly heard all the lights being suddenly snuffed out, and when it was pitch dark, he felt something like a smack in the face. Then he said, 'If anything like that happens again, I'm going to strike back.'

When he received a second smack in the face, he struck back, and so it went the whole night. He took nothing without paying it back generously, with interest, and kept himself busy by smacking anything that came near him. At daybreak, however, everything stopped. When the miller got up, he went by to see how the foreman was, and he was amazed to find him alive.

'I had a very fine meal,' said the foreman. 'Then I got some smacks in the face, but I also gave some in return.'

The miller was happy and said that the mill was now released from its curse, and he wanted to pay the foreman a reward.

'I don't want money,' said the foreman, 'I already have enough.' Then he took the flour on his back, went home, and told the bailiff he had done his job and now wanted to be paid the wages they had agreed upon.

When the bailiff heard that, he really became alarmed and upset. He paced up and down the room, and beads of sweat ran down his forehead. So he opened the window to get some fresh air, but before he knew it, the foreman had given him such a kick that he went flying through the window out into the sky. He flew and flew until he was completely out of sight.

Then the foreman said to the bailiff's wife, 'If he doesn't return, you'll have to take the other blow.'

'No, no!' she exclaimed. 'I won't be able to withstand it,' and she opened the other window because beads of sweat were running down her face also. Then he gave her a kick too, and she went flying out the window. Since she was lighter than her husband, she soared much higher.

Her husband called out to her, 'Come over here!'

But she replied, 'No, you come over here to me! I can't make it there.'

So they soared through the sky, and neither could get to the other. Whether they are still soaring, I don't know, but I do know that the young giant took his iron staff and continued on his way.

38
The King of the Golden Mountain

A MERCHANT had two children, a boy and a girl, who were still infants and could not walk. About this time the merchant had invested his entire fortune in richly laden ships that had gone out to sea. Just when he was about to make a lot of money through this venture, he received news that the ships had sunk. So now, instead of being a rich man, he was a poor one and had nothing left but a field outside the city. In order to take his mind off his troubles somewhat, he went out to his field, and as he was pacing back and forth a little black dwarf suddenly stood beside him and asked him why he was so sad and what was gnawing at his heart.

'If you could help me,' said the merchant, 'I'd certainly tell you.'

'Who knows,' answered the black dwarf, 'maybe I can help you.'

Then the merchant told him that he had lost his whole fortune at sea and had nothing left but the field.

'Don't worry,' said the dwarf. 'You shall have as much money as you want if you promise to bring me in twelve years the first thing that brushes against your leg when you return home. And you must bring it to this spot.'

The merchant thought, What else can that be but my dog? Of course, he did not think of his little boy and so said yes. Then he gave the black dwarf a signed and sealed agreement and went home.

When he returned to his house, his little boy was so happy to see him that he held himself up by some benches, toddled over to his father, and grabbed him around the legs. The father was horrified, for he remembered the agreement, and he knew now what he had signed away. Still, he thought the dwarf might have been playing a joke on him since he did not find any money in his chests and boxes. One month later, however, when he went up into his attic to gather some old tinware to sell, he saw a huge pile of money lying on the floor. Soon he was in good spirits again and bought new provisions, with the result that he became an even greater merchant than before and trusted in

God to guide his destiny. In the meantime, his son grew and learned how to use his brains wisely. As he neared his twelfth birthday, however, the merchant became so worried that one could see the anxiety written on his face. His son asked him what was bothering him, and the father did not want to tell him. But the son persisted until he finally revealed everything to him: how without thinking he had promised him to a black dwarf and received a lot of money in return, and how he had given the dwarf a signed and sealed agreement to deliver him to the dwarf on his twelfth birthday.

'Oh, Father,' said the son. 'Don't be discouraged. Everything will turn out all right. The black dwarf has no power over me.'

The son had himself blessed by the priest, and when the hour arrived, he went out to the field with his father. There he drew a circle and stepped inside it with his father. The black dwarf came then and said to the old man, 'Have you brought what you promised me?'

The father kept quiet, but the son said, 'What do you want here?'

'I've come to discuss matters with your father, not with you.'

'You deceived my father and led him astray,' replied the son. 'Give me back the agreement.'

'No,' said the black dwarf. 'I won't give up my rights.'

They bickered for a long time until it was finally agreed that, since the son no longer belonged to his father, nor did he belong to his arch-enemy, he was to get into a little boat and drift downstream on the river. His father was to shove the boat off with his foot, and the son's fate was to be decided by the river. The boy said farewell to his father, got into the little boat, and the father had to shove it off with his own foot. The little boat soon capsized with the bottom up and the top face down. The father thought his son was lost, and he went home and mourned for him.

However, the boat did not sink but continued to drift calmly downstream with the boy safely inside. Finally, it touched down upon an unknown shore and stood still. The boy went ashore, saw a beautiful castle lying before him, and went toward it. When he entered, he realized it was enchanted. He went through all the rooms, but they were empty except for the last chamber, where he found a snake all coiled up. The snake was an enchanted princess, who was glad to see him and said, 'Have you come at last, my saviour? I've been waiting now twelve years for you. This kingdom is enchanted, and you must release it from the magic spell.'

'How can I do that?' he asked.

'Tonight twelve black men wearing chains will come and ask you what you're doing here. You must keep quiet and refuse to answer them. Let them do whatever they want with you: they will torture you, beat you, and stab you. Let them do that, just don't talk. At midnight they must go away. The second night twelve other men will come, and the third night there will be twenty-four, who will chop off your head. But at midnight their power will be gone, and if you have held out until then and have not uttered a single word, I shall be saved and shall come to you carrying the Water of Life. I shall rub you with it, and you shall be alive again and as healthy as you were before.'

Now, everything happened just as she had said: the black men could not force a word out of him, and on the third night the snake turned into a beautiful princess who came with the Water of Life and brought him back to life. Then she embraced him and kissed him, and there was joy and jubilation throughout the castle. Soon thereafter they celebrated their wedding, and he was king of the Golden Mountain.

Thus they lived happily together, and the queen gave birth to a handsome boy. After eight years had passed, the king's thoughts turned to his father. His heart went out to him, and he wished he could see him again. But the queen did not want to let him go and said, 'I can tell that this will bring me bad luck.'

Still, he gave her no peace until she consented to let him go. Upon his departure she gave him a wishing ring and said, 'Take this ring and put it on your finger; with it you can transport yourself immediately to wherever you want to go. But you must promise me never to use it to wish me away from here to your father's place.'

He promised her, put the ring on his finger, and wished that he was home, outside the city where his father lived. Before he knew it, he actually found himself there and started to walk toward the city. However, when he reached the city gate, the sentries would not let him enter because he was wearing such strange clothes, even though they were rich and splendid. So he climbed a hill where a shepherd was tending his flock, changed clothes with him, and put on the shepherd's old coat. This time when he went into the city, the sentries did not challenge him. After he got to his father's house, he revealed his identity, but his father would not believe he was his son and said that, to be sure, he had had a son, but he was long since dead. Nevertheless, the father offered the man a plate of food since he saw he was a poor, needy shepherd.

'I'm really your son,' said the shepherd to his parents. 'Don't you remember any birthmarks you'd recognize me by?'

'Yes,' said his mother, 'our son had a raspberry mark under his right arm.'

He pulled up his shirt, and when they saw the raspberry mark, they no longer doubted that he was their son. Then he told them that he was king of the Golden Mountain and that he had a princess as his wife and a handsome seven-year-old son.

'Now that can't possibly be true,' said his father. 'What kind of a king would run around in a tattered shepherd's coat?'

Immediately the son got angry, and not thinking of his promise, he turned his ring and wished both his wife and son there, and within seconds they were with him. But the queen wept and accused him of breaking his promise and making her unhappy.

'I did it without thinking. There was nothing underhanded about my actions,' he kept saying, and he eventually convinced her. Indeed, she appeared to be satisfied, but there was evil on her mind.

Shortly thereafter he led her outside the city to the field and showed her the spot on the riverbank where the little boat had been shoved off. While they were there, he said, 'I'm tired now. Sit down next to me. I'd like to sleep a little on your lap.'

He laid his head on her lap, and she loused him a bit until he fell asleep. While he was sleeping, she took the ring off his finger and drew her foot out from under him, leaving only her slipper behind. Finally, she took her child in her arms and wished herself back in her kingdom. When he awoke, he was lying there all alone. His wife and child were gone, and the ring as well. Only the slipper, as a token, had been left behind. 'You can't go back home again to your parents,' he said to himself. 'They'd only say you were a sorcerer. You'd better pack up and get back to your kingdom.'

So he went on his way and finally came to a mountain where three giants were standing and quarrelling because they could not decide how best to divide their father's inheritance. When they saw him riding by, they called to him and said that since little people were shrewd, they wanted him to divide the inheritance among them. This inheritance consisted of three things: First, a sword that chopped off everyone's head except that of the person who held it and said, 'All heads off except mine!' Second, a cloak that made one invisible if one put it on. Third, a pair of boots that carried the person who wore them to any spot he wished in a matter of seconds.

'Give me the three objects,' said the king, 'so I can see if they're in good condition.'

They handed him the cloak, and when he had put it on his shoulders, he was invisible and then turned into a fly. After that he resumed his true form and said, 'The cloak is good. Now give me the sword.'

'No,' they said. 'We won't give it to you. If you say, "All heads off except mine!" we'd lose our heads, and you alone would keep yours.'

Nevertheless, they gave it to him on condition that he try it out on a tree. He did that, and the sword cut the trunk of a tree in half as if it were made of straw. Now he wanted to have the boots, but they said, 'No, we won't give them away. If you put them on and wish yourself on top of the mountain, then we would stand here below with nothing.'

'Oh, no,' he said, 'I would never do anything like that.'

So they gave him the boots as well. But, when he had all three objects, he could think of nothing but his wife and child and sighed to himself, 'Oh, if only I were on top of the Golden Mountain!' And he vanished right before the eyes of the giants. Thus their inheritance was divided.

When he drew near the castle, he heard cries of joy and the sounds of fiddles and flutes. The people at the court told him that his wife was celebrating her wedding with another man. So he got angry and said, 'That faithless woman! It was she who duped me and then left me while I slept!' He hung his cloak around his shoulders and went unseen into the castle. When he entered the hall, there was a large table covered with delicious food, and the guests were eating and drinking, laughing and joking. The queen was sitting in a royal chair at the centre of the table. She was wearing magnificent clothes and had her crown on her head. He went over to her, took a place right behind her, and nobody was aware of his presence. When they put a piece of meat on her plate, he snatched it and ate it. And, when they gave her a glass of wine, he snatched it and drank it. They kept giving her food and wine, but she would always end up with nothing because her plate and glass would vanish immediately. She became so upset and distraught that she left the table, went into her chamber, and began weeping, while he stayed behind her all the time.

'Has the devil got me in his power?' she asked. 'I thought my saviour had come.'

Then he smacked her in the face and said, 'Your saviour came! Now he's got you in his power, you faithless thing! Did I deserve to be treated the way you treated me?'

He made himself visible, went into the hall, and announced, 'The wedding is over! The true king has arrived!'

The kings, princes, and ministers who were assembled there began jeering and mocking him, but he wanted to make short work of them and said, 'Will you leave or not?'

At that they charged and tried to capture him, but he took out his sword and said, 'All heads off except mine!'

Then their heads rolled to the ground, and he alone was master and king of the Golden Mountain.

39

The Water of Life

ONCE upon a time there was a king who was
sick, and nobody thought he would live. His
three sons were very saddened by this and went down
into the palace garden, where they wept. There they
met an old man who asked them why they were so
distressed, and they told him that their father was so
sick that he would probably die. Nothing seemed to
help.

'I know of a remedy,' the old man said. 'It's the Water
of Life. If he drinks it, he'll regain his health. But it's
difficult to find.'

'Well, I'll find it,' said the oldest, and he went to the
sick king and requested permission to leave and search
for the Water of Life, for that was the only cure for his
illness.

'No,' said the king. 'The danger is much too great. I'd rather die instead.'

But the son pleaded so long that finally the king had to give his consent. Deep down the prince felt, If I bring him the water, I'll be my father's favourite and shall inherit the kingdom.

So he set out and, after he had been riding for some time, he came across a dwarf, who called to him and said, 'Where are you going in such haste?'

'You meddling twerp,' the prince said contemptuously, 'that's none of your affair!' And he rode on.

But the little dwarf became furious and put a curse on him. Meanwhile, the prince found himself travelling through a mountain gorge, and the further he rode, the more the mountains closed together until the way became so narrow that he could not proceed. Nor could he turn his horse or get out of his saddle. He sat there as if he were in a prison.

The sick king waited a long time for the prince, but he did not come back. Then the second son said, 'Father, let me go and search for the Water of Life,' and he thought to himself, If my brother's dead, then the kingdom will fall to me.

At first the king did not want to let him go either, but finally he gave in. So the prince set out on the same road that his brother had taken and met the dwarf, who

333

stopped him and asked where he was going in such haste.

'You meddling twerp,' said the prince, 'that's none of your affair!' And he rode off without turning around.

But the dwarf put a curse on him, and he ended up in a mountain gorge, where he became trapped like his brother. Indeed, that is what happens to arrogant people.

Now, when the second son also failed to return, the youngest offered to set forth and fetch the water, and eventually the king had to let him go too. When he met the dwarf and was asked where he was going in such haste, he stopped and answered, 'I'm looking for the Water of Life because my sick father is on the brink of death.'

'Do you know where to find it?'

'No,' said the prince.

'Well, since you've behaved yourself in a proper manner and are not arrogant like your faithless brothers, I'll tell you how to get to the Water of Life: you'll find it gushing from a fountain in the courtyard of an enchanted castle, but you'll never make your way inside unless I give you an iron wand and two loaves of bread. You're to knock three times on the castle gate with the iron wand, then it will spring open. Inside are two lions lying on the ground. They will open their jaws, but if you throw a loaf of bread to each of them, they will be quiet. Then you must hurry and fetch some of the Water of Life before the clock strikes twelve. Otherwise, the gate will slam shut, and you will be locked in.'

The prince thanked him, took the wand and the bread, and went on his way. When he arrived there, everything was just as the dwarf had said. After the third knock the gate sprang open, and when he had calmed the lions with the bread, he entered the castle and went into a big beautiful hall, where he found enchanted princes sitting all around. He took the rings from their fingers and also grabbed a sword and loaf of bread that were lying on the floor. Then he moved on to the next room, where he encountered a beautiful maiden, who was delighted to see him. She kissed him and said that he had set her free and could have her entire kingdom as reward. If he would return in a year's time, their wedding would be celebrated. Then she also told him where to find the fountain with the Water of Life, but that he had to hurry and draw the water before the clock struck twelve. So he went on and finally came to a room with a beautiful, freshly made bed, and since he was tired, he wanted to rest a little. Once he lay down, however, he fell asleep. When he awoke, the clock was striking a quarter to twelve, and he jumped up in a fright, ran to the fountain, and drew some water in a cup that happened to be lying on the ledge. Then he rushed outside, and just as he was running through the iron gate, the clock struck twelve, and the gate slammed so hard that it took off a piece of his heel.

Nevertheless, he was happy that he had found the Water of Life, and on his way home he passed the dwarf again. When the little man saw the sword and the bread, he said, 'You've managed to obtain some valuable things. With the sword you'll be able to defeat whole armies, and the bread will always replenish itself.'

But the prince did not want to return home to his father without his brothers, and so he asked, 'Dear dwarf, could you tell me where my two brothers are? They went out looking for the Water of Life before me and never came back.'

'They're trapped in between two mountains,' said the dwarf. 'I put them there with a magic spell because they were so arrogant.'

Then the prince pleaded until finally the dwarf decided to release them but not without a warning. 'Beware of them,' he said. 'They have evil hearts.'

When he was reunited with his brothers, he was happy and told them all that had happened: how he found the Water of Life and was now bringing back a cupful to their father, how he had rescued the beautiful princess and was going to marry her after waiting a year, and how he would receive a vast kingdom after their marriage. Once his story was told, he rode on with his brothers, and they came to a country plagued by war and famine. The king was already convinced that he would soon perish because the situation was so desperate. But the prince went to him and gave him the bread, which he used to feed his people and satisfy their hunger. After that the prince also gave him the sword, which he used to defeat the enemy armies, and he was then able to live in peace and quiet. So the prince took back the loaf of bread and the sword, and the brothers rode on. However, they passed through two other countries plagued by famine and war, and on each occasion the prince gave the king his bread and sword. In this way he was able to help save three kingdoms.

Later on they boarded a ship and sailed across the sea. During the trip the two older brothers plotted together against their brother. 'The youngest found the Water of Life, and we are empty-handed. So our father will give him the kingdom that is ours by right, and our brother will deprive us of our happiness.'

Overcome by a desire for revenge, they planned to put an end to their brother. They waited until he was sound asleep. Then they poured the Water of Life from his cup into their own and replaced it with bitter salt water. When they arrived home, the youngest brought the cup to the sick king and told him to drink it and he would get well. No sooner did the king drink the bitter salt water than he became sicker than ever. And as he began to moan the two oldest brothers came and accused the youngest of wanting to poison the king, while they, on the other hand, had brought the true Water of Life, and they handed it to their father. As soon as he drank some, he felt his sickness on the wane and became as strong and healthy as in the days of his youth. After that the two older brothers went to the youngest and belittled him. 'Oh, we know you found the Water of Life,' they said, 'but we're the ones who've received the reward for all your trouble. You should have been smarter and kept your eyes open. We took the water from you when you fell asleep at sea, and in a year's time one of us will fetch the beautiful princess. Still, you had better not expose us. Father will not believe you anyway, and if you breathe a single word about it, your life will be worth nothing. If you keep quiet, we'll let you live.'

The old king was angry at his youngest son because he believed that his son had wanted to take his life. So he summoned his ministers and ordered them to sentence his son to be shot in secret. So, one day, as the prince went out hunting, suspecting no danger, one of the king's huntsmen had to accompany him. When they were all alone out in the forest, the huntsman looked so sad that the prince asked him, 'Dear hunter, what's the matter?'

'I can't say,' answered the huntsman, 'and yet I should.'

'Tell me,' said the prince. 'Whatever it is, I'll forgive you.'

'Ah,' said the huntsman. 'The king has ordered me to kill you.'

The prince was taken aback by this news and said, 'Dear huntsman, let me live. I'll give you my royal garments, and you give me your common ones in exchange.'

'I'll gladly do that,' said the huntsman. 'I couldn't have shot you anyway.'

They exchanged clothes, and the huntsman went home, while the prince went deeper into the forest.

After a while three wagons loaded with gold and jewels arrived at the king's castle for his youngest son. They had been sent by the three kings who had defeated their enemies with the prince's sword and who had nourished their people with his bread. The wagons were an expression of their gratitude, and when the old king saw that, he began to think, Perhaps my son was innocent? And he said to the people at his court, 'If only he were still alive! Now I regret that I ordered him to be killed.'

'He's still alive,' said the huntsman. 'I didn't have the heart to carry out your order,' and he told the king what had happened.

The king felt greatly relieved, and he had it proclaimed in all the surrounding kingdoms that his son was free to return and was back in favour with the king.

In the meantime, the princess had decided to build a glittering gold road that would lead up to her castle. She told her guards that whoever came riding to her straight up the middle of the road would be the right man and they should let him enter. However, whoever rode up on the side of the road would not be the right man, and they were not to let him enter.

When the year of waiting was almost up, the oldest son thought he would get an early start and pass himself off as her saviour. Then he would get her for his wife and the kingdom as well. So he rode forth, and when he came to the castle and saw the beautiful road, he thought, It would be a terrible shame if you rode on it. So he turned off to the right and rode along the side. But when he got to the castle gate, the guards told him that he was not the right man and he had better go away. Soon thereafter the second prince set out, and when he came to the gold road and his horse set its hoof down on it, he thought, It would be a terrible shame if you damaged the road. He turned to the left and rode along the side. However, when he reached the gate, the guards told him he had better go away, for he was not the right man.

When the year was completely over, the third son prepared to ride out of the forest and hoped to forget his sorrows in the company of his beloved. As he set out he kept thinking about her and wishing he were already with her. When he arrived at the gold road, he did not even notice it, and his horse rode right down the middle of it. Once he reached the gate, it opened, and the princess welcomed him with joy. She pronounced him her saviour and lord of the realm, and they were blissful as they celebrated their wedding. When it was over, she told him his father had sent for him and had pardoned him. So he rode home and explained to his father how his brothers had deceived him and why he had kept quiet about it. The old king wanted to punish them, but they had taken flight on a ship, sailed away, and never returned as long as they lived.

40

The Wren and the Bear

ONCE, during the summertime, as the bear and the wolf were walking through the forest, the bear heard a bird singing a beautiful song and said, 'Brother wolf, what kind of bird can sing as beautifully as that?'

'That's the king of the birds,' said the wolf. 'We must bow down before him.'

However, it was nothing but the wren, popularly known as the fence king.

'If that's the case,' said the bear, 'I'd like very much to see his royal palace. Please take me there.'

'You can't go there just like that,' said the wolf. 'You'll have to wait until the queen comes.'

Soon thereafter the queen arrived carrying some food in her bill, and the king as well, and they began feeding their young ones. The bear wanted to run in right after them, but the wolf held him by his sleeve and said, 'No, you've got to wait until His Majesty and Her Highness have gone away again.'

So they took note of the place where the nest was and trotted off. However, the bear could not rest until he saw the royal palace, and after a short while, he went back to it. The king and queen had already flown away, and he looked inside and saw five or six young birds lying there.

'Is that the royal palace?' exclaimed the bear. 'It's a miserable palace. And you're not royal children in the least. You're a disgrace!'

When the young wrens heard that, they were tremendously angry and cried out, 'No, we're not! Our parents are honourable people. Bear, you're going to pay for your remarks!'

The bear and the wolf became frightened. They turned around, went back to their dens, and sat. But the young wrens kept crying and shrieking, and when their parents returned with food, they said, 'We're not going to touch so much as a fly's leg until you establish whether we're a disgrace or not. The bear was just here, and he insulted us.'

'Calm down,' said the old king. 'I'll settle this matter.'

He flew away with the queen to the bear's den and

called inside, 'Hey, you grumbly old bear, why did you insult my children? You'll pay for this. We'll have to settle this matter in a bloody war!'

So war was declared against the bear, who summoned all the four-legged animals: the ox, donkey, steer, stag, deer, and all those beasts that walk upon the earth. To counter this, the wren summoned everything that flies: not only the big and small birds, but also the gnats, hornets, bees, and flies had to come too.

When the time came for the war to begin, the wren sent out scouts to discover who the commanding general of the enemy forces was. The gnat was the wiliest of them all and roamed out into the forest, where the enemy had assembled. Then he hid under a leaf on the tree where the password was to be given out. The bear was standing right there, and he called the fox to him and said, 'Fox, you're the sliest of all the animals. I want you to be our general and to lead us.'

'Fine,' said the fox. 'But what shall we use as signals?'

Since nobody had any ideas, the fox said, 'I've got a nice long bushy tail that looks almost like a red plume. If I lift up my tail, that will mean everything's all right, and you should charge. But, if I let it droop, then run for your lives.'

Once the gnat heard that, he flew back to the wren

and reported everything down to the last detail. At daybreak, when the battle was to commence, the four-legged animals came thundering with such a clatter that the earth began to tremble. The wren and his army also came flying through the air. They buzzed, shrieked, and swarmed so much that everyone in the surrounding area was frightened to death. As both sides attacked, the wren sent the hornet out with instructions to dive under the fox's tail and to sting him with all his might. Now, when the fox felt the first sting, he twitched and lifted a leg, but he stood his ground and kept holding up his tail. With the second sting, he had to lower his tail momentarily. But by the third sting he could no longer stand the pain and had to howl and tuck his tail between his legs. When the other animals saw that, they thought all was lost and began to run, each to his own den. And so the birds won the battle.

The king and queen flew home to their children and called, 'Children, rejoice! Eat and drink to your heart's content. We've won the war.'

But the young wrens said, 'We're not going to eat a thing until the bear comes to our nest to beg our pardon and say that we're a credit to the family.'

Then the wren flew to the bear's den and cried out, 'Hey, you grumbly bear, I want you to go to my nest and ask my children for pardon. You'd better tell them they're a credit to the family; otherwise, your ribs will be broken to pieces.'

On hearing this, the bear became extremely frightened, and he crawled to the nest, where he apologized. Now the young wrens were finally satisfied, so they sat down together and ate, drank, and made merry till late in the night.

41
The Pea Test

ONCE upon a time there was a king whose only son was very eager to get married, and he asked his father for a wife.

'Your wish shall be fulfilled, my son,' said the king, 'but it's only fitting that you marry no one less than a princess, and there are none to be had in the vicinity. Therefore, I shall issue a proclamation and perhaps a princess will come from afar.'

Soon a written proclamation was circulated, and it did not take long before numerous princesses arrived at the court. Almost every day a new one appeared, but when the princesses were asked about their birth and lineage, it always turned out that they were not princesses at all, and they were sent away without having achieved their purpose.

'If everything continues like this,' the son said, 'I'll never get a wife in the end.'

'Calm yourself, my son,' said the queen. 'Before you know it, she'll be here. Happiness is often standing just outside the door. One only needs to open it.'

And it was really just as the queen had predicted.

Soon after, on a stormy evening when the wind and rain were beating on the windows, there was a loud knocking on the gate of the royal palace. The servants opened the gate, and a beautiful maiden entered. She demanded to be led directly before the king, who was surprised by such a late visit and asked her where she had come from, who she was, and what she desired.

'I've come from a distant country,' she answered, 'and I'm the daughter of a mighty king. When your proclamation with the portrait of your son arrived in my father's kingdom, I felt a strong love for your son and immediately set out on my way with the intention of becoming his bride.'

'I'm somewhat sceptical about what you've told me,' said the king. 'Besides, you don't look like a princess. Since when does a princess travel alone without an escort and in such poor clothes?'

'An escort would have only delayed me,' she replied. 'The colour of my clothes faded in the sun, and the rain washed it out completely. If you don't believe I'm a princess, just send a messenger to my father.'

'That's too far and too complicated,' said the king. 'A delegation cannot ride as fast as you. The people must have the necessary time for such a journey. Years would pass before they returned. If you can't prove in some other way that you're a princess, then fortune will not shine upon you, and you'd do well to head for home, the sooner the better.'

'Let her stay,' the queen said. 'I'll put her to a test and know soon enough whether she's a princess.'

The queen herself climbed up into the tower and had a bed made up for the maiden in a splendid room. When the mattress was carried into the room, she placed three peas on it, one on top, one in the middle, and one below. Then six other soft mattresses were stacked on top along with linen sheets and a cover made of eiderdown. When everything was ready, she led the maiden upstairs into the bedroom.

'After such a long trip, you must be tired, my child,' she said. 'Get some sleep. Tomorrow we'll continue talking.'

At the break of day the queen climbed up to the room in the tower. She thought the maiden would still be in a deep sleep, but the maiden was awake.

'How did you sleep, my little daughter?' she asked.

'Miserably,' replied the princess. 'I couldn't sleep a wink the whole night.'

'Why, my child? Wasn't the bed good enough?'

'In all my days I've never lain in such a bed. It was hard from my head to my feet. It seemed as if I were lying on nothing but peas.'

'Now I know for sure,' said the queen, 'that you're a genuine princess. I shall send some royal garments up to you with pearls and jewels. Dress yourself as a bride, for we shall celebrate your wedding this very day.'

42

The Lettuce Donkey

ONCE upon a time there was a young huntsman who went out into the forest to shoot some game. He was merry and lighthearted and whistled on a leaf as he marched along. Then he encountered an ugly old hag, who said, 'Good day, my dear huntsman, you're certainly cheerful and content, but I'm suffering from hunger and thirst. Would you give me some alms?'

The huntsman felt sorry for the poor woman, so he reached into his pocket and gave her whatever he could afford. As he was about to continue on his way, the old woman held him back and said, 'Listen to what I have to say, my dear huntsman. Since you've been so kind, I'm going to give you a gift. Just keep going straight ahead, and after a while you'll come to a tree. Nine birds will be sitting on it. They'll have a cloak in their claws and will be fighting over it. Take aim with your gun and shoot into the middle of them. They'll let go of the cloak for sure, and one of the birds will also be hit and drop dead at your feet. Take the cloak with you. It's a wishing cloak, and if you throw it around your shoulders, you need only wish yourself somewhere, and you'll be there in a split second. Take the heart out of the dead bird and swallow it whole. Then each and every morning, when you get up, you'll find a gold coin underneath your pillow.'

The huntsman thanked the wise woman and thought to himself, Those are great things she's promised me. If only they would come true! When he had gone about a hundred paces, he heard a great deal of screaming and squawking in the branches above him. As he looked up he saw a bunch of birds tearing at a piece of cloth with their beaks and claws. They screeched, tugged, and scuffled as if each wanted it for itself alone. 'Well,' said the huntsman, 'this is extraordinary. Everything's happening just as the old hag said it would.' He took the gun from his shoulder, aimed, and fired right into the middle of the birds so that their feathers fluttered about. Immediately the birds, with loud cries, took flight, but one fell to the ground dead along with the cloak. The huntsman then did what the old woman had told him to do: he cut the bird open, found the heart, swallowed it, and took the cloak home with him.

The next morning, when he woke up, he remembered the woman's promise and wanted to see if it had actually come to pass. As he lifted his pillow in the air the gold coin glimmered before his eyes. The following day he found another one, and so forth each time he got up. He collected a heap of gold but eventually began thinking, What's the use of all my gold if I stay at home? It's time I set out and see the world.

He took leave of his parents, swung his knapsack and gun over his shoulders, and went out into the world. One day he happened to pass through a dense forest, and when he reached the end of it, a stately castle stood on the plain before him. In one of its windows an old woman and a marvellously beautiful maiden were standing and looking down at him. The old woman, however, was a witch and said to the maiden, 'Someone's coming from the forest with a wonderful treasure in his body. We've got to get it out of him, my darling daughter, for it's really much more suited for us. You see, he's got a bird's heart in him, and every morning there's a gold coin under his pillow.' She told the maiden the whole story about the huntsman and what role she was to play. Finally, she threatened her and, with fury in her eyes, said, 'If you don't obey me, you'll regret it!'

As the huntsman came closer he spied the maiden and said to himself, 'I've been wandering around for so long that it's time to take a rest. I'll stop at this beautiful castle, for I've got plenty of money to pay.' But his real reason was that he had caught sight of the beautiful maiden.

He went into the castle and was received in a hospitable way and entertained courteously. It was not long before he fell in love with the witch's daughter. He thought of nothing else but her, had eyes only for her, and gladly did whatever she demanded. At that point the old woman said to her, 'Now we've got to get the bird's heart. He won't even notice it's missing.' She prepared a potion, and when it was ready, she poured it into a cup and gave it to the maiden, who had to hand it to the huntsman.

'Now, my dearest,' she said, 'drink to my health.'

So he took the cup, and after he had swallowed the drink, he vomited up the bird's heart. The maiden had to carry it off secretly and then swallow it herself, for that was what the old woman wanted. From then on the huntsman no longer found gold under his pillow, rather it lay under the maiden's pillow, and the old woman fetched it from there every morning. However, he was so much in love with the maiden and so infatuated that he had no other thought in his head than to spend time with her. Now the old witch said, 'We've got the bird's heart, but we must also take the wishing cloak from him.'

'Why not let him keep that?' answered the maiden. 'After all, he's already lost his wealth.'

The old woman became angry and said, 'Such a cloak is a wonderful thing. You won't find many like it in the world. I must have it, and I will have it.'

She gave the maiden instructions and told her that if she did not obey them, things would go badly for her. So the maiden did what the old woman told her to do; she stood at the window and gazed into the wide blue sky as if she were very sad.

'Why are you standing there so sadly?' asked the huntsman.

'Ah, my darling,' she replied, 'the Garnet Mountain lies over there, where precious jewels grow. Whenever I think about them, I get such a great longing for them that I become sad. But who can fetch them? Only the birds with their wings can fly there. A human being, never!'

'If that's all that's bothering you,' said the huntsman, 'I'll soon ease your woes.' Upon saying this, he spread his cloak over her and wished to be on top of the Garnet Mountain. Within a split second they were both sitting on top of it. The elegant jewels glimmered from all sides, and it was a joy just to look at them. Together they selected the most precious of the jewels. However, the old woman had used her witchcraft to make the huntsman's eyelids heavy, and he said to the maiden,

'Let's sit down and rest a bit. I'm so tired that I can't stand on my feet anymore.'

They sat down, and he laid his head in her lap and went to sleep. When he was sound asleep, she took the cloak from his shoulders and hung it around herself. She gathered the garnets and jewels together and wished herself back home.

After the huntsman had finished sleeping and awoke, he saw that his beloved had deceived him and had left him alone on top of the wild mountain. 'Oh,' he said, 'the world is full of treachery!' He sat there, overcome with sorrow and pain, and did not know what to do. The mountain, however, belonged to the wild and monstrous giants who dwelt there and who were always up to mischief. He had not been sitting there long before three of them came strolling toward him. He lay down as if he had fallen into a deep sleep. As the giants came by, the first one poked him in the foot and said, 'Who's this earthworm lying here and contemplating his navel?'

'Trample him to death!' said the second.

But the third one said contemptuously, 'He's not worth the trouble. Let him live. He can't survive here, and if he climbs higher, to the peak, the clouds will snatch him and carry him away.'

As they moved on they continued talking, but the huntsman had heard their words, and when they were out of sight, he got up and climbed to the peak. He sat there awhile until a cloud drifted by, grabbed him, and carried him away. For a long time it floated about in the sky. Then it began sinking and settled down on a large vegetable garden surrounded by walls, where the huntsman landed softly between the cabbages and vegetables. He looked around him and said, 'If I only had something to eat! I'm so hungry that it'll be hard to go anywhere from here, and there's nothing but vegetables. No apples or pears or any kind of fruit.' Finally, he thought, If need be, I can eat some of the lettuce. It doesn't taste very good, but it will refresh me.

So he picked out a fine head of lettuce and ate some of the leaves. No sooner had he taken a few bites than he had a strange sensation and felt completely changed: he sprouted four legs, a thick neck, and two long ears, and to his horror he saw that he had been transformed into a donkey. Nevertheless, since he still felt very hungry, and the juicy lettuce appealed to his present nature, he kept eating it with great zest. Eventually, he came to another kind of lettuce, and after he had swallowed a few leaves, he felt a new kind of sensation and returned to his human form.

Now the huntsman lay down and slept off his fatigue. When he awoke the next morning, he broke off a head of the bad lettuce and one of the good and thought, This ought to help me regain what belongs to me, and I'll be able to punish the treacherous women as well. He put the lettuce in his knapsack, climbed over the mountain, and set out to find the castle of his beloved. When he had wandered about several days, he was fortunate enough to find it again. Then he coloured his face brown so that his own mother would not have recognized him, went into the castle, and asked for lodgings. 'I'm so tired,' he said, 'that I can't go any farther.'

'Countryman, who are you, and what's your business?' asked the witch.

'I'm a royal messenger and was sent out to search for the most delicious lettuce under the sun. I was lucky enough to have found it, and I'm carrying it with me, but the heat of the sun has been so strong that the tender leaves are beginning to wilt, and I don't know whether I'll be able to carry it any farther.'

When the old woman heard of the delicious lettuce, she had a great yearning for it and said, 'My dear countryman, let me taste the wonderful lettuce.'

'Why not?' he answered. 'I've brought two heads with me, and I'll give you one.'

He opened the sack and handed her the bad one. The witch did not suspect anything, and her mouth watered so much for the new meal that she herself went into the kitchen to prepare it. When the lettuce was ready, she could not wait until it was on the table. She immediately took a few leaves and put them in her mouth. No sooner had she swallowed them than she too lost her human form and ran around in the courtyard as a donkey. Now the servant girl came into the kitchen, saw the lettuce all ready and wanted to serve it, but on the way she succumbed to her old habit of trying things and ate a couple of leaves. The magic power took effect immediately, and she too was changed into a donkey. She ran outside to the old woman, and the bowl with the lettuce fell to the ground. Meanwhile, the messenger sat with the beautiful maiden, and when nobody came with the lettuce and her longing for it also grew greater, she said, 'I don't know what's keeping the lettuce.'

The huntsman thought, The lettuce has probably worked, and so he said, 'I'll go to the kitchen and see what's happening.'

When he got there, he saw two donkeys running around the courtyard and the lettuce on the ground. 'Very good,' he said. 'The two have gotten their due,' and he picked up the remaining leaves, put them into the bowl, and brought them to the maiden.

'I've brought you the delicious food myself so that you won't have to wait any longer,' he said.

Then she ate some of the lettuce and was instantly robbed of her human form. Like the others, she ran out to the courtyard as a donkey. Next the huntsman washed his face so that the women as donkeys could recognize him, and he went down to the courtyard and said, 'Now you're going to get what you deserve for your treachery.' He tied all three to a rope and drove them ahead until they came to a mill, where he knocked on the window. The miller stuck his head out and asked what he wanted.

'I've got three bad animals, and I don't want to keep them anymore,' he responded. 'If you take them, feed them, and treat them as I tell you to, then I'll pay you whatever you want.'

'Why not?' said the miller. 'How do you want me to treat them?'

The huntsman told the miller to give the old donkey, actually the witch, three beatings a day and one feeding; the younger, actually the servant, one beating a day and three feedings; and the youngest, actually the maiden, no beatings and three feedings. He could not bring himself to have the maiden beaten. He then went back to the castle, where he found everything he needed.

After a few days the miller came and said he had to report the death of the old donkey that was supposed to receive three beatings and one feeding a day. 'The other two,' he continued, 'are not dead yet, to be sure, but they are so sad that they'll be dead before long.'

Then the huntsman took pity on them, forgot his anger, and told the miller to drive them back to the castle. When they arrived, he gave them some of the good lettuce to eat so that they became human beings again. The beautiful maiden fell upon her knees in front of him and said, 'Ah, my dearest, forgive me for the evil I've done you. My mother forced me to do it. Everything happened against my will, for I love you with all my heart. Your wishing cloak is hanging in a closet, and I'll drink something to make me throw up the bird's heart.'

But he had a change of heart and said, 'Just keep it. It doesn't make any difference now because I want to take you for my faithful wife.'

Then the wedding was held, and they lived happily together until they died.

43

The Four Skilful Brothers

THERE once was a poor man who had four sons.
When they had grown up, he said to them, 'My dear
children, you must now go out into the world, for I have
nothing to give you. Make your way to foreign countries.
Learn a trade and try to succeed as best you can.'

So the four brothers got ready for their journey, took
leave of their father, and went out of the town gate
together. After they had travelled for some time, they
came to a crossroads that led in four different directions.
Then the oldest son said, 'We must separate here, but let
us meet again at this spot four years from today. In the
meantime, we shall try our luck.'

So each one went his way, and the oldest met a man,
who asked him where he was going and what his plans
were.

'I want to learn a trade,' he answered.

'Then come with me,' the man said, 'and become a thief.'

'No,' the oldest son responded. 'That's no longer considered an honest trade, and one generally ends up dangling from the gallows.'

'Oh,' said the man, 'you needn't be afraid of the gallows. I'll just teach you how to get what nobody else can otherwise fetch, and I'll show you how to do this without ever being caught.'

So the oldest son let himself be persuaded, and the man taught him how to become a skilful thief. The young man became so adroit that nothing was safe from him once he wanted to have it.

The second brother met a man who asked him the same question about what he wanted to learn in the world.

'I don't know yet,' he answered.

'Then come with me and become a stargazer. You won't find anything better than this, for nothing will ever remain hidden from you.'

The second son liked the idea and became such a skilful stargazer that when he had finished studying and was about to depart, his master gave him a telescope and said, 'With this you'll be able to see everything that happens on the earth and in the sky, and nothing can remain hidden from you.'

The third brother served an apprenticeship under a huntsman and learned all there was to know about hunting, so that he became a full-fledged huntsman. His master gave him a gun as a gift upon his departure and said, 'You won't miss whatever you aim at with this gun. You'll hit it for sure.'

The youngest brother also met a man who spoke to him and asked him about his plans.

'Do you have any desire to become a tailor?'

'Not that I know of,' said the young man. 'I've never had the least desire to sit bent over from morning till night and to swing the needle or iron back and forth.'

'Oh, come now!' answered the man. 'You really don't know what you're talking about. With me you'll learn a totally different kind of tailoring that's respectable and decent and may even bring you great honour.'

The young man let himself be persuaded. He went with him and learned all the basics of the trade from the man, and upon his departure the master gave him a needle and said, 'With this you'll be able to sew together anything you find, whether it be as soft as an egg or as hard as steel. And you'll be able to make anything into one complete piece so that not a single seam will show.'

When the designated four years were over, the four brothers met together at the crossroads at the same time. They embraced, kissed each other, and returned home to their father.

'Well,' said the father delightedly, 'look what the wind has blown back to me again!'

They told him what had happened to them and how each had learned a particular trade. As they sat in front of the house under a big tree, the father then said, 'Well, I'm going to put you to the test to see what you can do.' After this he looked up and said to the second son, 'There's a chaffinch's nest up there in the top of this tree between two branches. Tell me how many eggs are in it.'

The stargazer took his telescope, looked up, and said, 'Five.'

Then the father said to the oldest son, 'Fetch the eggs without disturbing the bird that's sitting on them.'

The skilful thief climbed up the tree and took the five eggs from under the bird, who sat there quietly without noticing a thing. Then he brought the eggs down to his father, who took them and placed one on each corner of the table and the fifth in the middle and said to the huntsman, 'I want you to shoot the five eggs in two with one shot.'

The huntsman took aim with his gun and shot the eggs just as his father had demanded. Indeed, he hit all five of them with one shot, and he certainly must have had some of that powder that shoots around corners.

'Now it's your turn,' said the father to the fourth son. 'I want you to sew the eggs together again and also the young birds that are in them, and I want you to repair any damage that the shot has done to them.'

The tailor got his needle and sewed just as his father had demanded. When he was finished, the thief had to carry the eggs up to the nest again and put them back under the bird without it noticing anything. The bird sat on them until they hatched, and after a few days the young chicks crawled out of the eggs and had little red stripes around their necks where the tailor had sewn them together.

'Yes,' said the old man to his sons. 'I must praise you to the skies. You've made good use of your time and have learned something beneficial. I can't say which of you deserves the most praise, but if you soon have an opportunity to apply your skills, we'll find out who's the best.'

Not long after this there was a great uproar in the country: the king's daughter had been carried off by a dragon. Day and night the king worried over this, and he let it be proclaimed that whoever brought her back could have her for his wife. The four brothers discussed the situation together. 'This could be our chance to show what we can do,' and they decided to set out together to free the king's daughter.

'I'll soon find out where she is,' said the stargazer, and he looked through his telescope and said, 'I already see her. She's sitting on a rock in the sea very far away from here, and next to her is the dragon, who's guarding her.'

Then the stargazer went to the king and requested a ship for himself and his brothers. Together they sailed across the sea until they came to the rock. The king's daughter was sitting there, but the dragon was lying asleep with his head in her lap.

'I can't take a risk and shoot,' said the huntsman. 'I might hit the beautiful maiden at the same time.'

'Well, then I'll try out my skill,' said the thief, who crawled to the maiden and stole her from under the dragon so quietly and nimbly that the monster did not notice a thing and kept on snoring. The brothers joyfully hurried off with her, boarded the ship, and sailed away on the open sea. Upon awakening, however, the dragon discovered that the king's daughter was gone, and snorting furiously, it flew after them through the sky. Just as it was hovering above the ship, about to dive down upon the vessel, the huntsman took aim with his gun and shot it through the heart. The monster fell down dead, but it was so large and powerful that it smashed the entire ship to pieces in its fall. Fortunately those on board were able to grab hold of some planks and swim about on the open sea. Once again they were in terrible danger, but the tailor, who was always alert, took his marvellous needle and hastily sewed together the planks with a few big stitches. Then he sat down on the planks and collected all the parts of the ship, which he then sewed together in such a skilful way that in a short time the ship was seaworthy once again and they could sail home safely.

When the king saw his daughter once more, there was great rejoicing, and he said to the four brothers, 'One of you shall have the princess for your wife, but you must decide among yourselves which one it's to be.'

A violent quarrel broke out among the brothers then, for each one had a claim. The stargazer said, 'If I hadn't seen the king's daughter, all your skills would have been in vain. That's why she should be mine.'

The thief said, 'Your seeing her would not have helped much if I hadn't fetched her out from under the dragon. That's why she should be mine.'

The huntsman said, 'The monster would have torn all of you apart along with the king's daughter if my bullet hadn't hit the beast. That's why she should be mine.'

The tailor said, 'And if I hadn't patched the ship together for you with my skill, you'd all have drowned miserably. That's why she should be mine.'

Then the king made his decision known. 'Each of you has a just claim, and since it would be impossible to give the maiden to each of you, no one shall have her. Nevertheless, I shall reward each of you with half a kingdom.'

The brothers were satisfied with this decision and said, 'It's better this way than to be at odds with each other.' So each of them received half a kingdom, and they lived happily with their father as long as it pleased God.

44
The Fox and the Horse

A FARMER had a faithful horse that had grown old
and could no longer do his work. So his master
did not want to feed it anymore and said, 'You're of no
more use to me now, but I won't abandon you entirely:
show me that you're still strong enough to bring me
a lion, then I'll keep you. But for now, get out of my
stable!' And he chased the horse out into the open
field.

The horse was sad about this and went into the forest
to seek a little shelter from the weather. There he met
the fox, who asked, 'Why are you hanging your head and
moping about all by yourself?'

'Ah,' answered the horse, 'greed and loyalty can't live
side by side in the same house. My master has forgotten
how much work I've done for him over the years, and

since I can no longer plough properly, he won't feed me and has chased me away.'

'Without a word of consolation?' asked the fox.

'The consolation was meagre. He told me that if I was still strong enough to bring him a lion, he would keep me, but he knows full well that I can't do that.'

'Well, I'm going to help you,' said the fox. 'Just lie down, stretch yourself out, and don't move. Pretend you're dead.'

The horse did what the fox commanded, while the fox went to the lion, whose den was not far away, and said, 'There's a dead horse lying out there. If you want a great meal, come along with me.'

The lion went with him, and when they were at the horse's side, the fox said, 'It's not so comfortable for you here. You know what I'll do? I'll tie the horse to you by his tail so you can drag him and eat him in peace and quiet.'

The lion liked the idea, assumed a position for the fox to attach the horse to him, and kept still. However, the fox bound the lion's legs together with the horse's tail, and he tied and twisted it so tightly and firmly that the lion would not have been able to tear himself loose even if he used all his might. When the fox finally finished his work, he tapped the horse on his shoulder and said, 'Pull, horse, pull!'

All at once the horse jumped up and dragged the lion with him. The lion began to roar so loudly that all the birds in the forest flew away out of fright, but the horse let him roar and pulled and dragged him over the fields to his master's door. When his master saw that, he reconsidered everything in a better light and said to the horse, 'You shall stay here with me and shall be treated well.'

And he gave him all he wanted to eat until the day of the horse's death.

45
The Worn-out Dancing Shoes

ONCE upon a time there was a king who had twelve daughters, one more beautiful than the next. They slept together in a large room, where their beds stood side by side, and in the evening, when they went to sleep, the king shut and locked the door. However, when he opened it in the morning, he would see that their shoes were worn out from dancing, and nobody could discover how this kept happening. Finally, the king had it proclaimed that whoever could find out where his daughters danced during the night could choose one of them for his wife and be king after his death. But anyone who came and failed to uncover everything after three days and nights would lose his life.

Not long after this proclamation a prince came and offered to undertake the venture. He was well received, and in the evening he was conducted to a room adjoining the bedchamber of the king's daughters. His bed was set up there, and he was told to watch and find out where they went dancing. And, just to make sure they could not do anything in secret or go out anywhere else, the door of their room that led to his was kept open. Still, the prince's eyes became as heavy as lead, and he fell asleep. When he awoke the next morning, all twelve of them had been to a dance, for their shoes were standing there with holes in their soles. The same thing happened the second and third night, and his head was cut off without mercy. After that there were many who came to try their luck, but they were all destined to leave their lives behind them.

Now, it happened that a poor soldier, who had been wounded and could no longer serve in the army, headed toward the city where the king lived. Along the way he met an old woman, who asked him where he was going.

'I really don't know myself,' he said, and added jokingly, 'but I'd certainly like to find out where the king's daughters go dancing and where they wear out their shoes so I could become king.'

'That's not so difficult,' said the old woman. 'Just don't drink the wine that's brought to you in the evening, and then pretend that you've fallen asleep.' Then she gave him a little cloak and said, 'When you put this cloak on, you'll be invisible, and you'll be able to follow all twelve of them.'

After receiving such good advice, the soldier now became serious about the entire matter and plucked up his courage to present himself in front of the king as a suitor. He was welcomed just as cordially as the others had been and was given royal garments to put on. In the evening, at bedtime, he was led to the antechamber, and as he was preparing to go to bed the oldest daughter brought him a beaker of wine, but he had tied a sponge underneath his chin and let the wine run into it and did not drink a single drop. Then he lay down, and after lying there a little while, he began to snore as if in a very deep sleep.

When the princesses heard his snoring, they laughed, and the oldest said, 'He too could have done better things with his life.' After this they stood up, opened the closets, chests, and boxes, and took out splendid clothes. They groomed themselves in front of their mirrors and hurried about, eager to attend the dance. But the youngest said, 'I don't know. You're all happy, yet I have a strange feeling. I'm sure that something bad is going to happen to us.'

'You're a silly goose,' said the oldest. 'You're always afraid. Have you forgotten how many princes have already tried in vain? I didn't really need to give the soldier a sleeping potion. The lout would never have awakened even without it.'

When they were all ready, they first took a look at the soldier, but he had shut his eyes tight, and since he neither moved nor stirred, they thought they were definitely safe. So the oldest went to her bed and knocked on it. Immediately it sank into the ground, and they climbed down through the opening, one after another, with the oldest in the lead. The soldier, who had seen everything, did not hesitate long. He put on his little cloak and climbed down after the youngest. Halfway down the stairs he stepped on her dress slightly, causing her to become terrified and cry out, 'What's that? Who's holding my dress?'

'Don't be so stupid,' said the oldest. 'You've just caught it on a hook.'

They went all the way down, and when they were at the bottom, they stood in the middle of a marvellous avenue of trees whose leaves were all made of silver and glittered and glimmered. You'd better take a piece of evidence with you, the soldier thought, and broke off a branch, but the tree cracked and made a tremendous sound. Again the youngest called out, 'Something's wrong! Didn't you hear the noise?'

But the oldest said, 'That was just a burst of joy because we'll soon be setting our princes free.'

Then they came to another avenue of trees, where all the leaves were made of gold, and finally to one where all the leaves were made of pure diamond. The soldier broke off branches from each kind, and each time there was such a cracking sound that the youngest sister was terrified. But the oldest maintained that they were just bursts of joy. They went on and came to a large lake with twelve boats on it, and in each boat sat a handsome prince. They had been waiting for the twelve princesses, and each one took a princess in his boat, while the soldier went aboard with the youngest princess. Then her prince said, 'I don't understand it, but the boat is much heavier today. I'll have to row with all my might to get it moving.'

'It's probably due to the warm weather,' said the youngest. 'I feel quite hot too.'

On the other side of the lake stood a beautiful, brightly lit palace, and sounds of merry music with drums and trumpets could be heard from it. They rowed over there, entered the palace, and each prince danced with his sweetheart. The invisible soldier danced along as well, and whenever a princess went to drink a beaker of wine, he would drain it dry before it could reach her lips. The youngest sister was terribly concerned about this too, but the oldest continued to soothe her. They danced until three in the morning, when all the shoes were worn through and they had to stop. The princes rowed them back across the lake, and this time the soldier sat in the first boat with the oldest sister. The princesses took leave of their princes on the bank and promised to return the following night. When they reached the stairs, the soldier ran ahead of them and got into bed, and by the time the twelve princesses came tripping slowly and wearily up the stairs, he was again snoring so loudly that they could all hear it, and they said, 'We don't have to worry about him.' Then they took off their beautiful clothes, put them away, placed the worn-out shoes under their beds, and lay down to sleep.

The next morning the soldier decided not to say anything but rather to follow and observe their strange life for the next two nights. Everything happened just as it had on the first night: they danced each time until their shoes fell apart. However, the third time he took a beaker with him for evidence. When the time came for him to give his answer, he took along the three branches and beaker and went before the king. The twelve princesses stood behind the door and listened to what he said. When the king asked, 'Where did my daughters spend the night?' he answered, 'With twelve princes in an underground palace.' Then he reported what had taken place and produced the evidence. The king summoned his daughters and asked them whether the soldier had told the truth. When they saw that they had been exposed and that denying would not help, they had to confess everything. Then the king asked the soldier which princess he would like for his wife.

'I'm no longer so young,' he answered, 'so I'll take the oldest.'

The wedding was held that same day, and the king promised to make him his successor to the kingdom after his death. The princes, however, were compelled to remain under a curse for as many nights as they had danced with the princesses.

46

The Six Servants

LONG, long ago there lived an old queen who was a sorceress, and her daughter was the most beautiful maiden under the sun. The old woman, however, thought of nothing but how to lure people to their doom. Whenever a suitor came to her asking for her daughter's hand, she said that he would first have to perform a task and would die if he failed. Many men were tempted by the extraordinary beauty of the maiden and actually risked their lives, but none could perform the task given by the old woman, and she showed them no mercy: they had to kneel down, and their heads were cut off.

There was a prince who had also heard of the great beauty of the maiden, and he said to his father, 'Let me go and try to win her hand.'

'Never,' answered the king. 'If you go, it will be your death.'

The son then withdrew to his bed and became dangerously ill. He lay there seven years, and no doctor could help him. When the king saw that there was no more hope, his heart became filled with sadness, and he said to his son, 'Go there, and try your luck. I know of no other way to help you.'

When the son heard this, he left his bed, got well again, and went merrily on his way. As he was riding across a heath he happened to see something lying on the ground in the distance. It seemed like a big pile of hay, but as he came closer, he could see that it was the belly of a man who lay stretched out on the heath. However, the belly looked like a small mountain. When the fat man saw the traveller coming toward him, he stood up and said, 'If you need someone, then take me into your service.'

'What can I do with such a monstrosity as you?' the prince answered.

'Oh,' said the fat man, 'this is nothing. When I really want to expand, I'm three thousand times as fat.'

'If that's the case,' the prince said, 'then I can use you. Come with me.'

The fat man followed the prince, and after a while they found another man, who was lying on the ground with his ear glued to the grass.

'What are you doing there?' asked the prince.

'I'm listening,' answered the man.

'What are you listening to so intensely?'

'I'm listening to what's going on in the world right now, for nothing escapes my ears. I can even hear the grass grow.'

'Tell me,' asked the prince, 'what do you hear at the palace of the old queen who has the beautiful daughter?'

'I hear the swishing of a sword,' he answered. 'A suitor has just had his head cut off.'

The prince said, 'I can use you. Come with me.'

They continued on their way, and suddenly they saw a pair of feet lying on the ground, also part of the legs, but they could not see where they ended. When they had gone a good distance, they came to the body and finally to the head.

'My!' said the prince. 'I thought we'd never reach the end of you!'

'Oh,' responded the tall man. 'You haven't seen anything yet! When I really want to stretch out my limbs, I'm three thousand times as tall, taller than the highest mountain on earth. I'd gladly serve you if you'd have me.'

'Come with me,' said the prince. 'I can use you.'

They continued on their way and came across a blindfolded man sitting beside the road.

'Are your eyes so weak that you can't look into the light?' asked the prince.

'No,' answered the man. 'I don't dare take off the blindfold, for my glance is so powerful that it shatters whatever I gaze upon with my eyes. If something like this can be of use to you, then I'll gladly serve you.'

'Come with me,' answered the prince. 'I can use you.'

They continued on their way and came upon a man basking under the hot sun, but he was freezing and shivered so much that his entire body was shaking.

'How can you be freezing when the sun is so warm?' asked the prince.

'Ah,' answered the man, 'my nature is of a completely different kind. The hotter it is, the more I freeze, and the frost chills me to the bone. The colder it is, the hotter I am. In the midst of ice, I can't stand the heat, and in the midst of hot flames, I can't stand the cold.'

'You're a strange fellow,' said the prince, 'but if you'd like to serve me, then come along.'

They continued on their way and saw a man stretching his long neck way out and looking in different directions and over all the mountains.

'What are you looking for so eagerly?' asked the prince.

'I have such sharp eyes,' said the man, 'that I can see over all the forests and fields, valleys and mountains, and throughout the whole world.'

'If you want to,' said the prince, 'then come with me, for I've been in need of someone just like you.'

Now the prince and his six servants entered the city where the old queen lived. He did not reveal his identity to her but said, 'If you will give me your beautiful daughter, I'll carry out any task you give me.'

The sorceress was happy that she had snared such a handsome young man again and said, 'I'll give you three tasks. If you perform them all, you shall be my daughter's lord and master.'

'What's the first to be?' he asked.

'To bring back a ring that I dropped in the Red Sea.'

Then the prince went home to his servants and said, 'The first task isn't easy. A ring must be fetched out of the Red Sea. Now help me think of a way to do it.'

Then Sharp Eyes said, 'I'll see where it is.' After looking down into the sea, he said, 'It's caught on a sharp stone.'

Tall Man carried them there and said, 'I'd get it out if only I could see it.'

'If that's all there's to it, don't worry,' said Fat Man. He lay down, put his mouth to the water, and the waves rushed into it as if into an abyss. He drank up the entire sea until it was as dry as a meadow. Tall Man bent over a little and picked up the ring with his hand. The prince was happy when he got the ring, and he brought it to the old woman, who was astonished and said, 'Yes, that's the ring. You've performed the first task all right, but now comes the second. Do you see the three hundred oxen grazing on the meadow in front of my castle? You must devour them, skin and bones, hair and horns. Then, down in my cellar there are three hundred barrels of wine that you must drink up as well. If one hair is left from the oxen or one little drop from the wine, then your life will be forfeited to me.'

'May I invite some guests?' asked the prince. 'I don't enjoy my meals without company.'

The old woman laughed maliciously and answered, 'You may invite one person to keep you company, but no more than that.'

The prince then went to his servants and said to Fat Man, 'Today you shall be my guest, and for once you'll have your fill to eat.'

Fat Man expanded himself and ate the three hundred oxen without leaving a single hair anywhere. After that he asked what came after breakfast, and he proceeded to drink the wine right out of the barrels, without a glass, until the barrels were completely drained. When the meal was finished, the prince went to the old woman and told her he had completed the second task. She was surprised and said, 'No one has ever gotten this far, but there's still one task left.' And she thought to herself, You won't escape me, nor will you keep your head. Then she said aloud, 'Tonight I'm going to bring my daughter into your room, and you're to put your arms around her. While you sit there with her, be sure not to fall asleep. I shall come at midnight, and if she's no longer in your arms, you'll lose your life.'

This task is easy, the prince thought. I'll certainly be able to keep my eyes open. Nevertheless, he called his servants to him, told them what the old woman had said, and declared, 'Who knows what kinds of tricks she intends to play. It's wise to be cautious. So keep watch and make sure that the maiden doesn't get out of my room.'

At nightfall the old woman brought her daughter and put her into the prince's arms. Then Tall Man formed a circle around the two, and Fat Man placed himself in front of the door so that no living soul could enter. The couple sat there, and though the maiden did not say a word, the moon shone through the window on her face so that the prince could gaze at her marvellous beauty.

He was content just looking at her. His heart was full of joy and love, and his eyes did not tire at all. All this lasted until eleven o'clock. Then the old woman cast a spell on all of them, so they fell asleep. It was just at that moment that the maiden was carried off.

The others continued to sleep soundly until a quarter of twelve when the magic lost its power and they all awoke.

'Oh, what bad luck and grief!' exclaimed the prince. 'Now I'm lost!'

The loyal servants also began to moan, but Listener said, 'Be quiet, I want to see if I can hear something.' He listened for a minute and then said, 'She's being kept in a rock three hundred miles from here and is lamenting her fate. Tall Man, only you can help. If you stand up at your full height, you can be there in a couple of steps.'

'All right,' Tall Man answered, 'but Sharp Eyes must come with me so we can dispose of the rock.'

Then Tall Man lifted his blindfolded companion onto his back, and in no time they were in front of the enchanted rock. As soon as Tall Man took off the blindfold, Sharp Eyes needed only to look around, and the rock shattered into a thousand pieces. Tall Man took the maiden in his arms, carried her back to the prince in a split second, and then fetched his companion just as fast. Before the clock struck twelve, they were all seated again as they had previously been, and they were cheerful and in high spirits.

When the clock struck twelve, the old sorceress came creeping into the room with a scornful look on her face, as if she wanted to say, 'Now he's mine!' For she thought that her daughter was sitting in the rock three hundred miles away. However, when she saw her daughter in the prince's arms, she became horrified and said, 'I've more than met my match.' Hence, she could no longer object to the prince's bidding and had to give her daughter to him. Nevertheless, she whispered into her daughter's ear, 'It's a disgrace that you must obey a commoner and are not allowed to choose a husband to your own liking.'

Then the maiden's proud heart filled with anger, and she sought to avenge herself. The next morning she had three hundred cords of wood gathered together and said to the prince that, even though he had performed the three tasks, she would not become his wife until someone was ready to sit in the middle of the woodpile and withstand the fire. She was convinced that none of his servants would let himself be burned for the prince's sake and that the prince would have to sacrifice himself on the woodpile out of love for her. But the servants said, 'We've all done something with the exception of Frosty. Now he's got to do his share.'

They placed him in the middle of the heap of wood and set fire to it. The flames began to burn, and they burned for three days until all the wood had been consumed, and when the flames died down, Frosty stood in the middle of the ashes trembling like an aspen leaf and said, 'Never in my life have I endured such a frost, and if it had lasted much longer, I'd have been frozen stiff.'

Now there was no other way out: the beautiful maiden had to marry the young stranger. Still, when they left to drive to the church, the old woman said, 'I can't bear the disgrace,' and she sent her soldiers after them to bring back her daughter and to strike down anyone that opposed them. However, Listener had pricked up his ears and had heard the words spoken in secret by the old woman.

'What shall we do?' he asked Fat Man, who knew exactly what to do. He spat on the ground once or twice, and part of the sea water he had drunk came flowing out behind the carriage and formed a huge lake that stopped the soldiers, and they drowned. When the sorceress saw this, she sent her knights in armour, but Listener heard the rattling of the armour and undid the blindfold of Sharp Eyes, who took a piercing look at the enemy, and they shattered like glass. Thus the prince and his bride could continue on their way undisturbed, and when the couple had been blessed in church, the six servants took their leave. 'Your wishes have been fulfilled,' they said. 'So you don't need us anymore, and now we want to move on and seek our fortune.'

Half an hour from the prince's castle was a village, and outside the village a swineherd was tending his pigs. When the prince and his wife arrived there, he said to her, 'Do you know who I really am? I'm not the son of a king but a swineherd, and the man with the pigs over there is my father. You and I must now get to work and help my father look after the pigs.'

The prince took lodgings at the inn and secretly told the innkeeper and his wife to take away his wife's royal garments during the night. When she awoke the next morning, she had nothing to put on, and the innkeeper's wife gave her an old skirt and a pair of woollen stockings. At the same time the woman acted as if she were doing the princess a great favour and said, 'If it weren't for your husband, I wouldn't have given you a thing.'

After that the prince's wife believed that he really was a swineherd, tended the pigs with him, and thought, I've deserved this because of my arrogance and pride. All of this lasted a week, by which time she could no longer stand it, for her feet had become all sore. Then some people came and asked whether she knew who her husband was. 'Yes,' she answered.

'He's a swineherd, and he's gone out to do a little trading with ribbons and laces.'

'Just come with us,' they said. 'We want to take you to him,' and they brought her up to the castle.

When they entered the hall, her husband was standing there in his royal attire, but she did not recognize him until he took her into his arms, kissed her, and said, 'I suffered a great deal for you, and it was only right that you should also suffer for me.'

Now the wedding was truly celebrated, and you can imagine that the person who told this tale would have liked to have been there too.

47

The Turnip

ONCE upon a time there were two brothers, both of whom served as soldiers. One was rich, the other poor. Since the poor brother wanted to improve his circumstances, he left the army and became a farmer. He dug and hoed his little piece of ground and planted turnip seeds. As the turnips began to grow, one became large and strong and noticeably fatter than the others. It seemed as if it would not stop growing at all. Soon it was called the queen of all turnips, because nobody had ever seen one like it, nor will anybody ever see one like it again. At last it became so big that it filled an entire wagon by itself, and two oxen were needed to pull it. The farmer did not know what to do with the turnip, nor did he know whether it would bring him luck or misfortune. Finally, he thought, If you sell it, you won't get anything worth much. And, if you eat it, you might as well eat the small turnips, which are just as good. The best thing would be to bring it to the king. That way you can honour him with a gift.

So he loaded the turnip on his wagon, hitched up two oxen, brought it to court, and gave it to the king.

'What kind of a rarity do we have here?' asked the king. 'I've seen many strange things in my life, but I've never seen such a monstrosity as this. What kind of a seed did it grow from? Or do you have a green thumb and are lady fortune's favourite son?'

'Oh, no,' the farmer replied. 'I'm not fortune's favourite son. I'm just a poor soldier who gave up the army life because I could no longer support myself. Now I've taken up farming. You probably know my brother, Your Majesty. He's rich, but nobody pays attention to me because I have nothing.'

Then the king took pity on him and said, 'You shall be relieved of your poverty and shall receive such gifts from me that will make you the equal of your brother.' So he gave him a great deal of gold, fields, meadows, and herds, and made him so terribly rich that his brother's wealth could no longer match his at all.

When the brother heard what he had acquired with a single turnip, he became jealous and pondered ways to get fortune to smile on him too. However, he wanted to plan everything in a more clever way. So he took gold and horses and brought them to the king, for he was firmly convinced that the king would give him a much larger present in return. After all, if his brother had obtained so much for a turnip, he would certainly get many more beautiful things.

The king accepted his gifts and said that he could think of nothing better or rarer to give him than the large turnip. So the rich brother had the turnip loaded on his wagon and driven to his home. Once there he did not know on whom to vent his anger and frustration. Finally, some evil thoughts came to him, and he decided to kill his brother. He hired murderers and showed them a place where they were to ambush his brother. Afterward he went to his brother and said, 'Dear brother, I know where there's a secret treasure. Let's dig it up and divide it among us.'

The brother liked the idea and went with him without suspecting a thing. However, when they went out into the fields, the murderers fell upon him, tied him up, and were about to hang him from a tree when they heard loud singing and hoofbeats in the distance. They became frightened for their lives and hastily shoved their prisoner head over heels into a sack.

Then they hoisted it up on a branch and took flight. But soon the prisoner was at work and managed to make a hole in the sack through which he could poke his head. Then who should happen upon the way but a wandering scholar, a young fellow, riding along the road through the forest and singing a merry song. When the man up in the tree noticed that someone was passing below, he cried out, 'Welcome! You've come just at the right time.'

The scholar looked all around him but could not detect where the voice was coming from. Finally, he said, 'Who's calling me?'

The man in the tree answered from above, 'Lift your head. I'm sitting up here in the sack of wisdom, where I've learned great things in only a short time. Compared to this, all schools are like a bag of hot wind. Soon I shall have learned all there is to know. Then I'll climb down from the tree and be wiser than all other human beings. I understand the stars and the signs of the zodiac, the movements of the wind, the sand in the sea, the curses for sickness, and the power of herbs, birds, and stones. If you could be here in the sack just once, then you'd know the glorious feeling that flows from the sack of wisdom.'

When the scholar heard all this, he was astounded and said, 'Blessed be this hour in which I have found you! Would it be possible for me to get into the sack for a little while?'

The man in the tree answered as if he did not like this idea. 'I'll let you do it for a short time if you pay me and speak sweetly, but you'll have to wait another hour because there's still something more that I have to learn.'

The student waited a little while, but he became impatient and begged to be let in because his thirst for knowledge was so overwhelming. The man in the tree pretended to give in to the scholar finally and said, 'In order for me to leave the house of wisdom, you must lower the sack by the rope. Then you may climb in.'

So the scholar lowered the sack, untied it, and set the man free. Next he cried out, 'Now pull me up quickly,' and he sought to get into the sack feet first.

'Stop!' said the other. 'That's not the way.' He grabbed the scholar's head and shoved him upside down into the sack. After that he tied the sack and hoisted the disciple of wisdom up the tree by the rope. Then he swung him back and forth in the air and said, 'How's it going, my dear fellow? You see, I'm sure you already feel wisdom coming and are getting valuable experience. Sit there nice and quiet until you get wiser.'

Upon saying this, he mounted the scholar's horse and rode away. An hour later, however, he sent somebody to let the scholar down.

48
The Three Lazy Sons

A KING had three sons, and since he loved them equally, he did not know which to choose to be king after his death. When the time of his death drew near, he summoned them to his bedside and said, 'Dear children, I've been contemplating something for a while, and now I want to reveal it to you: I've decided that the laziest among you shall become king after me.'

'Then, Father,' said the oldest, 'the kingdom belongs to me, for I'm so lazy that, when I'm lying on my back and want to sleep and a drop of rain falls on my eyes, I won't even shut them so I can fall asleep.'

The second said, 'Father, the kingdom belongs to me, for I'm so lazy that, when I'm sitting by the fire to warm myself, I'd sooner let my heels be burned than draw back my feet.'

The third said, 'Father, the kingdom is mine, for I'm so lazy that, if I were about to be hanged and the noose were already around my neck and someone handed me a sharp knife to cut the rope, I'd rather let myself be hanged than lift my hand to cut the rope.'

When the father heard that, he said, 'You've outdone the others and shall be king.'

49

Snow White and Rose Red

A POOR widow lived all alone in a small cottage, and in front of this cottage was a garden with two rosebushes. One bore white roses and the other red. The widow had two children who looked like the rosebushes: one was called Snow White and the other Rose Red. They were more pious and kind, more hardworking and diligent than any other two children in the world. To be sure, Snow White was more quiet and gentle than Rose Red, who preferred to run around in the meadows and fields, look for flowers, and catch butterflies. Snow White stayed at home with her mother, helped her with the housework, or read to her when there was nothing to do. The two children loved each other so much that they always held hands whenever they went out, and when Snow White said, 'Let us never leave each other,'

Rose Red answered, 'Never, as long as we live.' And their mother added, 'Whatever one of you has, remember to share it with the other.'

They often wandered in the forest all alone and gathered red berries. The animals never harmed them and, indeed, trusted them completely and would come up to them. The little hare would eat a cabbage leaf out of their hands. The roe grazed by their side. The stag leapt merrily around them. And the birds sat still on their branches and sang whatever tune they knew. Nothing bad ever happened to the girls. If they stayed too long in the forest and night overtook them, they would lie down next to each other on the moss and sleep until morning came. Their mother knew this and did not worry about them.

Once, when they had spent the night in the forest and the morning sun had wakened them, they saw a beautiful child in a white, glistening garment sitting near them. The child stood up, looked at them in a friendly way, but went into the forest without saying anything. When they looked around, they realized that they had been sleeping at the edge of a cliff and would have certainly fallen over it if they had gone a few more steps in the darkness. Their mother told them that the child must have been the angel who watches over good children.

Snow White and Rose Red kept their mother's cottage so clean that it was a joy to look inside. In the summer Rose Red took care of the house, and every morning she placed two flowers in front of her mother's bed before she awoke, a rose from each one of the bushes. In the winter Snow White lit the fire and hung the kettle over the hearth. The kettle was made out of brass but glistened like gold because it was polished so clean. In the evening when the snowflakes fell, the mother said, 'Go, Snow White, and bolt the door.' Then they sat down at the hearth, and their mother put on her glasses and read aloud from a large book, while the two girls sat and spun as they listened. On the ground next to them lay a little lamb, and behind them sat a white dove with its head tucked under its wing.

One evening, as they were sitting together, there was a knock on the door, as if someone wanted to be let in. The mother said, 'Quick, Rose Red, open the door. It must be a traveller looking for shelter.' Rose Red pushed back the bolt thinking that it would be some poor man, but instead it was a bear. He stuck his thick black head through the door, and Rose Red jumped back and screamed loudly. The little lamb bleated, the dove fluttered its wings, and Snow White hid herself behind her mother's bed. However, the bear began to speak and said, 'Don't be afraid. I won't harm you. I'm half frozen and only want to warm myself here a little.'

'You poor bear,' the mother said. 'Lie down by the fire and take care that it does not burn your fur.' Then she called out, 'Snow White, Rose Red, come out. The bear won't harm you. He means well.'

They both came out, and gradually the lamb and dove also drew near and lost their fear of him. Then the bear said, 'Come, children, dust the snow off my coat a little.'

So they fetched a broom and swept the fur clean. Afterward he stretched himself out beside the fire and uttered growls to show how content and comfortable he was. It did not take them long to all become accustomed to one another, and the clumsy guest had to put up with the mischievous pranks of the girls. They tugged his fur with their hands, planted their feet upon his back and rolled him over, or they took a hazel switch and hit him. When he growled, they just laughed. The bear took everything in good spirit. Only when they became too rough did he cry out, 'Let me live, children.

> Snow White, Rose Red,
> would you beat your suitor dead?'

When it was time to sleep and the others went to bed, the mother said to the bear, 'You're welcome, in God's name, to lie down by the hearth. Then you'll be protected from the cold and bad weather.'

As soon as dawn arrived, the two girls let him go outside, and he trotted over the snow into the forest. From then on the bear came every evening at a certain time, lay down by the hearth, and allowed the children to play with him as much as they wanted. And they became so accustomed to him that they never bolted the door until their black playmate had arrived.

One morning, when spring had made its appearance and everything outside was green, the bear said to Snow White, 'Now I must go away, and I shall not return the entire summer.'

'But where are you going, dear bear?' asked Snow White.

'I must go into the forest and guard my treasures from the wicked dwarfs. In the winter, when the ground is frozen hard, they must remain underground and can't work their way through to the top. But now that the sun has thawed and warmed the earth, they will break through, climb out, search around, and steal. Once they get something in their hands and carry it to their caves, it will not easily see the light of day again.'

Snow White was very sad about his departure. She unlocked the door, and when the bear hurried out, he became caught on the bolt and a piece of his fur ripped off, and it seemed to Snow White that she saw gold glimmering through the fur, but she was not sure. The bear hurried away and soon disappeared beyond the trees.

Some time after, the mother sent the girls into the forest to gather firewood. There they found a large tree lying on the ground that had been chopped down. Something was jumping up and down on the grass near the trunk, but they could not tell what it was. As they came closer they saw a dwarf with an old, withered face and a beard that was snow white and a yard long. The tip of the beard was caught in a crack of the tree, and the little fellow was jumping back and forth like a dog on a rope and did not know what to do. He glared at the girls with his fiery red eyes and screamed, 'What are you standing there for? Can't you come over here and help me?'

'How did you get into this jam, little man?' asked Rose Red.

'You stupid, nosy goose,' answered the dwarf, 'I wanted to split the tree to get some wood for my kitchen. We dwarfs need but little food; however, it gets burned fast when we use those thick logs. We don't devour such large portions as you coarse and greedy people. I had just driven in the wedge safely, and everything would have gone all right, but the cursed wedge was too smooth, and it sprang out unexpectedly. The tree snapped shut so rapidly that I couldn't save my beautiful white beard. Now it's stuck there, and I can't get away. And all you silly, creamy-faced things can do is laugh! Uggh, you're just nasty!'

The girls tried as hard as they could, but they could not pull the beard out. It was stuck too tight.

'I'll run and get somebody,' Rose Red said.

'Crazy fool!' the dwarf snarled. 'Why run and get someone? The two of you are already enough. Can't you think of something better?'

'Don't be so impatient,' said Snow White. 'I'll think of something.' She took out a pair of scissors from her pocket and cut off the tip of his beard. As soon as the dwarf felt that he was free, he grabbed a sack filled with gold that was lying between the roots of the tree. He lifted it out and grumbled to himself, 'Uncouth slobs! How could you cut off a piece of my fine beard? Good riddance to you!' Upon saying this, he swung the sack over his shoulder and went away without once looking at the girls.

Some time after this Snow White and Rose Red wanted to catch some fish for dinner. As they approached the brook, they saw something like a large grasshopper bouncing toward the water as if it wanted to jump in. They ran to the spot and recognized the dwarf.

'Where are you going?' asked Rose Red. 'You don't want to jump into the water, do you?'

'I'm not such a fool as that!' the dwarf screamed. 'Don't you see that the cursed fish wants to pull me in?' The little man had been sitting there and fishing, and unfortunately the wind had caught his beard, so that it had become entangled with his line. Just then a large fish had bitten the bait, and the feeble little dwarf did not have the strength to land the fish, which kept the upper hand and pulled him toward the water. To be sure, the dwarf tried to grab hold of the reeds and rushes, but that did not help too much. He was compelled to follow the movements of the fish and was in constant danger of being dragged into the water, but the girls had come just in the nick of time. They held on to him tightly and tried to untangle his beard from the line. However, it was to no avail. The beard and line were meshed together, and there was nothing left to do but to take out the scissors and cut off a small part of his beard. When the dwarf saw this, he screamed at them, 'You birdbrains! You've disfigured my face like barbarians. It was not enough that you clipped the tip of my beard. Now you've cut off the best part. I won't be able to show myself among my friends. May you both walk for miles on end until the soles of your shoes are burned off!' Then he grabbed a sack of pearls that was lying in the rushes, and without saying another word, he dragged it away and disappeared behind a rock.

It happened that soon after this the girls were sent by their mother to the city to buy thread, needles, lace, and ribbons. Their way led over a heath which had huge pieces of rock scattered here and there. A large bird circled slowly in the air above them, flying lower and lower until it finally landed on the ground not far from a rock. Right after that they heard a piercing, terrible cry. They ran to the spot and saw with horror that the eagle had seized their old acquaintance the dwarf and intended to carry him away. The girls took pity on him and grabbed hold of the little man as tightly as they could. They tugged against the eagle until finally the bird had to abandon his booty. When the dwarf had recovered from his initial fright, he screeched at them, 'Couldn't you have handled me more carefully? You've torn my coat to shreds. It was thin enough to begin with, but now it's got holes and rips all over, you clumsy louts!' Then he took a sack with jewels and once again slipped under a rock into his cave.

The girls were accustomed to his ingratitude and continued on their way. They took care of their chores in the city, and when they crossed the heath again on their way home, they surprised the dwarf, who had dumped his sack of jewels on a clean spot, not thinking that anyone would come by at such a late hour. The evening sun's rays were cast upon the glistening stones, which glimmered and sparkled in such radiant different colours that the girls had to stop and look at them.

'Why are you standing there and gaping like monkeys?' the dwarf screamed, and his ash grey face turned scarlet with rage. He was about to continue his cursing when a loud growl was heard and a black bear came trotting out of the forest. The dwarf jumped up in terror, but he could not reach his hiding place in time. The bear was already too near. Filled with fear, the dwarf cried out, 'Dear Mister Bear, spare my life, and I'll give you all my treasures! Look at the beautiful jewels lying there. Grant me my life! What good is a small, measly fellow like me? You wouldn't be able to feel me between your teeth. Those wicked girls over there would be better for you. They're such tender morsels, fat as young quails. For heaven's sake, eat them instead!'

The bear did not pay any attention to the dwarf's words but gave the evil creature a single blow with his paw, and the dwarf did not move again.

The girls had run away, but the bear called after them, 'Snow White, Rose Red, don't be afraid! Wait. I'll go with you!'

Then they recognized his voice and stopped. When the bear came up to them, his bearskin suddenly fell off, and there stood a handsome man clad completely in gold. 'I am the son of a king,' he said, 'and I had been cast under a spell by the wicked dwarf who stole my treasures. He forced me to run around the forest as a wild bear, and only his death could release me from the spell. Now he has received his justly earned punishment.'

Snow White was married to the prince, and Rose Red to his brother, and they shared the great treasures that the dwarf had collected in his cave. The old mother lived many more peaceful and happy years with her children. Indeed, she took the two rosebushes with her, and they stood in front of her window, and every year they bore the most beautiful roses, white and red.

50

Puss in Boots

A MILLER had three sons, a mill, a donkey, and a cat. The sons had to grind grain, the donkey had to haul the grain and carry away the flour, and the cat had to catch the mice. When the miller died, the three sons divided the inheritance: the oldest received the mill, the second the donkey, and nothing was left for the third but the cat. This made the youngest sad, and he said to himself, 'I certainly got the worst part of the bargain. My oldest brother can grind wheat, and my second brother can ride on his donkey. But what can I do with the cat? Once I make a pair of gloves out of his fur, it's all over.'

The cat, who had understood all he had said, began to

speak. 'Listen, there's no need to kill me when all you'll get will be a pair of poor gloves from my fur. Have some boots made for me instead. Then I'll be able to go out, mix with people, and help you before you know it.'

The miller's son was surprised the cat could speak like that, but since the shoemaker happened to be walking by, he called him inside and had him measure a pair of boots for the cat. When the boots were finished, the cat put them on. After that he took a sack, filled the bottom with grains of wheat, and attached a piece of cord to the top, which he could pull to close it. Then he slung the sack over his back and walked out the door on two legs like a human being.

At that time there was a king ruling the country, and he liked to eat partridges. However, there was a grave situation because no one had been able to catch a single partridge. The whole forest was full of them, but they frightened so easily that none of the huntsmen had been able to get near them. The cat knew this and thought he could do much better than the huntsmen. When he entered the forest, he opened the sack, spread the grains of wheat on the ground, placed the cord in the grass, and strung it out behind a hedge. Then he crawled in back of the hedge, hid himself, and lay in wait. Soon the partridges came running, found the wheat, and hopped into the sack, one after the other. When a good number were inside, the cat pulled the cord. Once the sack was closed tight, he ran over to it and wrung their necks. Then he slung the sack over his back and went straight to the king's castle. The sentry called out, 'Halt! Where are you going?'

'To the king,' the cat answered curtly.

'Are you crazy? A cat to the king?'

'Oh, let him go,' another sentry said. 'The king's often very bored. Perhaps the cat will give him some pleasure with his meowing and purring.'

When the cat appeared before the king, he bowed and said, 'My lord, the Count'—and he uttered a long, distinguished name—'sends you his regards and would like to offer you these partridges, which he recently caught in his traps.'

The king was amazed by the beautiful, fat partridges. Indeed, he was so overcome with joy that he commanded the cat to take as much gold from his treasury as he could carry and put it into the sack. 'Bring it to your lord and give him my very best thanks for his gift.'

Meanwhile, the poor miller's son sat at home by the window, propped his head up with his hand, and wondered why he had given away all he had for the cat's boots when the cat would probably not be able to bring him anything great in return. Suddenly the cat entered, threw down the sack from his back, opened it, and dumped the gold at the miller's feet.

'Now you've got something for the boots. The king also sends his regards and best of thanks.'

The miller was happy to have such wealth, even though he did not understand how everything had happened. However, as the cat was taking off his boots he told him everything and said, 'Surely you have enough money now, but we won't be content with that. Tomorrow I'm going to put on my boots again, and you shall become even richer. Incidentally, I told the king that you're a count.'

The following day the cat put on his boots, as he said he would, went hunting again, and brought the king a huge catch. So it went every day, and every day the cat brought back gold to the miller. At the king's court he became a favourite, so that he was permitted to go and come and wander about the castle wherever he pleased. One day, as the cat was lying by the hearth in the king's kitchen and warming himself, the coachman came and started cursing, 'May the devil take the king and princess! I wanted to go to the tavern, have a drink, and play some cards. But now they want me to drive them to the lake so they can go for a walk.'

When the cat heard that, he ran home and said to his

master, 'If you want to be a rich count, come with me to the lake and go for a swim.'

The miller did not know what to say. Nevertheless, he listened to the cat and went with him to the lake, where he undressed and jumped into the water completely naked. Meanwhile, the cat took his clothes, carried them away, and hid them. No sooner had he done it than the king came driving by. Now the cat began to wail in a miserable voice, 'Ahh, most gracious King! My lord went for a swim in the lake, and a thief came and stole his clothes that were lying on the bank. Now the count is in the water and can't get out. If he stays in much longer, he'll freeze and die.'

When the king heard that, he ordered the coach to stop, and one of his servants had to race back to the castle and fetch some of the king's garments. The count put on the splendid clothes, and since the king had already taken a liking to him because of the partridges that, he believed, had been sent by the count, he asked the young man to sit down next to him in the coach. The princess was not in the least angry about this, for the count was young and handsome and pleased her a great deal.

In the meantime, the cat went on ahead of them and came to a large meadow, where there were over a hundred people making hay.

'Who owns this meadow, my good people?' asked the cat.

'The great sorcerer.'

'Listen to me. The king will be driving by, and when he asks who the owner of this meadow is, I want you to answer, "The count." If you don't, you'll all be killed.'

Then the cat continued on his way and came to a wheatfield so enormous that nobody could see over it. There were more than two hundred people standing there and cutting wheat.

'Who owns this wheat, my good people?'

'The sorcerer.'

'Listen to me. The king will be driving by, and when he asks who the owner of this wheat is, I want you to answer, "The count." If you don't do this, you'll all be killed.'

Finally, the cat came to a splendid forest, where more than three hundred people were chopping down large oak trees and cutting them into wood.

'Who owns this forest, my good people?'

'The sorcerer.'

'Listen to me. The king will be driving by, and when he asks who the owner of this forest is, I want you to answer, "The count." If you don't do this, you'll all be killed.'

The cat continued on his way, and the people watched him go. Since he looked so unusual and walked in boots like a human being, they were afraid of him. Soon the cat came to the sorcerer's castle, walked boldly inside, and appeared before the sorcerer, who looked at him scornfully and asked him what he wanted. The cat bowed and said, 'I've heard that you can turn yourself into any kind of an animal you desire. Well, I'm sure you can turn yourself into a dog, fox, or even a wolf, but I don't believe you can turn yourself into an elephant. That seems impossible to me, and this is why I've come: I want to be convinced with my own eyes.'

'That's just a trifle for me,' the sorcerer said arrogantly, and within seconds he turned himself into an elephant.

'That's great, but can you also change yourself into a lion?'

'Nothing to it,' said the sorcerer, and he suddenly stood before the cat as a lion. The cat pretended to be terrified and cried out, 'That's incredible and unheard of! Never in all my dreams would I have thought this possible! But you'd top all of this if you could turn yourself into a tiny animal, such as a mouse. I'm convinced you can do more than any other sorcerer in the world, but that would be too much for you.'

The flattery had made the sorcerer quite friendly, and he said, 'Oh, no, dear cat, that's not too much at all,' and soon he was running around the room as a mouse.

Then the cat ran after him, caught the mouse in one leap, and ate him up.

While all this was happening, the king had continued driving with the count and princess and had come to the large meadow.

'Who owns that hay?' the king asked.

'The count,' the people all cried out, just as the cat had ordered them to do.

'You've got a nice piece of land, Count,' the king said.

Afterward they came to the large wheatfield.

'Who owns that wheat, my good people?'

'The count.'

'My! You've got quite a large and beautiful estate!'

Next they came to the forest.

'Who owns that wood, my good people?'

'The count.'

The king was even more astounded and said, 'You must be a rich man, Count. I don't think I have such a splendid forest.'

At last they came to the castle. The cat stood on top of the stairs, and when the coach stopped below, he ran down, opened the door, and said, 'Your Majesty, you've arrived at the castle of my lord, the count. This honour will make him happy for the rest of his life.'

The king climbed out of the coach and was amazed by the magnificent building, which was almost larger and more beautiful than his own castle. The count led the princess up the stairs and into the hall, which was flickering with lots of gold and jewels.

The princess became the count's bride, and when the king died, the count became king, and the puss in boots was his prime minister.

Grimms' Fairy Tales

The Backstory

Learn how to make your own gingerbread!

The Ingredients for Fairy Tales

Take one beautiful princess, one handsome prince and an evil stepmother… abracadabra! You have a fairy tale! You may have noticed that similar characters turn up in each of the fairy tales by the Brothers Grimm. Let's meet them:

The Beautiful Daughter: Often a princess and the heroine of the tale, the beautiful daughter is sometimes spoilt and irritable (remember King Thrushbeard's wife) but more often they are beautiful *and* good, and this makes them easy prey to Wicked Stepmothers and the like.

The Handsome Prince: The poor Handsome Prince is also often the victim of enchantment or evil tricks (think of 'The Singing, Springing Lark' or 'The Frog King'), but just as often he arrives near the end of the story to rescue the Beautiful Daughter from a terrible fate – think of Snow White or Brier Rose.

The Wicked Stepmother: Jealous, spiteful and very bad-tempered, the Wicked Stepmother is unfortunately also very powerful – usually they are also witches or queens. The most famous of these is Snow White's terrifying stepmother with her magic mirror, or remember the Stepmother who torments poor Cinderella.

The Clever Poor Man: It's not all about princes and princesses, fairy tales are about ordinary folk and children, too. Think of Clever Hans, or the poor soldier who solves the riddle of The Worn-out Dancing Shoes, or poor starving Hansel and Gretel. These virtuous men and women may not have riches, but they usually end happily ever after.

The Marvellous Animal: Remember Puss in Boots? Or the Golden Goose? Our four-legged or feathered friends are sometimes the heroes (or villains) of the tale, but often they turn out to be unlucky humans under a spell.

Fairy Tale Folk: Lastly there are the very large, or the very small, or the very magical beings that only exist in fairy tales. This includes giants (such as the one defeated by the Brave Little Tailor), elves (remember the ones who made shoes so skilfully?), dwarves, devils and of course, witches.

Magic: All fairy tales involve a quantity of magic. Sometimes the magic is in wishing rings or rhyming spells, sometimes the magic turns princes into frogs or foxes, and princesses into snakes or birds.

Why not write your own fairy tale using a few of these key ingredients?

Test your knowledge of *Grimms' Fairy Tales*

(Turn to the back for answers. No cheating!)

1) How many flies did the Brave Little Tailor kill in one blow?

2) In the story of 'Hansel and Gretel', what is the roof of the witch's house made out of?

3) Can you remember the rhyme Cinderella repeats under the magic hazel tree when she needs a dress for the ball?

4) How does Thumbling end up inside a cow's stomach?

5) What kind of animal is Old Sultan?

6) According to the wise woman's spell, how long is Brier Rose to sleep for?

7) In the tale of 'Rumpelstiltskin', what does the king command the miller's daughter to do?

8) Where does Simpleton find the Golden Goose?

9) Which kind of bird is Jorinda transformed into by the powerful sorceress?

10) In the tale of 'The Worn-out Dancing Shoes', what three pieces of evidence does the soldier collect to prove where the princesses spend their nights?

Once There Were Two Brothers Named Grimm

by Jack Zipes

The fairy tales in this book were collected and written down by two brothers called Jacob and Wilhelm Grimm, who lived in Germany in the nineteenth century. Jack Zipes translated their stories from German into English, and here he tells the story of the Brothers Grimm:

A writer of fairy tales could not have created a more idyllic setting for the entrance of the Brothers Grimm into the world. Their father, Philipp, a lawyer, was ambitious and prosperous, while their mother, Dorothea, was a devoted and caring housewife. Jacob was born in 1785, followed by Wilhelm in 1786, and he was followed by three more brothers and a sister. At first the family lived in the village of Hanau in central Germany, but they later moved to a nearby town called Steinau, where Philipp became a judge and the family had a large comfortable home with servants to help with the domestic chores. All the children went to school, and Jacob and Wilhelm were particularly bright and hard-working, though they also loved playing in the countryside. The boys received strict religious training, and their father made sure they learnt his own motto by heart: *tute si recte vixeris* – which means 'honesty is the best policy in life'.

But everything changed when Philipp Grimm died suddenly in 1796 at the young age of forty-two. Dorothea and her children had to move out of their large house, say goodbye to their servants and live on a much smaller income. Fortunately, Dorothea's sister was a lady-in-waiting to a princess, and arranged for Jacob and Wilhelm to continue their studies at a prestigious high school.

Although the brothers were very different – Jacob was serious and strong, while Wilhelm was outgoing, cheerful and asthmatic – they were inseparable and totally devoted to one another. They were both determined to prove themselves to be the best students at their school, studying for more than twelve hours a day, though many of the teachers treated them as inferior because they were poorer than the other students. In fact, the brothers Grimm had to struggle against social prejudice and financial troubles for most of their lives – but they never forgot their father's motto, 'honesty is the best policy', and it served them well.

Both brothers graduated at the top of their class, and went on to study law at university. They learnt that the study of law must involve a study of the customs and language of ordinary people. This led Jacob and Wilhelm to devote themselves to the study of ancient German literature and folk tales – which is how they discovered the stories in this book. They both became librarians in the King's library, and together they wrote many books about German literature, language and folklore. The brothers hoped that all their books would help to encourage their readers to feel a sense of pride in ancient German customs and history.

Unfortunately, political unrest in Germany meant both brothers lost their jobs at the royal library and also had difficulties with a tyrannical king at the University of Goettingen in the 1830s. Eventually they found positions as professors in Berlin where they began to write a German dictionary about 1840 – they only got as far as the letter 'F', but you can imagine how complicated teaching and writing a dictionary must be! Wilhelm died in 1859, and Jacob became more solitary than ever, though he continued to work on the brothers' mutual projects until his own death in 1863.

How did the brothers collect their fairy tales?

For many years it was thought that Jacob and Wilhelm wandered around Germany and visited peasants' homes to hear their old tales. In fact, they would invite educated young women, usually friends of the family, to tell them the stories learnt from their nursemaids, governesses and servants. They learnt other stories from a tailor's wife, and still more from a retired soldier who passed on his tales in exchange for old clothes. In addition, the brothers found stories in old books and journals. They wrote everything down, and edited the stories according to their taste, often removing any details they found offensive. Their first collection of stories, called *Children's and Household Tales*, was published in 1812, with another volume following in 1815. By the end of the nineteenth century, their collection was a bestseller in Germany, many of the stories were taught in schools all over Europe, and the Brothers Grimm gradually became famous throughout the world.

Make a gingerbread house!

In the story of 'Hansel and Gretel', the wicked witch has built a house entirely of 'bread' to entice hungry children into her clutches. Often, when this story has been retold, the 'bread' is interpreted as gingerbread (because it's tastier). Below you'll find a recipe for gingerbread so you can make your own little house!

What you'll need:

360g plain flour   450g icing sugar

220g caster sugar   3 egg whites

4 tsp ground ginger   Smarties

200g butter   Chocolate buttons

240g golden syrup   Chocolate fingers

1 tsp baking powder   Jelly diamonds or jelly tots

Baking tray(s) and baking/greaseproof paper

A helpful adult!

1)   Heat oven to 180°C/350°F/Gas Mark 4.

2)   Sift the flour, ground ginger and baking powder into a large bowl.

3)   In another bowl, beat the butter and sugar together until the mixture is light and fluffy. Add the golden syrup and stir together.

4)   Add the butter-sugar-syrup mix to the flour mix and combine.

5)   Taste the dough and add more ginger if you like it spicy.

6)   If the dough is too soft to roll out, add a little more flour. Get a large sheet of baking paper and roll out the dough on top of it. The rolled-out dough should be about a centimetre thick.

7)   Cut out the sections of your house from the dough. You'll need two rectangles (14cm x 8cm) for the sides of the house, two rectangles (14cm x 8.5cm)for the roof, and a funny square-plus-triangle shape for the front and back of the house – see measurements below:

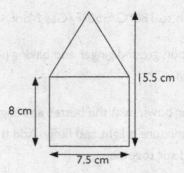

15.5 cm

8 cm

7.5 cm

8) Slide the sections, on the baking paper, onto the baking trays. Bake the sections for 12-15 minutes, then leave them to cool and harden.

9) In the meantime, combine about 300g of the icing sugar and 2 of the egg whites using an electric whisk. When the gingerbread is completely cool, smooth generous amounts of icing around the edges of the sections and stick them together to form your house. Use wooden blocks or a small bowl to support the sides of your house while the icing hardens. Leave it to harden for several hours – overnight if possible.

10) Make up some more icing using the remaining icing sugar and egg white. Use this as glue to stick chocolate buttons to the roof as tiles. Use chocolate fingers to make window and door frames, and smarties and jelly tots to make your house colourful!

Tip: Ask your helpful adult to transfer the gingerbread into and out of the oven, to help separate the egg whites, and to hold the sides of the house steady while you're sticking them together with icing.

Answers to the *Grimms' Fairy Tales* quiz – how did you do?

1) The Brave Little Tailor killed seven flies in one go.

2) The roof of the witch's house is made from cake.

3) The rhyme is: 'Shake and wobble, little tree!/Let gold and silver fall all over me.'

4) Thumbling falls asleep in some hay that turns out to be the cow's food!

5) Old Sultan is a dog.

6) Brier Rose sleeps for one hundred years.

7) The king tells the miller's daughter to spin straw into gold.

8) Simpleton finds the Golden Goose among the roots of an old tree.

9) Jorinda is transformed into a nightingale.

10) The soldier takes a branch each from the trees of silver, gold and diamonds.

Visit **www.worldofstories.co.uk**